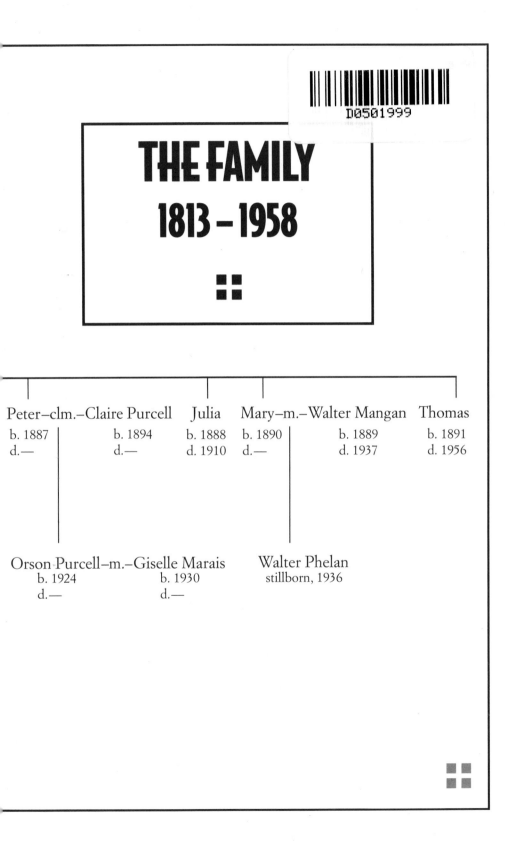

THE FAMILY
1813 – 1958

Peter–clm.–Claire Purcell   Julia   Mary–m.–Walter Mangan   Thomas

b. 1887   b. 1894   b. 1888   b. 1890   b. 1889   b. 1891

d.—   d.—   d. 1910   d.—   d. 1937   d. 1956

Orson Purcell–m.–Giselle Marais   Walter Phelan

b. 1924   b. 1930   stillborn, 1936

d.—   d.—

VERY OLD BONES

Also by William Kennedy

The Ink Truck
Legs
Billy Phelan's Greatest Game
Ironweed
Quinn's Book

NONFICTION

O Albany!
Improbable City of Political Wizards, Fearless Ethnics,
Spectacular Aristocrats, Splendid Nobodies,
and
Underrated Scoundrels

WITH BRENDAN KENNEDY

Charlie Malarkey and the Belly Button Machine

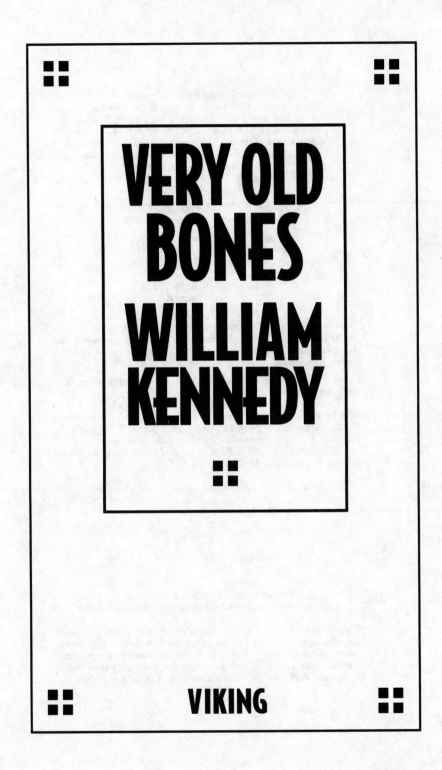

VERY OLD BONES

WILLIAM KENNEDY

VIKING

VIKING
Published by the Penguin Group
Viking Penguin, a division of Penguin Books USA Inc.,
375 Hudson Street, New York, New York 10014, U.S.A.
Penguin Books Ltd, 27 Wrights Lane, London W8 5TZ, England
Penguin Books Australia Ltd, Ringwood, Victoria, Australia
Penguin Books Canada Ltd, 10 Alcorn Avenue, Suite 300,
Toronto, Ontario, Canada M4V 3B2
Penguin Books (N.Z.) Ltd, 182–190 Wairau Road,
Auckland 10, New Zealand

Penguin Books Ltd, Registered Offices:
Harmondsworth, Middlesex, England

First published in 1992 by Viking Penguin,
a division of Penguin Books USA Inc.

Publisher's Note

This is a work of fiction. Names, characters, places, and incidents either
are the product of the author's imagination or are used fictitiously, and
any resemblance to actual persons, living or dead, events, or locales is
entirely coincidental.

Grateful acknowledgment is made for permission to reprint excerpts from
the following copyrighted works:
    Poem by Catullus translated by Edith Hamilton from *The Roman
Way* by Edith Hamilton. Reprinted by permission of the publisher,
W. W. Norton & Company, Inc. Copyright 1932 by W. W. Norton &
Company, Inc., copyright renewed 1960 by Edith Hamilton.
    "The Dwarf" from *The Palm at the End of the Mind* by Wallace
Stevens. By permission of Alfred A. Knopf, Inc.

LIBRARY OF CONGRESS CATALOGING-IN-PUBLICATION DATA
Kennedy, William.
Very old bones / William Kennedy.
p.   cm.
ISBN 0-670-83457-2
I. Title.
PS3561.E428V47   1992
813'.54—dc20   91-40723

Printed in the United States of America
Set in Simoncini Garamond · Designed by Francesca Belanger

This book is dedicated to the Hard Core (they know who they are), and to certain revered and not-so-revered ancestors of the author (they don't know who they are, for they are dead; but they'd know if they ever got their hands on this book).

Any one who has common sense will remember that the bewilderments of the eyes are of two kinds, and arise from two causes, either from coming out of the light or from going into the light . . . and he who remembers this when he sees any one whose vision is perplexed and weak, will not be too ready to laugh; he will first ask whether that soul of man has come out of the brighter life, and is unable to see because unaccustomed to the dark, or having turned from darkness to the day is dazzled by excess of light.

—Plato
The Republic

BOOK ONE

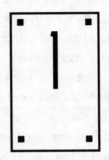

1

It is Saturday, July twenty-sixth, 1958, the sun will rise in about twenty-five minutes, the air is still, and even the birds are not yet awake on Colonie Street. There is no traffic on North Pearl Street, half a block to the east, except for the occasional auto, police prowl car, or the Second Avenue bus marking its hourly trail. A moment ago fire sirens sounded on upper Arbor Hill, to the west, their wail carrying down on the silent air, interrupting the dreams of the two sleeping occupants of this house, Peter Phelan, a seventy-one-year-old artist, and his putative son, Orson Purcell, a thirty-four-year-old bastard.

"Orson," Peter called out, "where are those sirens?"

"Not around here," I said.

"Good."

He knew as well as I that the sirens weren't close. His hearing was excellent. But he was reassuring himself that in case of fire Orson was standing by; for I was now the organizer of his life (not his art; he was in full command of that), the putative son having become father to the putative father. His health was precarious, a serious heart condition that might take him out at any instant; and so he abdicated all responsibility for survival and gave himself utterly to his work. I could now hear him moving, sitting up on the side of the bed in his boxer shorts, reaching for the light and for his cane, shoving his feet into his slippers, readying himself to enter his studio and, by the first light of new morning, address his work-in-progress, a large painting he called *The Burial*.

I knew my sleep was at an end on this day, and as I brought myself into consciousness I recapitulated what I could remember of my vanishing dream: Peter in a gymnasium where a team of doctors had just operated on him and were off to the right conferring about the results, while the patient lay on the operating table, only half there. The operation had consisted of sawing parts off Peter, the several cuts made at the hip line (his arthritic hips were his enemy), as steaks are cut off a loin. These steaks lay in a pile at the end of Peter's table. He was in some pain and chattering to me in an unintelligible language. I reattached the most recent cut of steak to his lower extremity, and it fit perfectly in its former location. But when I let go of it it fell back atop its fellows. Peter did not seem to notice either my effort or its failure.

"Are you going to have coffee, Orson?" he called out from his room. In other words, are you going to make my breakfast?

"I am," I said. "Couple of minutes." And I snapped on the light and sat up from the bed, naked, sweating in the grotesque heat of the morning. I put on a light robe and slippers and went down the front stairs and retrieved the morning *Times-Union* from the front porch. Eisenhower sending marines into Lebanon for mid-east crisis. Thunderstorms expected today. Rockefeller front runner for Republican nomination for Governor.

I put the paper on the dining-room table, filled the percolator, put out coffee cups and bread plates, and began plotting the day ahead, a day of significance to the family that had occupied this house since the last century. We would be gathering, the surviving Phelans and I, at the request of Peter, who was obeying a patriarchal whim that he hoped would redirect everybody's life. My principal unfinished task, apart from ridding the house of clutter, was to inveigle my cousin Billy to attend the gathering here, a place he loathed.

I first came here in 1934 for a funeral. Peter passed me off as the son of his landlady, Claire Purcell (which I was and am), whom he had never brought to this house even for tea, though he had been living with her then in Greenwich Village for more than fifteen years. I liked Albany, liked the relatives, especially my Aunt Molly, who became my nurse after I went crazy for the second time, and I liked Billy, who always tried to tell the truth about himself, a dangerous but admirable trait. I went to college in Albany before and after the war and came here for dinner now and again, slowly getting to know this ancestral place and its inhabitants: the Phelans and the McIlhennys, their loves, their work, their disasters.

I came to see how disaster does not always enter the house with thunder, high winds, and a splitting of the earth. Sometimes it burrows under the foundation and, like a field mouse on tiptoe, and at its own deliberate speed, gnaws away the entire substructure. One needs time to see this happening, of course, and eventually I had plenty of that.

Colonie Street in Arbor Hill was the neighborhood where these people had implanted their lives in the last century. The first Phelans arrived from Ireland in the 1820s to finish digging the Erie Canal and by mid-century were laborers, lumbermen, railroad men, and homemakers of modestly expanding means. The McIlhennys came in the late 1870s, poor as turkeys and twice as wild.

Michael Phelan inherited twenty-one thousand dollars upon the death of his father, a junior partner in a lumber mill, and in 1879 Michael built this house for his bride, Kathryn McIlhenny, creating what then seemed a landmark mansion (it was hardly that) on a nearly empty block: two parlors, a dining room, and seven bedrooms, those bedrooms an anticipatory act of notable faith and irony, for, after several years of marriage, Kathryn began behaving like an all-but-frigid woman. In spite of this, the pair filled the bedrooms with four sons and three daughters, the seven coming to represent, in my mind, Michael Phelan's warm-blooded perseverance in the embrace of ice.

The siblings were Peter and Molly; the long-absent Francis; the elder sister, Sarah; the dead sister, Julia; the failed priest, Chick; and the holy moron, Tommy. Peter had fled the house in the spring of 1913, vowing never to live here again. But the family insinuated itself back into his life after a death in the family, and he came home to care for the remnant kin, Molly and Tommy.

Peter's pencil sketches of his parents and siblings (but none of his putative son) populated the walls of the downstairs rooms in places Peter thought appropriate: Francis in his baseball uniform when he played for Washington, hanging beside the china closet, the scene of a major crisis in his life; Julia in her bathing costume, standing in the ankle-deep ocean at Atlantic City, where her mother took her to spend two months of the summer of 1909, hoping to hasten her recovery from rheumatic fever with sea air, this sketch hanging over the player piano; Sarah, without pince-nez, in high-necked white blouse, looking not pretty, for that wasn't possible for the willfully plain Sarah, but with an appealing benevolence that Peter saw in her, this sketch hanging on the east wall of the front parlor, close to the bric-a-brac Sarah had accumulated through the years, the only non-practical gifts the family ever gave her; for her horizon of pleasure in anything but the pragmatic was extremely limited. Molly hung in the back parlor also, with one foot on the running board of her new 1937 Dodge, looking very avant-garde for that year.

Peter sketched Chick at sixteen, in the black suit, Panama hat, and priestly collar he wore in the seminary, and hung the sketch in the front hallway, next to the autographed photo of Bishop T. M. A. Burke, former pastor of St. Joseph's, whose sermon in 1900, on the fortieth anniversary of the church, inspired the fourteen-year-old Chick to devote his already pious life unreservedly to God. The parental sketches hung between the two windows of the dining room: Kathryn in the laundry of St. Peter's Hospital on Broadway, which she worked in as a girl, then supervised for three years until the birth of Peter, after which she never worked; and Michael in his coveralls, at trackside with his gandy dancers, and with the same engine that killed him sitting benignly on the tracks behind him.

Only Tommy's sketch was upstairs (Peter did numerous self-portraits but hung none of them), hanging in his old room, which I occupied when I moved in to take care of Peter. Tommy is moon-faced and young and has already gone bald in the sketch, and his mouth is screwed rightward in a smile that makes him look both happy and brainless at the same time. Sarah was Tommy's caretaker, and though Tommy went to work every day as a sweeper in the North Albany (water) Filtration Plant, a major achievement in coherence for Tom, Sarah viewed it otherwise. She had a theme: "Oh God let me outlive Tommy, for he can't survive alone." But then she died and Tommy didn't, and Peter became his brother's keeper.

This was in the fall of 1954 and Peter was nearly destitute, a recurring condition; and so he welcomed a place to live rent-free. He moved up from Greenwich Village and settled back into the homestead. His old bedroom fronted on Colonie Street and, because its three bay windows offered the best light in the house, he turned it into his studio. He took down all the drapes, curtains, and dark green shades with which his mother and Sarah had kept out the light of the world for so long, and by so doing he let in not only the sunshine but also the nonplussed gazes of Arbor Hill rubbernecks who went out of their way to watch crazy old Peter Phelan, artist without a shirt, standing morning and afternoon with his expansive back to the open windows, forever dabbing paint onto his great canvases. Not like it used to be, the Phelan place.

When I moved into Tommy's room I swept out the cobwebs and dingbats, took off the old Tommy bedclothes, heavy with dust, and discovered the Tommy treasure under the bed: dozens of packages just as they'd been when he'd bought them at Whitney's and Myers' and other Downtown stores where he spent his wages. I opened one box and found white kid gloves, size four, petite, lovely, brand new in white tissue paper; opened another and found a beige slip with lace bodice; opened a third, a fourth, found pink panties, a pink brassiere.

"He gave them away to ladies," Peter told me. "He did that all his life until he ran out of ladies."

Did you buy on spec, Tom, you old dog? Did you then walk the town till you found the hand, the bodice, the thighs that fit the garment?

—*Excuse me, ma'am, but I bought you a little gift.*

—*A gift, for me? Who are you? I don't know you.*

—*That's all right, ma'am, you don't have to know me.*

And you tip your cap and move on, leaving the woman holding the bra.

"The three Foley sisters up the street," Peter said. "They were his ladies before the war." And I tried to imagine what they gave Tommy in return for his gifts. Did they model the garment? Give him a bit of stocking, a bit of white thigh? Could he have handled more? Whatever the Foley sights, they were not unfamiliar sights to many men in Arbor Hill, or so Peter said. But then one day Tommy's Tommy-love went unrequited by all Foleys—the sap bereft—and the gifts piled up under the bed.

I began to create this memoir five years ago among the pines and hemlocks of a summer hotel on the shore of Saratoga Lake, not knowing what its design would be. It began as a work of memory, passed through stages of fantasy, and emerged, I hope, as an act of the imagination. Freud wrote of imaginative artists that they could, through artistic illusion, produce emotional effects that seemed real, and so, he said, they could justly be compared to magicians.

Never mind art or justice, but I am a bit of a magician, having been exposed to the wisdom of the hand, the innocence of the eye, at an early age: when my mother was an assistant to Manfredo the Magnificent, a mediocre illusionist in the age of vaudeville. But I also learned magic by studying Peter Phelan, for, while Manfredo played tricks on the gullible, fantasy-ridden public, Peter pursued freedom from cheap illusion and untrustworthy instincts by trying for a lifetime to find magic in what was real in the world and in his heart, ultimately reaching a depth of the self that others rarely achieve. I tried this myself, went through my theatrical double breakdowns in Germany and Manhattan in the process, and have now produced this cautionary tale of diseased self-contemplation—my own and others'.

I've often used my talent as a magician, that is as a card manipulator, to entertain, but only rarely for personal gain. The first time I did that I was finishing my bachelor's degree at Albany State after the war and found myself welcome at the tables of Fobie McManus's blackout poker game on Sheridan Avenue.

Fobie was a mean-spirited erstwhile burglar who ran a saloon that catered chiefly to newspaper people. He furnished them with drink and warmth until closing, then offered them the solace of dollar-limit poker until dawn. I was working weekends as a nightside rewrite man on the *Times-Union,* trying to pay my tuition. But the wages were puny and I would've quit if I hadn't discovered Fobie's game.

It was peopled with printers, reporters, and copy editors who fancied themselves gamesters of a high order. But there was only one minor-league thief (he hid cards) among them, a few anal retentives who nurtured their secret straights with confessional glee, and an assortment of barflies whose beer intake spurred them to ever greater mismanagement of their hands.

9

I was light-years beyond them all in handling both the deck and myself, for I had learned from Manfredo that a magician is also an actor; and so I considered my financial gain from those ink-stained wretches to be fair exchange for a thespian's risky performance. Some nights I chose to lose heavily at the outset, though good luck would usually stalk my later play. On occasions I might even drop thirty dollars on the night to prove my vulnerability, but by so doing was then free at the next sitting to fleece again those good- and well-tempered suckers. Thus did I move ever closer to my degree in education.

I interrupted my college career to enlist in the army in 1942, when I turned eighteen, gained a lieutenancy, and in '44 I landed at Normandy with replacement troops after the heroes and martyrs had taken the high ground as well as the beach. I was seldom in danger from then on but could not let go of the universal fantasy that death was a land mine ten steps ahead. I walked the wrong way to die, it turned out, and after the war I went back to Albany to finish my degree in three years instead of four. After graduation, instead of teaching, I found a job with the Manhattan publishing house where my father had worked as an illustrator.

Idiotically, I'd stayed in the reserve after the war, so when Korea erupted I turned into a retread. We started at Fort Benning, creating an infantry division from scratch. The Captain who had been assigned to establish the Public Information Office, the division's press section, liked my record: precocious scholar, sometime newsman, editor of books, working on a book of my own, and, on top of it all, a line officer in the big war. What can I say?

We went to Germany instead of Korea, the first troops to go back to Europe since the war, and we headquartered in the Drake *Kaserne,* a comfortable old Nazi Wehrmacht barracks outside Frankfurt, which brings me to Giselle, my somewhat excruciating wife, and the cause of my using my talent with cards for the second time in my life to enhance my net worth.

The enlisted men of our PIO section were throwing a Christmas party that year (it was 1951) and invited the Captain and me to stop by for a bit of wassail. I was already there when the Captain arrived with this remarkable beauty on his arm. They'd have a drink, then go to dinner; that was their plan. The men had hired a belly dancer named Eva to elevate the lust factor at the party and she was dancing when the Captain and Giselle arrived. The troops were yelling at Eva to remove garments, but she wouldn't even lower a strap. She did a few extra bumps, but that didn't cut the mustard with the boys, and half a dozen of them backed her into a corner. Because of who knows what reason, Giselle spoke up.

"Leave her alone," she said. "I'll take over."

The Captain looked stricken as Giselle picked up a high stool from a corner and carried it to the center of the room. All eyes went to her as she sat on the stool with her hands in her lap, evaluating her audience. Then she undid the two top buttons of her blouse, revealing a contour—the quartering of a small moon. She lifted one leg, pointed her toe, her instep arched inside her elegant black pump, the heel of her other shoe hooked over the stool's bottom rung. One up, one down. The upward motion of her right leg moved her skirt a bit above the knee. She swept the room with her eyes, engaging everyone like a seductive angel: madonna of the high perch.

The swine who had been attacking Eva suddenly realized that Giselle's panorama seemed to be accessible. They didn't even notice Eva backing off to a corner, snatching up her coat, and running out the door.

The swine grunted when Giselle brought her right leg back and hooked her shoe on the highest rung, her skirt going higher still. Oh how they grunted, those swine. They were all in uniform, their Ike jackets swinging loose. They jostled each other to solidify their positions. They knew, as others jostled *them,* that their turf nearest Giselle had become valuable. They could have rented it out.

One of them leaped into a crouch, inches away from Giselle's knee, and he stared up the central boulevard of her shadow. But no one dared to touch her, for they intuited that vantage was all they would ever get, and the jostling grew stronger.

They moved in an ellipse, the ones with a clear view of the boulevard being the first to be shoved out of the vista.

Shoved out of the vista, imagine it.

Poor swine.

But they ran around the ellipse, got back into line, and shoved on. "Keep it moving" was the unspoken motto, and on they shoved, those in the best position always trying to retain the turf. But they'd lose it to the needy, then circle back again.

Giselle started to sing, in French, "Quand Madelon."

"*Et chacun lui raconte une histoire, une histoire à sa façon . . .*" she sang.

Then she moved her blouse to the right and exposed more of that region. My impulse was to photograph her from a low angle, but when I told her this later she said she'd have considered it rape. She touched her breast lightly and I thought, "Phantom queen as art object."

"*La Madelon,*" Giselle sang, "*pour nous n'est pas sévère.*"

The swine kept moving round and round, like the old ploy of running from one end of the photo to the other in the days when the camera panned so slowly you could put yourself into the photo twice. I see those piggies still, moving in their everlasting ellipse— that piggy-go-round—shouldering one another, hunkering down as they moved to their left for a better view of that boulevard, lowering themselves, debasing all romance, groveling to Giselle's secrets with bend of knee and squint of eye.

I still can't blame them.

And what *did* the swine see? Quite amazing to talk about it afterward. One saw wildflowers—black-eyed Susans. Another said she wore a garment. Yet another no. A sergeant who'd been in the

Fourth Armored during the war said he saw a landscape strewn with crosses and corpses, the reason why the war was fought.

And then she gave one final rising of the knee, stood up, and put herself back together. Slowly the troops started to applaud, and it grew and grew.

"More, more," they called out, but Giselle only buttoned the last button, threw them a kiss, and returned to the Captain's side. The troops shook the Captain's hand, congratulated him on his taste in women, and when he went for their coats I asked Giselle her name but she wouldn't tell me. Then the Captain came and said, "All right, Giselle, let's go."

"Ah, Giselle," I said.

It took me only a few days to track her to the office where she worked as a translator for diplomats and army bureaucrats.

"I've come to rescue you from old men," I told her.

"I knew you would," she said with a foxy smile.

But she resisted me, and professed fidelity to the Captain, who, though twice-and-a-half her age and going to fat, was flush with money from his black-market adventures in coffee and cigarettes.

"Can you take me to Paris for the weekend as he does?" she asked me. "Can you fly me to the Riviera?"

"How direct the mercenary heart," I said. "I understand your point. I suspect we are much alike."

But the truth was that I never valued money except when I had none. And Giselle's hedonist remarks were a façade to keep me at bay. You see she was already starting to love me.

Each day I sent her a yellow rose—yellow the color of age, cowardice, jaundice, jealousy, gold, and her own radiant hair. In a week the flowers softened her telephone voice, in two weeks she agreed to dinner, and in three to a Heidelberg weekend, which was the first stop on my road to dementia.

We stayed at a small pension and left it only for meals. Otherwise we inhabited the bed. She put all of her intimate arenas on display and let me do with them what I pleased, with a single exception: I could enter none of them with my principal entering device.

I had never been more excited by a woman's body, though I know the relative fraudulence of memory in such matters. Denial of entry was of small consequence to a man of my imagination, given the beatific pot of flesh to which I had access in every other way. Giselle said she was fearful of pregnancy, of disease, of sin, even of vice, can you imagine? But I know she was actually testing my capacity to tolerate her tantalizing. I've known exhibitionistic women, several, but none with the raw, artistic talent for exposure that Giselle demonstrated in Heidelberg. This was my initiation into the heavenly tortures of Giselle-love.

In the days that followed, she and I moved together in a delirium, I sick with love. When I was away from her I fell into what I came to think of as the coma of the quotidian, my imagination dead to everything except the vision of her face, her yellow hair, and the beige, angelical beauty of her sex, though that describes only the look of it, not the non-angelical uses to which she put it.

One understands addiction, obsession. It begins as the lunacy of whim, or desire, but ends as the madness of need, or essence. I could not be without her, and so all my waking movements were the orchestration of our next meeting.

I bought her gifts: Hummel dolls, a cuckoo clock, a Chanel suit, Italian shoes, cultured pearls (I could not afford diamonds). I bought her books. She'd never heard of Kafka, or Christopher Marlowe, or Philip Marlowe, for she was a visual animal, fascinated by art and photography, the twin provinces of her mother, who ran an art gallery in Paris.

I bought her a camera, took her to Versailles, Mont St. Michel, and other spectacles for the eye, took her to Omaha Beach and tried to explain to her some of the war and my puny part in it. She'd lived in Paris the entire war and saw no fighting, only occupation, during which her father had been executed by the Nazis. Her mother, a paragon of independence and survival, raised this very willful daughter.

There was much more, but, to get to the point, Giselle-love broke me. I ran through my paychecks and small savings account, and got a bit of money from my mother. But I soon went through it all, and it was out of the question to ask Peter for money. He never had any.

Then I remembered Walt Popp, captain of Special Services, mentioning a game of poker. That was a month after I met Giselle, the days when I had no time for any other game but her. Now I tracked down Popp at the officers' club and bought him a drink.

"I thought you were getting a poker game together," I said.

"I did ask a few guys. Are you ready?"

"I could use a little action."

"I thought you had this beauty, this cover-girl type."

"Hanging out with you mugs, I'll appreciate her even more."

"I'll round up a crowd for Friday night," Popp said.

So I practiced. There'd never been a time I hadn't, really. Manfredo's wisdom was that once you lose your touch it will never come back with quite the same delicacy. Any talent must be husbanded or else we diminish in the breach; and so I spent two hours a week, maybe three, handling the cards, cutting them for aces, dealing seconds, bottoms, reading the deck when I shuffled. I practiced in bed, in the latrine, anytime I was alone. Almost nobody after Fobie's knew about me and cards. My magic was still in my hat.

Popp told the Captain there'd be a game and I'd be playing, and the Captain brought it up the next day in the office.

"Cards? You mean you aren't seeing Giselle any more?"

"Matter of fact I am," I said.

"I don't see her any more."

"Is that so?"

"You damn well know it's so."

"I don't follow you around, Captain."

"You follow Giselle around."

"I wouldn't deny it."

"She likes 'em young."

"She's young." She was twenty.

"I miss her," he said.

"I'd miss her too."

"You took her away from me."

"That's not how it happens. People do what they want."

"She liked me."

"We all like you, Captain."

"You do good work, Orson. It's a good *thing* you do good work."

"I try not to disappoint."

"That's smart. Never disappoint. What time is the game?"

"Seven o'clock."

"I'll see you across the table," he said.

It sounded like an invitation to a duel.

"Is the coffee ready, Orson?" my father called.

"It is," I said. "Come on down."

I heard him shuffling toward the stairs in his slippers, and I remembered when as a child I shat in one of his slippers, a moment of my precocious psychosis. It is a thief's traditional trick to shit in the victim's lair, and I had been a thief of vision—of my father's and mother's private life. The occasion was an argument over love. Whose property was Claire Purcell? Was she owned body and soul by Peter, her live-in lover, or was she the intimate assistant to Manfredo the Magnificent?

I awoke in the middle of the night to find my father home after a two-week absence, heard his voice, moved toward it comprehending no words, closed on the parental bedroom to see my naked father standing over my supine, naked mother, and hear him say: "Why don't you take your cunt back to Manfredo and have him give you another one?"

I, at the age of eight, had never heard the word "cunt" uttered other than once in schoolboy talk: Why do they call it a cunt? . . . You ever see one? . . . Yeah . . . Well, then, what else would you call it? Nor did I understand the import of the phrase "another one," until time had passed and I had dwelled sufficiently on the overheard words to conclude that my father had been talking about me, the only *one* there was: Orson Purcell, son without siblings (living or dead) of Claire Purcell-never-Phelan. I was "son," "sonny," "Orse," and "Orsy-Horsey" to Peter Phelan, the only father I'd ever known. But when I at last understood the meaning of his assault on my mother (I soon began to use the term "father" in an ambiguous way, and eventually abandoned it), then it occurred to me that bastardy might be an enduring theme of my life. I grew angry at Peter for not (*if* not) being my father, grew angry also at Manfredo, who was unacceptable as a father.

This latter anger prevailed after I entered a dressing room of the Palace Theater in Albany, just after Manfredo had finished his act on stage. There sat Mother on the dressing-room vanity, naked legs akimbo. There stood Manfredo in top hat, tux jacket, and pants around ankles, thrusting his magic wand into her rabbit, and giving moon to all visitors who did not know they were not wanted, just as the magic couple did not realize that they had not locked the door until after the Orse was gone.

Orson the adventurer, Orson the thief of vision. I waited a week before making the assault on my father's slipper (I should have shat in Manfredo's hat) as an ultimate gesture of rebellion

17

against his verbal cruelty. My mother rejected my act of solidarity with her, terming it loathsome, and my father, whose anger with Claire had abated, took off his belt and said, "Now I'm going to whip you until you bleed," and did. I then brooded myself into a dream of being attacked by crocodiles and, while pulling myself out of the water, of being consumed by the crocs up to the neck, my head floating away to live a disembodied life of its own.

That, more or less, is the truth of my head.

Peter finally reached the bottom of the stairs and shuffled toward the dining room.

"I never thought my bones would turn into my enemy," he said with a great wheezing sound. "Skeletons are not to be trusted."

He sat at the dining-room table and I put the toast and butter on the table and poured his and my coffee.

"Are you going to go to work?" I asked him.

"I have no alternative."

"You could take it easy. Take the day off. It's a special day, isn't it?"

"That's like cheating at solitaire. Who gets cheated?"

"Are you nearing the end of this painting?"

"There's distance to go, but there's even more to do after this one."

"You always talk about dying but you don't behave like a dying man."

"As soon as you behave like a dying man, you're dead."

"You're a man with a mission."

"A man with curiosity. I come from a long line of failed and sinful flesh, and there's a darkness in it I want to see."

"Speaking of sin," I said, "isn't today the day that Adelaide comes to give you your therapy?"

"You have an abrasive tongue in your head this morning."

"I just want to make sure I'm here to let her in."

"You're a thoughtful boy, Orson."

18

"I used to be a boy," I said.

We looked at the window at the beginning of the day, a grudging gray light, no sunbeam to color it brilliant.

"They say it's going to rain," I said.

"They always say that," said Peter. "And they're always right."

Those who do the great heroic work of being human never work solely from experience. My father, for instance, could never have painted his *Malachi Suite,* that remarkable body of paintings and sketches that made him famous, without having projected himself into the lives of the people who had lived and died so absurdly, so tragically, in the days before and after his own birth. I am not implying here that *any* historical reconstruction is heroic, but rather that imaginative work of the first rank must come about through its creator's subordination of the self, and also from the absorption into that self of what has gone on beyond or before its own existence.

Clearly there is no way to absorb the history of even one other being wholly into oneself; but the continuity of the spirit relies on an imagination like my father's, which makes the long-dead world, with a fine suddenness, as Keats put it, fly back to us with its joys and its terrors and its wisdom. Keats invented the term "negative capability" to define what he saw in the true poetical character: a quality of being that "has no self—it is everything and nothing . . . it enjoys light and shade; it lives in gusto, be it foul or fair, high or low . . ." The poet should be able to throw his soul into any person, or object, that he confronts, and then speak out of that person, or object. "When I am in a room with people," wrote Keats, "if I ever am free from speculating on creations of my own brain . . . the identity of every one in the room begins to press upon me [so] that I am in a very little time annihilated . . ."

I speak with some authority when I say that it is a major struggle for anyone to annihilate his or her own ego, to cure the disease of self-contemplation, for as you will see there is ample attention paid to myself in this memoir. But I believe it could not be otherwise, for only through what I was, and became, could the family be made visible, to me, to anyone. And so I invoke Keats, without any claim to art of my own, both to drain myself of myself, and to project myself into realms of the family where I have no credentials for being, but am there even so; for I do know the people in this memoir, know where and how they lived, or live still.

I know, for instance, what is going on in the Quinn house on North Pearl Street in North Albany this morning at a little past five o'clock. Two sleeping men are nearly naked, and three sleeping women are ritually modest in their shorty summer nightgowns. In each of three bedrooms a crucifix hangs on a nail over the sleepers' beds and, in a luminous print looking down at Peg and George Quinn in their double bed, the Christ exposes his sacred heart, that heart encircled by tongues of fire.

The house normally rouses itself from slumber at seven o'clock, except on Sunday, when late rising is the rule. As the milkman sets foot on the front stoop next door at this crepuscular hour, that house's resident chow disturbs all light sleepers here with his murderous bark from the back yard. Under the quietest of circumstances it is not easy to achieve sleep on this infernal morning, but after the chow's bark, George Quinn, vigorous still at seventy-one, raises himself on one elbow, rolls himself onto his wife's body, and then, with high comfort and the expertise that comes with practiced affection, he rides the lovely beast of love.

Dead heat was saturating the room, the sheet and pillowcases under the two bodies soaked from the long and humid night, no breeze at all coming in the fully opened window, no leaf moving on the trees of North Pearl Street; nor was any cross-ventilation possible, for the bedroom door was closed now in these moments of hot waking love, all nightclothes strewn on the floor beside the bed, the top sheet kicked away.

As they moved in their naked heat toward mutual climax the door creaked open, its faint crack a thunderclap to both lovers. George knelt abruptly up from his wife's soft and sodden body, grabbed for his pajama bottoms as Peg felt for the lost topsheet to cover herself; and the door creaked again, the gap between its edge and its jamb widening, the hall light striping the room with a sliver of brilliance, then a board's width; and there, in the foot-wide opening, appeared Annie Phelan's face, ghostly inquisitor with flowing white hair, her face growing larger and more visible as she pushed the door open and stared into the bedroom of interrupted love.

"What is it, Mama?" Peg asked.

Behind the door George was stepping into his pajamas, and Peg, with the use of one deft arm, the other holding the found sheet in front of her breasts, was threading herself into her nightgown.

"What time is it, Margaret?" Annie asked.

"It's too early," said Peg. "Go back to bed."

"We have to make the coffee and set the table."

"Later, Mama. It isn't even five-thirty yet. Nobody's up except you."

From his darkened bedroom Billy Phelan inquired: "Is Ma all right?"

"She's all right," Peg said. "She's just off schedule again."

Billy raised his head, flipped his pillow to put the wet side down, and tried to go back to sleep, thinking of how he used to work the window in Morty Pappas's horseroom, but no more.

Standing in the doorway of the third bedroom, where she and Annie Phelan slept in twin beds, Agnes Dempsey, wearing a pink knee-length nightgown, and yawning and scratching her head with both hands, said to Peg, "I didn't hear her get up, she doesn't have her slippers on"; and then to Annie Phelan: "What kind of an Irishman are you that you don't put your slippers on when you walk around the house?"

"Oh you shut up," Annie said.

"Go in and get your slippers if you want to walk around."

Annie went into the bedroom. "The bitch," she muttered. "The bitch."

"I heard you," Agnes said.

"You did not," said Annie.

"I could stay up and make the coffee," Agnes said.

"No, it's too early," said Peg. "She'd stay up too, and then we'd never get her back on schedule."

"You go to bed," said Agnes. "I'll keep her in the room. I'll put the chair in front of the door."

George was already back in bed, eyes closed and trying for sleep as Peg lay on her back beside him and hoisted her nightgown to thigh level to let her legs breathe. Her interrupted climax would probably nag her at odd moments for the rest of the day, but she wouldn't dispel that now with her own touch. She wondered when the day of no more climaxes would arrive, wondered whether it would be her failure or George's. How long before George was as senile as Mama? When was Mama's last orgasm? When did she last feel Poppy's hand on her? Peg had no memory of anything sexual in Annie's life, never caught them at it the way Danny caught her and George up at the lake. We thought he was swimming for the afternoon, but in he came, George doing great, and me on the verge. He opens the door with the key and we both look at him. "I didn't know you were sleeping," he says, and out he goes, and that's that for that.

Peg charted the day to come: office till noon, the boss, and Basil, probably. Work will be light, all their attention on the strike vote in the shop this morning. I hope there's no fights. Then Roger. He wants to drive me down to Peter's luncheon. It'd be easy to go along with Roger. He has a way about him, and funny too. Smart and funny and so young. It's so silly. The important thing is to turn George around.

"Are you asleep, George?"

"Nobody can sleep in this stuff. It's like sleeping in pea soup."

"We have to buy this house."

"We do like hell."

"Think about it, damn it all, *think about it!* Where could we *ever again* find this much space for that kind of money?"

"Who needs all this space? Danny's not home any more."

"He comes home sometimes. And we still have Mama."

"Yeah, and we also got Agnes. Jesus Christ."

"She's a big help."

"She's also another mouth."

"If she wasn't here we'd have to pay *somebody* to watch Mama, unless *you* want to stay home and do it."

"Why can't Billy take care of his own mother?"

"Billy can't do that sort of thing. And he wouldn't. The personal things, I mean."

"You always got an answer," George said.

"So do you. And the answer's always no."

Peg pushed herself up from the bed, pulled off her nightgown, thrust herself into a cotton robe, and strode briskly to the bathroom, leaving the bedroom door ajar. The hall light would fall directly into George's eyes. Good. George stood up, walked to the door and closed it, sat back on the bed, and looked at his dim reflection in the dresser mirror.

"You're gonna die in the poorhouse of bullshit and other people's generosity," he said to himself.

In her chair by the parlor window Annie Phelan monitored the passing of neighbors, sipping her first cup of tea of the day from

24

the wheeled serving table, popping white grapes into her mouth, chewing them with great vigor, coming to an end of chewing, organizing her lips and tongue, and then spitting the grape seeds onto the oriental rug.

Billy, in the kitchen breakfast nook, was reading the baseball results (the Red Sox and the Albany Senators had both lost) in the morning *Times-Union,* his right leg stretched kitchenward, its plaster ankle cast covered by the leg of his navy-blue Palm Beach trousers, the toes of his shoeless foot covered by half a white sock, his hickory cane standing in the corner of the nook next to a paper bag containing his right shoe.

Agnes Dempsey, practical nurse and Billy's special friend, who'd been a now-and-then overnight guest for years, and who became a full-time live-in member of the household a year ago April, when Annie's feebleness and vagueness were becoming a family problem, Agnes Dempsey at forty stood at the counter by the sink, breaking soft-boiled eggs into coffee cups with broken handles.

Peg, dressed perfectly, as usual, in high heels and blue flowered dress, stood at the gas stove pouring a cup of coffee, the only breakfast she would allow herself, except for one bite of Billy's toast, she in such a high-energized condition that we must intuit some private frenzy in her yet to be revealed.

Agnes brought Annie her breakfast before serving anyone else, stirred up the eggs with a teaspoon, topped them off with a touch of butter, salt, and pepper, then set them in front of Annie along with two pieces of toast. Annie looked at the eggs.

"They got bugs," she said.

"What's got bugs?"

"Those things. Get the bugs off."

"That's not bugs, Annie. That's pepper."

Annie tried to shove the pepper to one side with a spoon.

"I don't eat bugs," she said.

"That's a new one," Agnes said when she set Billy's eggs in front of him on the oilcloth-covered table. "She thinks pepper is bugs."

"Then don't give her any pepper," Billy said.

"Well, naturally," said Agnes, and Peg saw a pout in Agnes's lips and knew it had more than pepper in it. They all ate in silence until Agnes said, "I've got to get a room someplace."

"You don't have to go noplace," Billy said.

"Well, I do, and you know I do."

"Let's not create a crisis," Peg said.

"I'm not creating a crisis," Agnes said. "I'm saying I've got to get out of here. Father McDevitt said it, not me. But I've been thinking the same thing."

"Then why didn't you ever say anything?" said Billy.

"Because I didn't know how to say it."

"Well, you've said it now," said Peg. "Do you mean it, or is this just a little low-level blackmail?"

"What's that mean, blackmail?"

"Agnes," said Peg, "go on with your tale of woe."

"I'm saying only what the Father said. That we can't go on living this way, because it doesn't look moral."

"Very little in this life looks moral to me," Peg said. "When are you leaving?"

"She's not leaving," Billy said. "Who'll take care of Ma?"

"We can't let Ma interfere with Agnes's new moral look," Peg said.

"You heard the Father," Agnes said. " 'How long have you been here, my dear?' 'A little over a year, Father.' I felt like I was in confession. 'You did that? How many times did you do it, dear?' They always want the arithmetic."

"I'm surprised the Vatican hasn't sent in a team of investigators to get to the bottom of this," Peg said.

26

"Whataya talkin' about, *this*?" Billy said. "There's nothin' goin' on."

"Then you don't have anything to worry about," said Peg.

"Worry? Why should I worry?"

"You shouldn't," Peg said. "You're clean."

"Look, I know what you're gettin' at," Billy said, "and I'm not gettin' married, so change the subject."

"Changed. When do you move out, Ag?"

" 'We don't want to give scandal,' the priest says. What does he think we do here?"

"He imagines what you do," said Peg. "It probably keeps him peppy. What else did he say?"

"He says we have to create the sacrament."

"What sacrament?" Billy said.

"I don't think he meant baptism," said Peg. "Do you?"

"I don't know what's he mean sacrament," Billy insisted.

"No more profane love in the afternoon, maybe? Make it sacred?"

"You'd better watch what you say," Agnes said.

"You better organize this act you've got going here," Peg said. "And you too," she said to Billy. "I really don't give a rap what the priest says, or the bishop either. This is our house and we do what we like in it. But I think you ought to make a decision about your own lives for a change. I've got to get to work." She bolted her coffee and stood up.

"I'll call about supper," she told Agnes. "I've got that luncheon with Peter and Orson. The lawyer's picking me up and I suppose the whole gang will be there. I want to go down early and help with the lunch."

"We've got a roasting chicken and lamb chops," Agnes said.

"Better be careful about lamb chops," George Quinn said, coming through the swinging door into the kitchen. "That's why

Annie had her stroke. Always showin' off eatin' lamb-chop fat."

"I'm going where there's no lamb chops," Peg said. She gave George a quick kiss and went out.

The phone rang and George, the closest to it, answered: "Hello there, who's calling this early? . . . Who? . . . Oh, yeah . . . Well, no, Peg's gone to work. Any message? . . . Yeah, Billy's right here," and he handed Billy the phone with the words, "It's Orson, that floo-doo."

"What's the prospect, Orson?" Billy said into the phone.

"I need to get out of this goddamn house," I said. "What are you up to?"

"I gotta go to the doctor's."

"When?"

"This morning."

"I'll take you," I said.

"What's your problem down there?" Billy asked.

"It's a big day today. I need to get out from under for a while."

"So come have breakfast and we'll go down to Sport Schindler's for an eye-opener. I gotta meet a guy there owes me money."

"Always a pleasant prospect," I said. "I'll see you in five minutes."

"You can't get here sooner?"

George Quinn sprinkled a teaspoon of sugar on his eggs, his tie tied tight on his lightly starched collar on this day that was headed into the high nineties: sartorial propriety, impervious to weather.

"So how's the numbers business, George?" I asked as I sat across the breakfast table from him and Billy.

"It don't exist," George said.

"What?"

"Where you been, Orson?" Billy said. "George has been out of business for a year."

"I thought that was temporary," I said.

"A few of the big boys went to work by phone after it all closed down. But not me," George said.

"I blame Dewey for starting it," Billy said. "That son of a bitch, what the hell's the town gonna do without numbers? Without Broadway."

"Broadway? Broadway's not gone."

"It ain't gone," Billy said, "but it ain't got no life to it. You can't get arrested on Broadway any more. Town is tough as Clancy's nuts. Even if you get a bet down you don't know the payoff. No phone line with the information any more. You gotta wait for to-morrow's newspaper. I blame Kefauver."

"Forget I asked," I said. "Tell me about the house, George. Peg says you may buy this place after all these years."

"Peg said that?"

"She said you might cash an insurance policy. Seven grand for this house sounds like the bargain of the century."

"Not buyin'," George said.

"It's fifteen hundred down," Billy said.

"Fifteen hundred down the bowl," George said. "Who's got money to buy houses when you're seventy-one years old? I'm not waitin' for my ship to come in. It's not comin' and I know it."

"What're you gonna do, move?" I asked.

"Yeah. We'll find a place."

"Probably not at this rent," Billy said.

"Then we'll pay what it takes," George said.

"Why not put that into owning the house?" I said. "It'd make more sense."

"I'm not buyin' a house!" George yelled, standing up from the table. "Has everybody got that? No house. Period."

"You ready to go, Orson?" Billy asked softly, reaching for his cane.

"I guess I'm ready. I haven't had any coffee but I guess I'm ready."

"Let him have his coffee," Agnes said.

"I don't know if I'll make it for dinner," George said to Agnes. "Depends on when the picnic ends."

"Picnic? I thought it was a political meeting," Agnes said.

"It's a political picnic."

"What's not political in this town?" Billy said.

"Buyin' a house," George said.

Agnes collected Annie's breakfast dishes and her untouched eggs and put them on the counter by the sink, gave Peg's African violets by the windowsill of the nook their weekly watering, then sat across from me to finish her second cup of coffee. As she sat, Billy rose up on his cane.

"I gotta do a wee-wee before we leave," he said.

"Good," I said. "Time to worry is when you can't."

"Stop that talk," Agnes said.

I stared at her and decided she was a looker. Lucky Billy. Agnes had bottled blond hair, the color of which she changed whimsically, or maybe it was seasonally. She'd put on a few pounds since I'd last seen her, but she could handle them. She looked crisp and fresh in a red-and-white-check house dress with a box neck and two-inch straps over bare shoulders.

"I couldn't butt in on that conversation about the house," Agnes said, "but I'd be glad to give a hand with the down payment. I've got some dollars tucked away."

"That's real nice, Agnes," I said. "Did you tell Peg?"

"Nobody yet. I'm just sayin' it now 'cause it occurred to me. But if Billy hears he'll think I'm proposin'."

"Have you done that before?"

"Twenty times, how about. But he can't see himself married. He's been single too long."

"Everybody's single till they marry."

"Billy'd be single even *after* he got married, *if* he ever got married, which I don't think."

"He loves you, though," I said. "Anybody can see that."

"Sure. But what's he done for me lately?"

"Maybe you ought to go out together more often, be alone. I know you're in a lot with the family, taking care of Annie."

"We go to the movies once a week, and dinner after. But you're right. We should. I also got another obligation, a patient. An old man I sit with one night a week. And another night I take piano."

"How long you been taking?"

"Twenty-four years."

"You must be good."

"I'm terrible. Maybe I'll be good some day, but I don't practice enough."

"It's hard without a piano."

"Yeah. But I get a thrill playing the teacher's. I always do a half-hour alone, before and after the lesson. And once or twice a week I play in the church basement in the afternoons. It fills me up, excites me. You know how it is when you feel young and you know you still got a lot to learn, and it's gonna be good?"

"You're a graceful person, Agnes."

"Yeah, well, George shouldn't be afraid of lettin' people do him a favor. That down payment's not a whole lot of money, really. But I heard him tell Peg, 'They don't give loans to people like me.' "

"What's he mean, 'people like me'?"

"He doesn't know about credit," Agnes said. "He's got no credit anyplace. He paid cash all his life, even for cars. Doesn't wanna owe anybody a nickel. He thinks credit's bad news."

"So's not having a place to live."

"He said he'd live in a ditch before he bought a house."

"He's batty."

"Could be. Wouldn't be a first in this family." She looked up at me. "I didn't mean that personally," she said.

Billy expected to have his cast removed but that didn't happen. After Doc McDonald read the X-rays he decided the cast should stay in place another three weeks at least, and so Billy had to carry his right shoe around in a paper bag the rest of the day. We were in my car, Danny Quinn's old 1952 Chev that I'd bought from Peg. Billy mentioned an eye-opener at Sport Schindler's, but it was only ten-fifteen, and that's a little early for my eye.

"You been to the filtration plant since they started that dig?" I asked Billy.

"I ain't been there in years. My grandfather used to run that joint."

"I know, and Tommy was the sweeper. You see in the paper about the bones they found?"

"Yeah, you think they're still there?"

"It's worth a look."

The old plant, which had changed the health of Albany in 1899, was being torn down. The chronic "Albany sore throat" of the nineteenth century had been attributed to inadequate filtering of Hudson River water. But after the North Albany plant opened, the sore throats faded. Still, river water was a periodic liability until the late 1920s, when the politicians dammed up two creeks in the Helderberg Mountains and solved all city water troubles forever. The filtration plant relaxed into a standby item, then a useless relic. Now it stood in the way of a superhighway's course and so it was time to knock it down.

Construction workers had found bones in their dig, near the mouth of the Staatskill, the creek that ran eastward from Albany's western plateau and had long ago been buried in a pipe under North Pearl Street and Broadway. When the dig reached the glacial ledge where the creek made its last leap into the Hudson River, half a dozen huge bones were found. Workers didn't inform the public until they also found two tusks, after which a geologist and biologist were summoned. No conclusions had been reported in the morning paper but everybody in town was saying elephants.

I drove down the hill from the doctor's office and into North Albany. When I reached Pearl Street Billy said "Go down Main Street. I want to see what it looks like."

Billy's grandfather Joe Farrell (they called him Iron Joe because two men broke their knuckles on his jaw) had lived at the bottom of Main Street, and also had run a saloon, The Wheelbarrow, next to his home. The house was gone but the saloon building still stood, a sign on it noting the headquarters of a truckers' union. Trucking companies had replaced the lumber yards as the commerce along Erie Boulevard, the filled-in bed of the old canal.

"I wouldn't know the place," Billy said. "I never get down here any more." He'd been born and raised on Main Street.

"Lot of memories here for you," I said.

"I knew how many trees grew in those lots over there. I knew how many steps it took to get from Broadway to the bottom of the hill. The lock house on the canal was right there." And he pointed toward open space. "Iron Joe carried me on his shoulder over the bridge to the other side of the lock."

Implicit but unspoken in Billy's memory was that this was the street his father fled after dropping his infant son and causing his death. I was close to Billy, but I'd never heard him mention that. He and I are first cousins, sons of most peculiar brothers, I the unacknowledged bastard of Peter Phelan, Billy the abandoned son of Francis Phelan, both fathers flawed to the soul, both in their errant ways worth as much as most martyrs.

Billy was still looking at where his house had been when I turned onto the road that led to the filtration plant. It was busy with heavy equipment for the dig; also a police car was parked crossways in the road. A policeman got out of the car and raised his hand to stop us. Billy knew him, Doggie Murphy.

"Hey, Dog," Billy said. "We came to see the elephants."

"Can't go through, Billy."

"What's goin' on?"

"They found bones."

"I know they found bones. I read the paper."

"No, other bones. Human bones."

"Oh yeah?"

"So nobody comes or goes till the coroner gets here."

"Whose bones are they?"

"Somebody who don't need 'em any more," Doggie said.

And so I swung the car around and headed for Sport Schindler's, where I would have my eye opened whether it needed it or not. Sport was pushing sixty, a retired boxer who had run this saloon for thirty-five years, keeping a continuity that dated to the last century. The place had a pressed-tin ceiling, a long mahogany bar with brass rail, shuffleboard, dart board, and years of venerable grime on the walls. Apart from the grime it was also unusually clean for a saloon, and a haven for the aging population of Broadway. A poster at one end of the bar showed two sixtyish, wrinkled, white-haired naked women, both seated with hands covering their laps, both wearing glasses, both with an enduring shapeliness and a splendid lack of sag. Centered over the back bar was the mounted head of a cow, shot in Lamb's lot by Winker Wilson, who thought it was a rabbit.

Billy had lived for years in the night world of Broadway, where Schindler's was a historic monument. But times were changing now with the press of urban renewal by squares and straights who had no use at all for Billy's vanishing turf. Also, the open horserooms of Albany had moved underground when the racing-information phone line was shut off by pressure from the Governor, and the only action available now was by personal phone call or handbook. Bookies, to avoid being past-posted, paid off only on the race results in tomorrow's newspaper. What the hell kind of a town is it when a man can't walk in off the street and bet a horse?

Sport Schindler's looked like an orthopedic ward when we settled in. Billy sat at the end of the bar, his right foot in his plaster cast partially covered by white sock and trouser cuff, his hickory cane dangling from the edge of the bar. Up the bar was a man whose complete right leg was in a cast elevated on another stool, a pair of crutches leaning against the bar beside him.

Billy earned his cast riding in a car whose windshield somebody hit with a rock, scaring hell out of the driver, who drove into a tree. Billy broke his ankle putting on the brakes in the back seat. "You ain't safe noplace in this world," Billy concluded.

The man with the crutches was Morty Pappas, a Greek bookie who had been a casualty of the state-police crackdown on horse-rooms. Instead of booking on the sneak, Morty took his bankroll and flew to Reno with a stripper named Lulu, a dangerous decision, for Lulu was the most favored body of Buffalo Johnny Rizzo, the man who ran the only nightclub strip show in town. Morty came back to Albany six months after he left, flush with money from a streak of luck at the gaming tables, but minus Lulu and her body. Rizzo welcomed Morty back by shooting him in the leg, a bum shot, since he was aiming at Morty's crotch. Rizzo went to jail without bail, the shooting being his third felony charge in four years. But it had come out in the morning paper that by court order he was permitted bail; and so Buffalo Johnny was back in circulation.

Billy was offering Morty even money that the bones found up at the filtration plant were not elephant bones, Billy's argument based in his expressed belief that they never let elephants hang around Albany.

"Whataya mean they never let 'em hang around," Morty said. "Who's gonna tell an elephant he can't hang around?"

"You want the bet or don't you?" Billy asked.

"They found tusks with the bones."

"That don't mean nothin'," Billy said.

"Who else got tusks outside of elephants?"

"Joey Doyle and his sister."

"You're so sure gimme two to one," said Morty.

"Six to five is all I go."

"You're right and the newspaper's wrong, is that it?"

"What I'm sayin' is six to five."

"You got a bet," said Morty, and Billy looked at me and winked.

I couldn't figure out why Billy was so hot to bet against elephants, but neither could I bet against Billy, for I was his kinsman in more ways than one. Someone once remarked that Billy had lived a wastrel's useless life, which struck me as a point of view benightedly shrouded in uplift. I always found this world of Broadway to be the playground of that part of the soul that is impervious to any form of improvement not associated with chance, and relentlessly hostile to any conventional goad toward success and heaven. I remember years ago standing with Billy and Sport Schindler as a Fourth of July parade went past Sport's place on Broadway. A stranger beside us, seeing a Boy Scout troop stepping along, remarked, "What a fine bunch of boys." Sport took his cigar out of his mouth to offer his counterpoint: "Another generation of stool pigeons," he said.

That was years ago, and now here I was again with Sport and Billy and their friends, and those Scouts had grown up to become the lawyers, bankers, and politicians who had forced Sport to sell his saloon so they could level the block and transform it into somebody else's money. The Monte Carlo gaming rooms were gone, another victim of the crackdown: end of the wheel-and-birdcage era on Broadway; Louie's pool room was empty, only Louie's name left on the grimy windows; Red the barber had moved uptown and so you couldn't even get shaved on the street any more; couldn't buy a deck of cards either, Bill's Magic Shop having given way to a ladies' hat store. A ladies' hat store. Can you believe it, Billy?

Also Becker's Tavern had changed hands in the early fifties, and after that nobody paid any attention to the photographic mural behind the bar, mural of two hundred and two shirtsleeved men at a 1932 clambake. Nobody worried any more about pasting stars on the chests of those men after they died, the way old man Becker used to. One by one the stars had gone up on those chests through the years; then sometimes a star would fall and be carried off by the sweeper. Stars fell and fell, but they didn't rise any more, and so now the dead and the quick were a collage of uncertain fates. Hey, no star on his chest, but ain't he dead? Who knows? Who gives a goddamn? Put a star on him, why not? Put a star on Becker's.

One by one we move along and the club as we know it slowly dissolves, not to be reconstituted. "Broadway never sleeps," Sport always said, but now it did. It slept in the memories of people like him and Billy, men who wandered around the old turf as if it wasn't really old, as if a brand-new crap table might descend from the sky at any minute—and then, to the music of lightning bolt and thunder clap, the dice would roll again.

But no. No lightning. No thunder. No dice. Just the memory of time gone, and the vision of the vanishing space where the winners and losers, the grifters and suckers, had so vividly filled the air with yesterday's action.

"They want me to get married," Billy said to me.

"Who does?"

"Peg. The priest. Agnes."

"What's the priest say?"

"He says we're givin' scandal with Agnes livin' in. She's been with us a year maybe."

"Then you're already married, basically."

"Nah. She's got her own room. She's a roomer."

"Ah, I get it," I said.

" 'Doesn't look moral,' the priest says."

"Well he's half right, if you worry about that sort of thing."

"I don't worry. They worry."

"What's Peg say?"

"Peg says she doesn't give a damn whether I marry the girl or not. But yeah, she wants it too. It'd get the priest off her back."

"So get married, then," I said. "You like the girl?"

"She's great, but how the hell can I get married? I'm fifty-one years old and I don't have a nickel and don't know where to get one. I scrounge a little, deal now and then, but I haven't had steady work since Morty closed the horseroom. And the chiselin' bastard owes me back wages and two horse bets."

"How much?"

"About a grand. Little less, maybe."

"That's a lot."

"He said he went dry, couldn't pay off, said he'd pay me later. But then he went off with Lulu and now he's runnin' a floatin' card game and he don't listen. I oughta cut his heart out, but it's even money he don't have one."

Billy stopped talking, stopped looking me in the eye. Then, with his voice in a low register and on the verge of a tremolo, he said, "You know, Orson, I never could hold a job. I never knew how to do nothin'. I couldn't even stay in the army. I got eye trouble and they sent me home after eight months. The horseroom was the longest steady job I ever had."

"Something'll turn up," I said.

"Yeah? Where? I could always get a buck around Broadway but now there ain't no Broadway."

Yeah.

Put a star on Billy's Broadway.

I drank the beer Billy bought me, drank it in silent communion with his unexpected confession. Billy—who had been inhaling money for years in bowling alleys, pool rooms, and card games—was he unemployable? Was he really a man who "never knew how to do nothin' "? It's true Billy found straight jobs laughable, that he left as many as he was fired from, once even calling the foreman of a machine-shop paint gang a moron for presiding over such labor. Liberated by such words, Billy invariably wended his way back to the cocoon of Broadway, within whose bounds existed the only truly usable form of life; or so Billy liked to believe.

I was making a decision about telling him my own tribulations when the door opened and Buffalo Johnny Rizzo walked in, a fashion plate in blue seersucker suit and white Panama hat with a band that matched his suit. He stood in the doorway, hands in his coat pockets, looked us all over, opened his coat and took a pistol from his belt, then fired two shots at his most favored target: Morty Pappas's crotch, which was forked east toward Broadway, from whence Johnny was just arriving.

Billy saw it all happening and so did I, but Billy acted, lifting his cane from its dangle on bar's edge into a vivid upthrust and sending Johnny's pistol flying, but not before Johnny got off two shots. Morty fell from his bar stool with a crumpling plaster thud, his crotch intact but one bullet hitting his good leg, and the other lodging in the neck of the stuffed cow over the back bar, victim yet again of inept shooters.

Sport quickly retrieved the flown pistol and Johnny just as quickly moved toward the aging Sport to get it back and try again for Morty's gender. Billy and I both stepped between the two men, and Sport, still a formidable figure with the arms and fists of the light heavyweight he had once been, said only, "Better get outa here, John."

Buffalo Johnny, his failed plan sinking him into the throes of social wisdom, looked then at the fallen and bleeding Morty; and he smiled.

"Boom-boom, fucker," he said. "Boom-boom. Boom-boom."

And then he went out onto Broadway.

Except for Billy and me, the customers at Sport's saloon exited with sudden purpose after Buffalo Johnny left the premises. Sport drew new beers for us as we gave aid and comfort to Morty Pappas in his hour of pain. Sport then called an ambulance and together Billy and I organized Morty on the floor, propping him with an overcoat someone had left on a hook during the winter. Sport made a pressure pack on the wound with a clean bar towel.

"So, ya bastard, ya saved my life," Morty said to Billy between grimaces of agony.

"Yeah," said Billy. "I figure you're dead you'll never pay me what you owe me."

"You oughta pay him," Sport said, putting a new beer in Morty's grip.

"I'll pay him all right," and Morty put down the beer and reached for his wallet, a hurtful move. "What do I owe you?"

"You know what you owe me," Billy said.

"Six hundred," Morty said.

"That's wages. Plus the bets, three eighty, that's nine eighty."

Morty fumbled with his wallet, took out his cash. "Here. It's all I got with me," he said. He yelped with new pain when he moved. Billy took the money, counted it.

"Count it," said Morty.

"I'm countin'."

"Four hundred, am I right?"

"Three sixty, three eighty, four."

"That wacky bastard Rizzo," Morty said. "They'll lock him up now. Put him in a fucking dungeon."

"If they find him," said Sport.

"He's too stupid to hide out," Morty said. "Stupidest man I ever know. He ain't got the brains God gave a banana."

"He knows somethin'," Sport said. "He knows how to shoot you in the leg."

"How was his broad?" Billy asked.

"She wasn't his broad."

"He thought she was."

"She was hot," Morty said. "Hot for everybody. Gimme his gun."

"Whataya gonna do with it?" Sport asked.

"Give it to the cops."

"I didn't call the cops," Sport said.

"They'll turn up at the hospital."

"Cops'll want witnesses," Billy said. "You got any?"

"You saw," Morty said.

"Who, me?" Billy said.

"Who's your friend there?" Morty said, looking at me.

"I never saw him before," Billy said.

"What's your name, bud?"

"Bud," I said.

"All I can remember is my money," Billy said.

"I was out in the kitchen when it happened," Sport said.

"You bastards."

"Pay the man, Morty," Sport said.

"I got no more cash," Morty said. "You come to the game, Billy, I'll back you for what I owe you." He turned to Sport. "He comes to the game I'll back him for what I owe him."

"You on the level?" asked Billy.

"Would I lie at a time like this?"

"You only lie when you move your lips. Where you playin'?"

"Tuesday eight o'clock, Win Castle's house."

"Win Castle, the insurance guy?"

"He asked me to run a game for him. He likes to play but he needs players. You play pretty good."

"You'll back me?" Billy asked.

"Up to what I owe you," Morty said.

"Here's the ambulance," Sport said.

After they packed Morty off to the hospital I told Billy, "You get me into that card game and I'll make sure you get your money from Morty." Then I explained my talent with cards to him, the first time I ever told anybody about it. Giselle knew I gambled but she didn't know there was no risk involved, that I could cut aces and deal anybody anything. I told Billy how I'd practiced for months in front of the mirror until I could no longer see myself dealing seconds, or bottom cards, and that now it was second nature. Billy was mesmerized. He never expected this out of me.

"They shoot guys they catch doin' that," Billy said.

"They shoot guys anyway. Haven't you noticed?"

"You really good? You know I can spot cheaters."

"Come over to the house I'll show you. I can't show you in public."

When we got to Colonie Street Billy was vigorously aloof, refused to look at anything in the parlor in a way that would give the thing significance. He came here only when he was obliged to, and left as soon as possible. Now he let his gaze fall on the chandeliers, and sketches, and ancestor paintings, the framed old photos, dried flowers, the bric-a-brac on the mantel, the ancient furniture, the threadbare rugs, and the rest of the antique elegance, and it was all dead to him. He sat in the leather chair by the window where Peter always sat to watch the traffic on Colonie Street, took a sip of the beer I gave him, and then I told him, "You look like your father."

"They always told me that," he said.

"I met him just once, in 1934, when your grandmother died.

I have some old photos of him upstairs. He's in a baseball uniform, playing with Chattanooga in the Southern League."

"He managed that team," Billy said.

"I know. You want to see the pictures?"

"It don't matter," Billy said. "I know what he looked like."

"He looks very young. My father did a sketch from one of them, a good sketch. In the dining room."

"Never mind that stuff. Your father wouldn't let him in this joint when he came home in '34."

"That's not how it was," I said.

"Just get the cards," said Billy, and I knew we'd come back to Francis before long. Billy was intimidated by the house, by the memories of his father's exile from it after his marriage to Annie Farrell, and by his inexact knowledge of Francis's peculiar visit here when Kathryn died. But here he was, on deck for the family luncheon with the lawyer that would take place in another hour or so. My father, when we organized this luncheon, thought it essential that Billy be present to hear whatever was going to be said, even if he didn't care about any of it.

The gathering had to do with money, but Peter was tight-lipped about specifics. He knew he was seriously ill and he was putting what was left of his life in order, the way I had put his *Malachi Suite* in order (with the Leica I'd given Giselle in Germany, and which she gave back to me when I undertook the job), numbering and photographing the hundreds of sketches, watercolors, and oils that my father was obsessively creating, and which had sprawled chaotically in all the upstairs rooms until I put everything into categories.

Peter did not consider the *Malachi Suite* finished, and I wasn't sure he ever would. Two days ago he had asked me to hang one of the oils over the dining-room table, the first time he'd exhibited any of the work anywhere in the house outside his studio. It was the painting he called *Banishing the Demons,* and it showed Malachi

43

and his co-conspirator, Crip Devlin, shooing invisible demons out of Malachi's cottage, with five others, including a woman in bed, as terrorized witnesses. It is a mysterious and eerie painting, but Peter gave me no explanation of why he wanted it on the dining-room wall.

"Where's your old man now?" Billy asked me.

"Upstairs sleeping," I said. "He gets up at dawn, works till he drops, then goes back to bed."

"Another screwball in the family."

"Without a doubt. You gettin' hungry?"

"In a while."

"We'll have lunch. Molly is bringing food, and Giselle's due in on the noon train. You never met Giselle, did you?"

"I heard about her. I seen that stuff she did about your father in a magazine."

"She'll be here. So will Peg."

"What's happening?"

"A get-together."

"I'll get outa your hair," Billy said.

"Not at all. You stick around. You should be here."

"Who says I should?"

"I do."

"You wanna show me your card tricks, is that it?"

"Right," I said, and I found the cards in a cabinet and we went to the dining-room table, site of two notable crises in the life of Billy's father; and I wondered if Billy knew anything about the day Francis fell into the china closet. Billy took a long look at the sketch Peter had done of Francis and then we sat down with the cards. When I started to shuffle the deck I realized Billy was the only man I trusted totally in this life. After he confessed to me that he never knew how to do nothin', I felt bonded to him, and to his father, in a way that seemed new to me; and as I performed for him with the cards, I knew I was going to tell him about my nosedive in Germany. I dealt us both a hand of blackjack.

"Was that straight or seconds?" I asked him.

"Seconds?"

"Wrong." And I turned up the cards to show him the ordinary cards I'd dealt. Then I dealt again, asked again.

"Straight," he said.

"Wrong again," and I showed him the ace and king I'd dealt myself.

"You're good," he said. "I can't see anything."

"The best ones you never see."

"Why you doin' this shit? You got a brain. You don't hafta cheat cards."

"You're right, Billy," I said. "I don't have to cheat at cards. But it's a talent I acquired early, the way you learned how to play pool when you were in short pants. We tend to use our talents, don't we? We also tend to follow our demons. We'll do anything to gain a little power over life, since none of us know our limits until we're challenged—and that's when the strangeness begins."

Billy just stared at me. He didn't know what I was getting at, but he'd understand. He was uneducated, but he was smart as hell.

"There I was," I said, "a little kid backstage, watching Manfredo organize his magic, putting birds in the hat, rabbits in the armpit, cards up both sleeves. He was a whiz, and I wanted to know his secrets. He'd shoo me away so he could be alone with my mother, but I'd insist on another trick, more know-how, and he'd always give in to get rid of me. By the time I was seven I was learning the key-and-lock trick, and by nine I could deal seconds and read the marked decks Manfredo used in his act. He even taught me how to palm cup-poker dice, control two out of five dice in your hand, but I never liked the game.

"Cards were my game and look where they led me. You knew

I'd gotten into trouble in Germany, but you didn't know I was part of an international currency scam, did you?" Billy looked at me as if he'd never seen me before. I was rising in his esteem: more of a screwball than he thought.

"It all started with an army card game I played in," I said, "first to finance my love affair with Giselle, and then to support our marriage, all of which led me to conclude that there are no rules; that anything can develop out of anything, chaos out of conjugality, madness out of magic . . ."

3

I'll talk now about that game and its consequences, because that's where things started going down. My fellow players were the Captain, Walt Popp (we played at his apartment), Archie Bell, a warrant officer with the worst body odor I'd ever smelled, Herm Jelke, a nasty second-lieutenant runt with a Clark Gable mustache that made him look like a wax dummy, and my kid cousin, Dan Quinn, Peg and George's son, who had written about poker as a sports writer and for which reason the Captain, considering him an expert, invited him.

I'd gotten Quinn into our section after he'd finished basic training in a heavy-weapons company. He was a corporal, the only enlisted man in the poker game, and he played well and honestly and had a good time and lost. I didn't want him playing at all, but there he was.

I won money regularly for months, not a great deal, but enough to handle my scaled-down plan for keeping Giselle dazzled. She and I focused on the restaurants of Frankfurt, all of them within range of my military wages, even the Bruckenkeller and the outdoor café with violins at the Frankfurter Hof. We took day trips to Wiesbaden and Bad Nauheim for the baths and the Spielbanks, where we swam, bathed in steam, and spectated at the roulette and baccarat. We wandered the ruins of Frankfurt and took pictures of

each other standing in the rubble of the opera house, or in somebody's exploded parlor, or on the altar of a church with no roof,
or in Goethe's bedroom, or trying to find Schopenhauer's old digs
in Sachenhausen. I recounted Schopenhauer's argument for Giselle:
that the body is the objectification of the will. Tooth and penis, eye
and vagina, were all created by the needs of the soul, no? Well,
maybe. But Schopenhauer loathed women and called his white poo-
dle Atma, the Soul of the World. I told Giselle she was the soul of
my world, vividly isolating life for me: golden hair with violin, perfect
knees crossed for wild arousal as taxi moves along Hauptwache.
Phantom queen as art object. Clearly an existence such as hers was
not happenstance. Clearly some arcane will had divined this glorious
object in order to reflect what will demanded beauty must become.
Schopenhauer had a point.

"I love the way you talk to me," she said.

In these rapturous days she and I came to understand each
other ever more intimately, finding where our intensities lurked,
how soon boredom enveloped us, and why. Her goal, she said, was
freedom, and she felt free with me.

"I think I want to be with you from now on," she said.

I took kindly to this idea.

"Life traps you," she said. "It trapped my father when the
Gestapo shot him for hiding two Jews. But they didn't kill him;
they just shot him and left him there in the courtyard, and he became
an invalid and made my mother his bedside prisoner for three years,
until he finally died."

"You don't want to be a prisoner," I said.

"I think not."

"Did you love your father?"

"Tremendously. But it was pitiful how my mother withered.
My brothers took her gallery away from her in 1948. She had Pi-
cassos, Van Goghs, Mirós she'd kept hidden all during the war years

and she wouldn't sell them. My brothers couldn't stand that money being there, inaccessible to them."

"You didn't want the money?"

"I wanted my mother to keep everything, but they got the paintings away from her and sold them. And then she died too. A prisoner with no money."

"But she loved your father."

"I suppose she did."

"Then she was a willing prisoner."

"I couldn't say. She did her duty, as you military people say."

I vowed not to become a prisoner. I vowed not to let Giselle become one. I vowed I would have money enough for us to live idyllic lives of love and freedom. I vowed to keep her with me now and tomorrow; always now, always tomorrow. That was my best-laid plan, and the reason I again became a poker player.

I preferred five players to six or seven, for I handled the cards more often. I told my fellow gamesters how great a player I was, how I knew cards. I told them how Nick the Greek, by the third card in a five-card-stud game, could call everybody's hole card, and that I was Nick's spiritual disciple. I intimidated them, and I became the one to beat. When I lost they were buoyant at the braggart's fall. That was my method, of course, putting their money where my mouth was.

I didn't mind keelhauling Popp, who could afford it, or Jelke, who was a schmuck, but I trod lightly with the Captain when I nailed him ("With all due respect for your rank and position, Captain, I must raise you thirty dollars"), for he was angry enough at me already and I didn't want to be sent down to a line company. I had to keep an eye on Quinn's earnestness, and watch over Archie too, but Arch was a sap gambler who didn't mind losing.

The game went on for months and slowly I built a bankroll to finance my addiction to Giselle's joys. We played for scrip, the dollar-equivalent currency the army had used since 1946, but sometimes players used German marks, at the legal rate of four marks to the dollar. The Captain often played with marks, for he was getting fat from his black-market deals. His sisters in Bridgeport sent him huge cartons of tea, coffee, cocoa, and cigarettes, and he'd sell it all to Germans at quadruple his investment. I'd done a bit of that too, but it smacked of grocery clerking, and so I concentrated on the game and sold my scrip winnings for the street price of five marks to the dollar, a modest profit, but the way to go as long as Giselle and I were cultivating rapture on the German economy.

And then Italy loomed, for I'd proposed to Giselle and told her we'd honeymoon in Venice. To do this right I needed dollars, not marks, and I mentioned during the game that because of stateside publicity on military black marketeering, the army was hovering over us all, their gumshoes noting who exchanged how many marks for how many dollars in excess of our monthly wages. I wondered out loud where to change marks for bucks outside army channels.

"I know somebody," Archie said. "Not a very savory character."

"Who is he?" asked the Captain before I could ask.

Archie said his street name was Meister Geld, and that he could be reached through the Rhineland Bar, off Kaiserstrasse near the Hauptbahnhof, an arena of whores, beer halls, and black marketeers. But, said Arch, if you're in uniform they won't let you in. I was ready for that. The uniform was required everywhere in Germany but I'd picked up civilian clothes for traveling, and had also bought a cheap blue German suit, a chalk-stripe double-breasted with ridiculously wide lapels. I'd bought it one size too small so whenever I put it on I ceased looking American and could pass for a working-class German. The suit seemed just right for living anonymously, or hanging out in an off-limits bar, which is what the Rhineland was.

Six years after the surrender Germany remained treacherous, full of entropic hatred. Some of the hate eventually found outlets: packs of GIs breaking fascist heads during binges of vengeance; GIs found face down in the gutter with two broken arms, or floating in the river with a knife in the back, or a slit throat. Too many killings and maimings took place in or near the Rhineland, a watering hole for unreconstructed Nazis, so the MPs put it off limits. A weathered sign in English was tacked to the door of the club:

Dear Mr. G.I. Sorry but you cannot come in.
Tonight is open only to club members.

The Manager

I went in and ordered a schnapps and sat across from a chesty, frizzy-haired woman I took to be a whore. She smiled at me and I smiled back and shook my head no. When the bartender brought my drink I asked him about Meister Geld and he said, "*Nicht verstehen.*" I repeated the question in French and invoked Archie Bell as my contact, but the barman still didn't get me. The woman came to my table and asked in French what I wanted and when I told her she said the barman didn't know anybody by that name but she did, and then in English asked, "What you want with Meister Geld?"

"It has to do with money," I told her.

She made a phone call and came back and said she would take me to him. I drank my schnapps and we went out. It was April in Frankfurt, a sunny day with a bit of a nip to it, and I made a mental note to buy a lighter-weight German suit for the summer.

"You speak bad French," the woman said, taking my arm. "Why not speak you English to the man?"

"I didn't want him to know I was American."

"But you look like American, speak German like American, have American haircut. The man said polite, please leave, American."

I shrugged and wondered was my disguise also transparent to the MPs? I walked with the young woman, who, erect, had a provocative shape and sprightly gait. The phrase "abundantly frolicsome" occurred to me. I asked her how long she'd been a whore and she said she'd worked as a mechanic for the Luftwaffe during the war, now repaired auto engines, and only sometimes worked as a whore.

"Where are we going?" I asked her.

"It does not matter," she said. "He follow us where we go."

"Who does?"

"Meister Geld. He always look to people before he meets. We go here," and she pointed to a café with a window full of seven-layer chocolate cakes, cream tarts, glazed Apfelkuchen, and other ambrosial wonders. She said she loved sweet food and then ordered two kinds of chocolate cake. She was rosencheeked, a characteristic in many German women that I took to be seasonal, or perhaps dietetic. Her face, with very modest makeup, was a map of sensuality, her eyes wizened with what I construed to be sexual wisdom. Her tight sweater covered only unencumbered natural uplift. Was there a reason beyond money that she became a whore?

"Only money," she said. "For money I used to carry a piece of carpet so when I lay down in the ruins to fuck my boys I would not tear my clothes. I made much money but later I am unhappy that I will die in disgrace. Now I want to live only old and please self, so I eat sweet cake. I hungry now. In war days I only sometimes hungry, sometimes whore. Now I always hungry, always whore. Now I live to eat."

I nodded and asked when Meister Geld was coming. She looked in my eye and said, "I know you do not want me, but I always pay for cake."

She opened her blouse and presented her naked breasts to my gaze. They were abundant and firm, underlined below by a long, jagged horizontal scar on her stomach. "Gift from lover," she said, touching the scar. She closed her blouse and stood up.

"I know nobody with name Meister Geld," she said. "It is silly name." Then she left the café.

What was I to make of that? Conned out of two pieces of cake by a sugar whore? Was that all there was to it? I paid the check, and as I left the café, thinking about my next move, a black Mercedes pulled alongside me; and from the rear seat came a greeting.

"Good afternoon, Lieutenant. I have your tidings from Archie Bell," this in very good English from a man in a dark blue leather coat, and a dark suit of color and cut not unlike the suit on my back. The man was corpulent, with the red beard of a Viking warrior. I judged him to be forty.

"Meister Geld?" I asked, and when he smiled and opened the car door I got in beside him.

In my hierarchy of personal demons at the time of the fall, Meister Geld holds a position of eminence. He had been wounded by the weather in December, 1941, on the day the Russians stopped Hitler at Stalingrad. Forty-two degrees below zero, and his left foot froze into the similitude of marble; a frozen foot as good as a bullet in the chest. He ran barefoot in the snow to gain circulation, then stole a felt shoe from a Russian soldier who lay dead in the street, needless of the shod life. He did not steal the Russian's right shoe but kept his own, a piece of cracked leather. His foot of marble recovered in the felt, but his right foot congealed and died inside the sodden leather. Also a hole in his glove cost him his right thumb.

The Meister told me all this when he saw me staring at that peculiar ersatz thumb: an unlikely length of glove-covered hard rubber, tied with a finger-threading thong. And, in the shoe where the front half of his foot used to be, a piece of toe-shaped wood. Why had the Meister not understood his thumb was freezing? Why had he not stolen the Russian's right shoe along with the left? Look to the minor devils of war for answers.

My simple task, to change two thousand marks for dollars, was achieved in the first moments of talking, the Meister excavating from a vast interior coat pocket a leather bag thick with banknotes, and giving me the going street rate of exchange.

"A formidable amount of marks, Lieutenant," the Meister said. "You have been saving your pfennigs."

"Some belong to an associate of mine," I said.

"Archie Bell?"

"No. Archie handles his own."

"So you not only deal in money, you are also a courier for others. And out of uniform. You have the air of the adventurer about you, Lieutenant."

The thought pleased me. I began to think of myself as Orson-at-large, Orson-on-the-town. Other than manipulating cards and a few black-market cigarette sales, I had done very little in life that could be construed as illegal. My moral stance on cards was that it was a survival tactic; also I gave back as much as I stole, although not always to the same citizens. I knew I was an adept, a figure of reasonable power in an unreasonable world, flush now with money, love awaiting at the other end of a taxi ride, Europe at my doorstep, needful only of a weekend or three-day pass to know the glories of civilized empire, including the empires of love, lust, beauty, and freedom (temporal for the moment, but longitude will develop; all things wait on the man who embraces the muse of freedom). And now, as I rode in the Mercedes with an underworld figure of notable dimension, I moved into a realm of possibility that included illegalities permissible to The Man Who Is, always stopping short of what might be considered serious criminality, of course. No need to venture *that* far into a new career.

Meister Geld took me to a small movie theater where we stood in the back and watched a scene from a German melodrama in black and white: A woman in a kitchen backs away from a threatening man and reaches for a knife. Close on the knife, as man of menace, undeterred, comes toward her. She thrusts. Close on knife entering his stomach. He crumples. She backs away, runs out of house. Close on man, dead. He opens eyes, removes knife from his stomach, no wound visible, rises, puts knife in sink, no blood visible on it, opens cabinet, takes down whiskey, pours self a drink, drinks, looks toward door, smiles.

The Meister grew bored and climbed the stairs to a second-floor office beside the windowed projection booth, the office similarly windowed to give access to the screen. The office was cluttered with German movie posters and photographs of naked women. The Meister hung his coat upon a hook, sat in his leather chair, and asked: "Do you like to travel, Lieutenant? May I call you Orson?"

"Travel pleases me. Orson is my name."

"One may make a great deal of money by traveling, especially if one is an American officer like yourself."

"I'm in the mood for money," I said.

"From the black market?"

"Everybody does it."

"The army frowns on it."

"But they do very little to discourage it, especially among officers. My partner in this deal is another officer."

"I can't tell you how it pleases me to hear this," said the Meister. "I sense an alliance of substance."

In agreeing to travel for the Meister, I perceived a change in my attitude toward myself and others. Clearly, I thought and acted faster and with more resolution than other men, knew what others would think before they thought it, knew, for instance, when I caught the Captain biting his nails, and he then guiltily hid his hands, that he was behaving like a recidivist thumbsucker, which is to say an autoeroticist. How swift the demon Orson—or is it Oreson-Whoreson?—faster by a whisker than old Freud devoid.

55

As he listened, the Meister unfolded the tale of his childhood in the war, early soldierhood in the Wehrmacht, surviving the bombings of Frankfurt, aiding in their aftermath (his half a foot then only a stump), putting out fires, carrying wounded to belowground shelters. The boy into man became the peddler who could get anybody anything at a price by the time he was twenty-three. He crossed into the British, French, and Russian zones during the early occupation years with great ease and casualness, owning papers of four nations, fluent in five tongues, and with a sixth sense for survival.

He stole an artificial leg from the hospital where he recuperated, sold the leg to an amputee for two hundred cigarettes, bartered the cigarettes for a live pig, traded the pig to a butcher who supplied the mayor of Darmstadt in exchange for the loan of a Leica and a roll of film, bided his time until he had secretly photographed an American lieutenant colonel in bed with three Fräuleins and a Doberman pinscher, blackmailed the colonel into lending him his automobile, drove to the officers' quarters and cleaned out another colonel's vast hoard of medicine, chocolate, uniforms, military insignia, and whiskey, imposed these gifts on a black marketeer known as the King of Mannheim, and earned himself the right to deal in currency for the King, which was his goal from the outset.

The Meister carried a pistol, which was visible in the crotch of his left arm, and as he dropped references to this killing, that murder attempt, I grew wary of getting thick with his mission, which I had yet to understand. But as he unraveled the operation, I again grew comfortable, because I would be dealing with *legitimate* life: buying money at banks, using legitimate dollars that I could easily have come by legally. I lost my fear and entered into the brilliance of a solvent future, one in which I would crown Giselle the queen of all fortune, and where we would reign as sovereigns of a postmilitary life in the *haut monde*.

The Meister's method was a complex cycle of money in motion. On the street he sold marks to Americans for scrip, turned the scrip into greenbacks through a network of American army associates (like myself) by legal means, buying money orders, for instance; then sent me and others to Switzerland with the greenbacks, where we bought German marks at considerably less than their value in the American sector of Germany. Back in Frankfurt we'd take our cut, and the Meister would then sell the marks for scrip at a profit, turn the scrip into greenbacks, and off we'd go again to Switzerland on our moneycycle.

The danger was minimal. Military personnel underwent baggage inspection at the American zone's exit points, but I had educated luggage and also the inspection of officers was usually perfunctory, for officers are honest—except the Captain, who was a grand thief in his heart, a petty thief in his skin. It was he who owned half the marks I first changed with the Meister, and it was he who saw dollar signs in his dreams after I told him of the Meister's scheme.

What can I say of international currency violation? Not much more than that it's the rape of the system. The Swiss have been fucking the rest of the world with their secret vaults for generations. What the Meister and I did was to join the game.

It would have taken me years to get rich on this arrangement, but I did finance my marriage and honeymoon, did fulfill the vision of Venice as altar and nuptial bed—Giselle and I afloat on the Grand Canal, stroked along in our gondola of desire, knowing that today is tomorrow, and tomorrow is forever, and that we will be in ecstasy, we will be rich and free, and we will manifest our own destiny forever; and not only will we never die, we will not even grow old. That's what I told Giselle the night before we returned to Germany and I was arrested by the Military Police.

They interrogated me for two days, then let me go but confined me to quarters, not as a total prisoner, but restricted to one room and the grounds at headquarters *Kaserne,* where the MPs were billeted.

They escorted me to chow and kept checking to see that I hadn't gone off. Being a married officer, I'd had my own apartment in an army housing project close to the center of the city, but I could no longer live there.

They knew that two other officers were involved with the scam—my boss, the Captain, and Warrant Officer Archie Bell. They transferred Archie to Korea but sent the Captain to cushy London, which led me to believe that the Captain was the informer in the case. Vengeance is my estimate of his motive, since I took Giselle away from him. The police must have known he was dealing, confronted him, and he ratted. And there I was, an upstanding citizen, suddenly thrust among outcasts, thrown into an underworld role for which I had small talent and less stomach.

Right after they checked on me I dressed and left the *Kaserne,* walked past the guard at the gate and took his salute, then caught a taxi to my apartment, where I changed into my German suit. Giselle was at work and I decided not to leave her a note. I've always quested after mystery, and as I studied myself in the mirror I realized that the Orson of the past was gone forever. I took all the cash I had in the drawer, slicked my hair with Vaseline, put on the leather coat I'd bought in emulation of Meister Geld, and stepped out into the Teutonic darkness.

I went looking for the Meister, my first stop being his movie theater. The usher said he'd never heard of anybody named Meister Geld and I realized then that I didn't know the man's real name, or if he had one. The usher grew impatient and said if I wanted to go inside I'd have to buy a ticket, and I did.

A military hanging was in process in the film. A much-decorated warrior wearing his uniform and medals ascends to the gallows, and disdains the hood that covers a hanged man's death gasp. Hangman loops rope around his neck, man proudly strokes his medals, and hangman weeps as trapdoor springs. Close on face of hanged man:

tongue out, eyes all but exploded. Hold on face as eyes return to normal, tongue recedes into mouth. View on military guards weeping as they look at hanging man. Close on hanged man, dead and smiling. His eyes suddenly open, his smile widens, and he laughs.

I went up the stairs toward the office by the projection booth. It was as I remembered, but empty: no movie posters, no naked women, no furniture, telephone, or rug. Meister the Magnificent had made himself disappear. The usher came in behind me, said I shouldn't be up here, and ushered me out into the night. I circled several blocks, looking for the Meister's car, my peregrinations bringing me eventually to the only other place where I knew to look for him, the Rhineland Bar. It was busy with a mix of men and women, whores and pimps, and I sought my main connection, the sugar whore, but without success. I wanted to see her again expose her scar, the validity of which I had begun to doubt. Was it pasted on? Tattooed? Drawn? Would it run during sex, or come off on your stomach? Would *you* then be scarred?

Sitting with a whore who was not as attractive as my sugar whore was a corporal from Seventh Army who had worked as a courier for the Meister. All I knew him by was Bosco, which may or may not have been his name. And when I had this thought I realized how very little I knew about any of my co-conspirators. I'd met Bosco in Switzerland, where the Meister had sent him with greenbacks—to deliver to me—for the purchase of German marks, the Meister reasoning that I was the more suave, more cosmopolitan figure to deal with bankers.

Bosco, now in civilian clothes, looked like a character out of the funny sheets of my childhood, Wash Tubbs. He was short with glasses and wiry black curls all over his head. I found him a mix of regular-army rube and bright, wily skuldugger. We'd had drinks on two occasions and talked of the Meister, about whom Bosco was mysterious but portentous. What I took home from him was that the Meister not only dabbled in the black market, the currency conduit, and the flesh exchange, but Bosco also hinted vaguely at the more exalted intrigue of politics. And that implied politics. Was the Meister an agent? A double agent? A provocateur? A hired political killer? I couldn't say. But that's how the imagination went.

I went over to Tubbs-Bosco and greeted him with a question: "*Zigarette, bitte?*" He smiled, proffered a Lucky Strike, and asked me to sit down beside his whore, whom I glanced at with a certain shock to the system, for she looked very like my Aunt Molly, one of the grand people of the universe. I squinted at her, disbelieving my eyes, and saw she looked not like Molly at all but really like Juliette Levinsky, a blond Jewess of great beauty who was the love of my life for a year or more, and yet this woman was not a blonde; and when I looked at her from another angle she resembled neither Molly nor Juliette. Clearly this face required further scrutiny.

"Have you seen the Meister?" I asked Bosco.

"Not since before the fall," he said.

"Which fall is that?" I asked.

"Fall? Fall? What do you mean fall?" he asked.

"I mean fall. It's what *you* said. Whose fall? What fall are you talking about?"

"That's my question," he said.

"The Meister," I said. "Where is he?"

"I wish I knew the answer to that," Bosco said.

"When did you see him last?"

"Last week. We had a meal together. We both had *Heilbutt vom Rost, mit Toast.*"

"What do I care what you ate? Where is he? He's no longer at the theater."

"He sold the theater," Bosco said.

"*Heilbutt vom Rost* is my favorite German dish," I said. "I had it on Good Friday, with *Krauterbutter.*"

"The Captain threw you in, of course. You knew that."

"I suppose I did," I said.

"I'd have him killed, if I were you," said Bosco.

"That's extreme," I said. "Not my way. I admit I considered it, however."

"The Captain's in London," Bosco said. "Living it up at the Strand and the Ritz, dining out at the Connaught and Brown's Hotel, shopping on Savile Row, screwing all the girls in Soho. And you call yourself a spy?"

"I never call myself a spy," I said.

I looked at the whore. She looked like my third-grade teacher, who used to rub herself against the edge of the desk while lecturing us. A beautiful woman. A tall redhead with long blond hair. She was smitten with me. Followed my career all through grammar school. No one quite like her, the sweet little dolly.

"*Heilbutt vom Rost* I could go for right now," I said.

"I can get it for you half price," Bosco said.

"Where's Geld?" I asked.

"Geld is where you find him," Bosco said. "In the Russian zone by this time, I'd venture."

"You always said he was a double agent."

"No, I merely suggested that he was a provocateur-killer with a finger in every political honeycomb in Europe. Even his toenails are illegal. He's a great man. He's entitled to finger anything or anybody he pleases. You know who the greatest man in the world is?"

"Of course," I said. "Harry Truman. For dropping the bomb on Hiroshima. I never thought so many were undoable."

"And the second-greatest man in the world?"

"The pilot who bombed Hiroshima. Think of the night sweats and headaches he's had to put up with ever since."

"In my opinion," Bosco said, "there's only one war, with intermissions."

"That's how it should be," I said. "Let me tell you the greatest bunch of men I ever came across. The glory brigades who landed

61

at Normandy on D Day, pissy with fear, climbing that fucking cliff into the path of those fortified Nazi cocksuckers, soaked to the soul in blood, brine, sand, and shit, choking with putrescible courage and moving ahead into the goddamn vortex of exploding death. Who's got balls? Those guys had *cojones* big as combat boots. I arrived two weeks after Normandy, a goddamn latecomer, a slacker, a shitassed mewling little yellowbelly, and I got separated from my outfit for three days with no food or water and then I saw a Nazi, a fat fucking killer of women and children and newborn baby Jews, an asswipe shitface murdering swine of a fucking Nazi prick, and I got him in my sights and shot him through the nose. Then somebody shot at me. It was dusk. I couldn't see where the shot came from, but obviously he had a *Kamerad* on his flank, and so I went back into my cave, my earthworks, and laid low. Four days without food by this time, and we piss and moan when we miss a meal. I crawled as far into my earthworks as earth would allow and I heard someone up there walking around calling, "Here, doggie, come on, nice little doggie," all this with a kraut accent, of course, thinking I'd fall for the old dog-biscuit offer. He probably didn't even have a dog biscuit. Then it grew silent and I went dead out, probably slept two more days. It might've been a month. Who knows how long, or how well, or how deeply, or how significantly, or how richly, or how comfortably we sleep when we're fucking asleep? We're asleep, aren't we? So how the hell are we supposed to know how well, or how deeply, and so on? But to get to the point—are you with me?"

"Dogfood," said Bosco.

"Good," I said. "So I came up from the earthworks, crawling out like some goddamn creature of the substructure, some toad of the underground river, some snake of the primeval slime, some cockroach from the cooling ooze of creation. I came up and looked out into the sky and saw it was fucking dawn or fucking twilight, what you will. Another fucking crepuscular moment, let's call it.

And I said to myself, it's going to be all fucking right in half an hour. But *what* was going to be all right?"

"There's a question on the floor," Bosco said.

"Exactly," I said. "What is it?"

"Crepuscularity," he said.

"Of course. So I surveyed the scene as best I could and saw that the Nazi I'd shot through the nose was still there in the distance. I had a perfect vision of how he'd fallen, how his helmet went up on the right ear, how the blood coursed down his ex-nose into his mouth, et cetera. I listened for any telltale sign of that sly fucker with the goddamned dog biscuits and I stayed put but made de-marcative notations in my brain of what lay between that Nazi son of a bitch and myself, what approximate distance I had to traverse, for I had already decided, with a form of self-defense made known to me by every cell in my body, that if I did not eat within several minutes I would die.

"I have no stomach for death, especially my own, and so I calculated the hectares, the rods, and the metrical leftovers between the Nazi and me, and I slithered on my belly like a lizard up from the putrid slush, the foul paste, the vomitous phlegm of a slop-jar swamp, and in time I reached my target, of whose freshness I was assured, unless I had been asleep for several days. I took his helmet off, cut off his head and let it roll, sliced his clothing, ripped him up the middle and cut a split steak off his stomach, turned him over and cut two chops off his buttocks, stuck him in the gizzard and ripped him sideways just so he'd remember me, slithered back to my cave with the steak and chops in his helmet, waited till dark, sealed up the cave so no fire would be seen, cut out a chimney for the smoke, then dined on filet of Nazi, chops on the Rhine, and lived to tell the tale."

The whore looked me in the eye.

"You made steak and chops out of a German soldier?" she inquired.

"Where'd you ever get an idea like that?" I asked her.

"You just said it."

"I wasn't talking to you. Whores should be fucked but not heard."

She signaled to a man at the bar who was a perfect double of the hanged man in the film I'd just seen. Clearly there is a problem of identity here, I thought, as four of the men at the bar (one looking incredibly like the Captain) moved toward our booth and separated me from Bosco and the blond whore forever.

The hanged man came for me, while the other three converged on Bosco. We all went down as they stomped and punched us, then dragged us to our feet with the intention, I presume, of taking us elsewhere to cut our throats. But the hanged man could not resist punching me one more time while one of his fellows held me. Incredibly, I wrenched myself loose, though not in time to escape the punch, which sent me reeling backward toward the front door of the bar.

"You Nazi carbuncle," I said to the hanged man, and the thought came to me then of how well I used the language, and that if I pursued the writing life seriously I might become as successful in one art form as my father had been in another. The sugar whore came into the bar as I was reeling toward the door and when she saw me falling she let me fall, then took me by the arm and raised me up. This interrupted my beating and I gathered my wits and kicked the hanged man in the vicinity of the scrotum, causing him what I'd estimate to be moderate pain. While two thugs dragged Bosco toward the back room, I grabbed the sugar whore by the hand, thinking how our visions, even in dreams, define us, how we are products of the unfathomable unknown, how, for instance, I knew that my sugar whore was not a whore at all but a transpositional figure—Joan of Arc, Kateri Tekakwitha, St. Teresa of Avila—sent to ferry me out of danger; and, knowing this, I realized how superior I was to all in this barroom, how few people in the world could have such a beatific vision in this situation, and I pitied the crowd of them as I grabbed the whore by the wrist and ran with her out into the night streets of Frankfurt, where we would romp as lovers should, I, a prince of this darkness, about to embrace the saintly and virginal lark.

"Will they come after us?" I asked the whore.

"There is time and chance in all things," she said.

When she said that, I could not resist putting my hand under her blouse to touch the scar I had seen, if it was a scar. I felt the ridges of it, let my fingers move upward between her mounds, touch her tips.

"Not here, not now, my darling," she said, her voice a chorus of holy venereal rhapsodies.

We walked on dark streets, in time coming to the banks of the Main River. On an embankment where grass grew amid the rubble, a figure dressed as a bat knelt over a supine blond woman whom I recognized as the librarian I unrequitedly loved for two years during adolescence. What retribution, I thought. How cruelly the Godhead dispenses justice. The librarian was bleeding from several orifices.

"Don't look," my sugar whore said, and so I kissed her opulent mouth and put my hand under her skirt, stroking the naked thigh, the tender curve of her posterior puffs.

"Not here, not now, my darling," she said.

I began to see the pattern: Bosco in the pay of the Meister, who was in the pay of Archie Bell of G-2, the main connection to army intelligence, Archie's cover blown by my arrest and so he is shipped to Korea to bide his time for subsequent return; and the Meister moves to the Russian zone, where he is at home, and will now be viewed as a fugitive from the very structure to which he still gives allegiance; though naturally he is a double-bladed allegiant, without pride, without pity, the pluperfect hypocrite with yet a third face toward any allegiance that offers him the solace of money, or pudenda. There he will sit, accumulating slaves in his icecap of Slavic disorder, a Pharaoh, a Buddha, a slavering three-headed Cerberus, lackey to the gluttonous, glutinous garbagemasters of east and west, the accumulators, the suppurating spawn of cold-war politics, putrid fiscality, and ravenous libido.

"Not here, not now, my darling," said my sweet whore of this magical night as I raised her blouse for a bit of a suck.

We walked hand in hand toward the riverbank and both of us pointed to the same thing in the same instant. There, bobbing on the surface of the water, moving slowly with the current, came Bosco-Tubbs, minus his glasses, his head rotating as it bobbed, and for a moment I thought of leaping in and saving the man from drowning. But then, when he bobbed sideways, I perceived clearly that his head was connected to no body, only skull flesh, with livid neck fractions dangling free, and I knew it was pointless to effect a rescue. He was too far gone.

"Not here, not now, my darling," said my honeypot, pushing my hand away from the concatenation of her thighs.

"May we go somewhere, then," I asked, "and spend a gentle hour together?"

"We can go where my pimp lives," she said. "Would you like that?"

"Is it far?" I asked.

"About ten miles," she said.

"That's a long walk," I said.

"We could take the *Strassenbahn*. You take the number four and then transfer to the number six, then take the yellow bus and transfer to the red bus, and there you are."

"It would be easier if we drove," I said, and with my Swiss knife I slit the canvas top of an old Mercedes convertible parked in front of us, hotwired it as a detective had taught me when I was covering the police beat, and away we went into the rosy-fingered dawn, moving out of fucking crepuscularity at last.

4

It was about an hour before dawn when I called Giselle to tell her I'd stolen a German policeman's car and was with a whore named Gisela at a place called Fritz's Garden of Eden. I said I'd fallen in love with the whore because her name was the German correlative of Giselle. I think this miffed Giselle, but she nevertheless got out of bed and dressed, and as she was going out the door she thought of her camera.

I'd given her that Leica thirty-five-millimeter with wide-angle lens, filters, light meter, the works, infecting her with light and shadow. She had moved well beyond the usual touristy snaps of me at the Köln Cathedral, or the Wurzburg Castle, and had come to think of the camera as her Gift of Eyes, the catalyst for her decision to seek out the images that lurk on the dark side of the soul. She was beginning to verify her life through the lens of her camera, while I, of a different order, was pursuing validation through hallucination, which some have thought to be demonic; and I suppose I have courted the demonic now and again.

I once told Giselle she was the essence of the esemplastic act, for as she was giving me the curl of her tongue at that moment, she would pause to speak love words to me in three languages. That spurred me to lecture her on unity, a Greek derivation. "There is no shortage of unity but much of it is simulated," I began. "The one from the many is no more probable than many from the one. Only sea life propagates in solitude. But here, behold the esemplastic! . . . the unity of twain—I speaking, you comprehending, I delivering, you receiving, I the supplicant, you the benefactor, I me, you thee (I was within her at that moment), and yet we are loving in a way that is neither past, present, nor future, but only conditional: a time zone that is eternally renewable, in flux with mystery, always elusive, and may not even exist."

She didn't know what I was talking about, but here I was, back in that elusive time zone at Fritz's Garden of Eden, melting with the heat of love and penance when she arrived. I was standing on what passed for a bar in this hovel of depravity, holding a glass of red wine, in shirtsleeves, delivering a singsong harangue to my audience, and biting myself on the right hand. Giselle wondered: Is he really biting himself?

"Jesus was the new Adam, and I report to you that I am the new Jesus," I proclaimed, and then bit myself just below the right shoulder, and everybody laughed. A stain spread on my sleeve as I talked. Giselle thought it was a wine stain.

"Jesus descended into hell, and what did he find? He found my wonderful, lascivious mother, my saintly, incestuous father. He found all of you here, this carnival of panders and half-naked whores, scavenger cripples, easy killers, and poxy blind men. He found you burglars and dope fiends, you crutch thieves and condom salesmen, you paralytic beggars and syphilitic hags, all doomed and damned to this malignant pigmire for an eternity of endless and timeless sin."

The audience hooted and whistled its approval of my sermon (Giselle took a photo of them) and I laughed wildly and bit myself on the palm of my left hand, then dripped blood from my thumb into my wineglass (Giselle took another photo, sending the carnival into a new eruption of applause). What she had thought to be wine was obviously my blood, and so she moved closer to where I could see her, and when she came into view I stopped my harangue. I snatched up my coat, jumped down from the bar, sucking my hand and balancing my wine, and I kissed Giselle on the mouth with my bloody lips. She backed off from me and raised her camera.

"I want you to see yourself as you are tonight," she said to me, and I opened both palms outward to show her where I had invested myself with the stigmata of the new Jesus.

"We must leave," I said to her. "They all want to kill me for my coat and suit. And they'll kill both of us for your camera."

"Where is your whore?" she asked me.

"She's working, over there," I said, and I pointed to the table where my Gisela was fellating the handless wrist of a one-eyed beggar whose good hand was somewhere inside her blouse.

Giselle rapidly snapped photos of this, and of the entire mob, as the rabble eyed us and whispered. I broke my wineglass on the floor as we retreated, insuring that at least the barefoot and shoeless freaks would think twice before following us. We fled Fritz's Garden, leaped into the stolen Mercedes, and I then drove through the dark streets and woodlands of Frankfurt, zigzagging at wild speed, turning on two wheels (or so it felt) into a place that seemed to be a wall and certain death but was an alley, as I saw, though Giselle didn't, and she chose to scream.

"Let me out!" she yelled, and I slowed the car.

"Are you bored?" I asked.

"I find death boring. Why should I die because my husband wants to? I find it boring."

"You certainly have style, Giselle, to think about death when we're out for a joy ride."

I reached behind the driver's seat and found a small package, then deftly, with one hand, unwrapped it to reveal four bratwurst afloat in mustard, and I offered the mess to Giselle. She set it on her lap and I then found my bag of *Brötchen,* and while holding the steering wheel with my knee, I split a *Brötchen,* stuffed a brat-wurst into its crevice, hot-dog style, and handed it to her.

"Is this today food?" she asked.

"As I recall."

"How long since you bought this?"

"Time means nothing to me."

"It means everything to bratwurst."

"Trust me."

"Are you in your right mind?"

"No, nor have I ever been. My life is a tissue of delirious memory."

"What do you remember?"

"Peculiar things. The Captain's hypocritical face when we met at MP headquarters after my arrest. The smell of my father's whiskey-and-tobacco breath when I was twelve. The desire to raise a handlebar mustache like my father's. The spasms of bliss that always punctuate the onset of love with you. Why do you ask?"

"I was curious about your saintly incestuous father."

"Did I speak of my saintly incestuous father?"

"You did."

"I can't account for it. May I take off your clothing?"

"It remains to be seen."

"I would stop the car, of course."

"That would improve our chances of not dying a hideous death."

I stopped the car and went for the back of her neck, running one hand under her hair and with the other seeking blouse buttons. She pushed me away and got out and I instantly broke into a fit of sobbing. The sobs choked me, my body twisted, my face fell into the bratwurst, and I made the noises a man makes when he knows that the sorrows of the world are his alone.

Giselle came round to my side of the car and opened my door, tugged me up and out. I stopped sobbing, rubbed the mustard off my face, and she and I walked together on strange streets, she silent, I smiling with what came to be known as my zombie joy. Giselle didn't know where to take me. I'd been a fugitive now for two days and she feared premature contact with the military. My wounds, though not serious to look at, were a problem; for she envisioned the Military Police ignoring them and throwing me into a cell where I'd molder in my zombie coma, oblivious to the venomous impact my own morbid bites might be having on my body.

"You bit yourself, Orson," she said to me.

"Bit yourself," I said.

"Our mouths are full of poison," she said.

"Yes. Pyorrhea. Gingivitis."

"What if you bit your own hand and infused the pyorrhea into your fingers?"

The thought gave me pause. I stopped walking and looked at my hand.

"Pestilential saliva," I said.

"Exactly."

"Bronchial methanes, colonic phosgenes. Can they become agents of involuntary suicide?"

"I think you're getting the idea," she said.

The perception raised my spirits and Giselle decided to call Quinn, who would be getting ready for reveille, the sun now breaking through the final moments of the night. Quinn had access to a Jeep and had contacts with German newspapermen who would know where to get me treated. I liked Quinn and trusted him, which certainly proves something. I didn't know he'd been in love with Giselle since the night she performed on the high stool at the Christmas party. Quinn went to dinner with us now and again and I saw that Giselle found him appealingly innocent.

Quinn did know a doctor, an ex–medical officer in the Wehrmacht who had a small general practice in the suburb of Bonames.

He treated my five bite wounds and then we went back to our apartment, where Giselle bathed me, washed the pomade out of my hair, and dressed me in my uniform so I would surrender as a soldier, not a madman. I was contrite at the surrender, but in a moment of messianic candor I told the officer of the day I had been to hell and back and was now prepared to redeem the world's sins, including his.

They put me in tight security and limited my visitors to Giselle and an army psychiatrist, Dr. Tannen, who saw the condition I was in and transferred me to an army hospital. It became clear I was not fit to stand court martial.

"The man seems to have had a psychotic episode, but I would not say he's psychotic," the doctor told Giselle in my presence, as if I didn't exist. "He is living in the very real world of his second self, where there is always an answer to every riddle. He believes he is a bastard, an unwanted child. He was seriously neglected by mother and father, though he exudes love for them both. He is so insecure that he requires a façade to reduce his anxieties to manageable size; and so every waking moment is an exercise in mendacity, including self-delusion. He has found no career direction, and has completed nothing of significance to himself. He left the publishing world, rejects teaching and journalism, loathes the army, and rues the inertia that allowed him to be called back to active duty. He sees nothing worth doing, including completing the last contorted sentence of his unfinished book, which now ends on a high note of suspense with a comma. He is a man for whom money means nothing, but who has wrapped himself inside a cocoon of such hubris that he centers his life at the apex of the *haut monde,* as he calls it, a world for which there is no equivalent in reality, at least not without much more money than he possesses. Seated beside him at this apex is you, my dear, his goddess of the unattainable moon. He never quite believes you are really his wife, and so, when he reaches out to impose love upon you and you push him away, his moon explodes, and he drops into near catatonia, his so-called zombie condition."

I nodded my agreement, which amused Giselle and also the doctor, who continued: "To finance his life with you in the *haut monde,* he thrust himself into the petty criminality that now threatens his freedom. Further, after his arrest, and being simultaneously abandoned by his mentor in corruption, Meister Geld, a man about whom he knows almost nothing, he is once again the bereft bastard, without parent, without salvation. He is the unredeemable, loathsome, fear-ridden orphan of the storm, living in the shadow of an achieved father, crippled, he thinks, by the genes of unknown ancestors, and now with a future that holds only degradation, possibly of a lifelong order. And so he descended into a neurotic abyss, and resurrected from it in the guise of a blasphemous new Jesus, the only saviour available in this profane world he now inhabits. The army would be as mad as he is to put him on trial in this condition."

The army, citing my illness and my sterling war record, moved me toward a medical discharge. Dr. Tannen also announced that his tour of army duty was at an end, and that he was returning to private practice in Manhattan. This news plunged me into a new depression.

As I slowly came out of it, I was released from the hospital, and at the sunny lunch hour of the third day I told Giselle I wanted to go to the Künstler Klause to dance. It was the first time I'd expressed interest in doing anything since my collapse. The dismissal of the charges buoyed my spirit, but the impending loss of my therapist weighed on me. Giselle asked him if he would take me as a patient back in Manhattan, and he said of course. She then made the private decision to send me home alone.

Eva the belly dancer was one of the Künstler Klause's attractions, along with a magician and a four-piece band—trumpet, drums, violin, and accordion. The club was cheap glitz with a marine decor. Fishnets adorned with anchors, marlin, and mermaids formed the backdrop for the small stage and modest dance floor. The waiter lit the table candle when we sat down, and as we listened to the music I became intensely happy. The club's crowd was mostly Germans, with a few GIs. Quinn came in while the band played.

"I didn't know you were coming," I said to him.

"I asked him," Giselle said. "I thought we'd celebrate your first night out."

"That's a fine idea," I said.

"I'd like some wine," Quinn said to the waiter. "Moselle."

"Moselle all around," I said and I took a fifty-mark note out of my pocket.

"Put your money away," Quinn said.

Quinn looked very young. He had large even teeth and a handsome, crooked smile that gave him a knowing look.

"I saved the good news for our party," Giselle said.

"What good news?" I asked.

"Quinn started it," she said. "He sent my photographs to *Paris Match* and they bought them. Isn't that something?"

"That's quite something," I said. "What photographs?"

"The photos of you at Fritz's Garden, you and all those freaks. The editors said they hadn't seen anything like this out of Germany since the early thirties. Isn't that remarkable?"

"Photos of me?" I said.

"No one could recognize you," she said. "You were biting yourself. *Paris Match* is using four pictures and they have an assignment for me in Berlin."

I said nothing.

"I did very little," Quinn said. "I just put her in touch with the editors. The pictures sold themselves. Not only that, the magazine's art director knew Giselle's mother very well."

"She knew everybody in art," Giselle said.

"So Giselle comes by her talent naturally," Quinn said.

"She's a natural, all right," I said, and I heard that my voice had gone flat.

Eva the belly dancer came on, dancing close to the ringside tables so men could stuff money into her belt, which rode well below the belly.

"I remember her," I said when I saw Eva. "People insulted her at the Christmas party." I took my fifty marks out of my pocket again and tucked it into Eva's belt, just under the navel.

"Orson," Giselle said, grabbing the bill as Eva spun away from us, "you can't afford to give money away."

"We have to pay for insulting the girl."

"I already paid," Giselle said. "Remember?"

"Ah," I said.

"I remember," said Quinn.

We didn't speak until Eva had finished her dance and the magician came on. He gave his patter in German and then did a few simple tricks with handkerchiefs and flowers. Boring. He lit a cigarette and made it disappear to his left, then picked it out of his right pocket, smoked it, threw it, lit, from hand to hand, and smoked it again.

"That's a fake cigarette," I said. "It's not lit. Watch what he does with it."

The magician put the cigarette inside his shirt collar, against his neck.

"He gets rid of the real cigarette right away and holds its smoke in his mouth to use for the fake one," I explained.

"You know all the tricks," Giselle said.

The magician had relaxed me and I asked Giselle to dance. We danced well, like old times.

"I'm sorry I'm sick," I said.

"You're not sick. Things just got to be too much."

"I'll come out of it."

"Dr. Tannen thinks he can help you. He said he'd continue treating you."

"How? By mail?"

"You could go to New York."

"*I* could."

"Yes, you."

"Not you?"

"One of us has to work. I've got another six months in my contract with the government. And now there's the photo assignment in Berlin, and I really want that."

"So. You go your way, I'll go mine."

"Wrong, wrong, wrong. I'll come to New York to stay in six months' time."

I let my arm fall and walked back to the table and drank my wine. "I have no place to live in New York," I said.

"I called your father yesterday and again this morning. He has space in his apartment. He also called your old publisher and they'll give you free-lance editing work."

That widened my smile. "My father," I said. "My father, my father, my father. I could sleep on my father's couch anytime. I could sleep on his couch or I could sleep in his bathtub, in his sink. He'd give me his bed, two beds. Two beds and a couch. Three beds, two tubs, and six couches. Take your choice, boy, the sky's the limit, anything you want. Dad. My dad. Symbiotic, that's what we are. He's the symbi, I'm the otic, together we're a great team. It's just like this place, look around you. Ever see a more homey, more beautiful place? Look at those fishnets, listen to that music, straight from the angels, straight from the fish. And Eva, what a beauty. I thinks she wants to fuck me. Why don't we go back and tell her it's okay? She's such a sweetheart, nobody like her in Germany. Like my mother, a great dancer. Like my father, a great dancer. Dance is the thing, the ticket, the flow, the flood. Dance is manse and pants and ants in your prance. High kicking, watch those shanks and pasterns, folks, watch those hocks and fetlocks. Nothing like mothers and fathers dancing together, nothing like fucking beautiful women who love you and dance so well while they're doing it, wishing it, wishing will make it so, wish you were here, it is true if you think it is, true love, it's true, it's blue, it's you, it's moo moo *mulieribus in aeternitatem, ein Prosit, ein Prosit,* Herr Ober, more Moselle, more Moselle, more Moselle . . ."

And on I went until Giselle leaned over and kissed me with her Judas kiss. Then she and Quinn took me home. Dr. Tannen came the next afternoon and the way to New York was arranged, the charges against me buried in the army's dead-case file, my troop ship awaiting. Quinn and Giselle took the train with me to Bremerhaven and we had a fine time while I said my farewells to Germany. We ate in the first-class dining car, ordered champagne to toast our reunion in six months, and the beginning of our new lives. I put Quinn in charge of Giselle, told him to report anyone who tried to move in on her while I was away. Quinn and I shook hands on it. On the way back to Frankfurt I have no doubt that Quinn, being in charge of Giselle, bought a first-class sleeper for their trip.

BOOK TWO

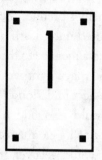

When Kathryn Phelan died in her sleep of oblivion on December 9, 1934, her son and my father, Peter, after twenty-one years of part-time exile from his mother's influence, was at the brink of the success to which his exile had led him. The Greenwich Village gallery that had paid him seventy-five dollars for every painting he created during his first two years in New York, and which doubled that amount after he returned from the Great War, decided that the time for Peter's elevation into the stratosphere of artistic repute and solvency was at hand, and so its owners gave over all their wall space to an exclusive showing of his work. Peter's mother would neither know, nor, if she had known, care, whether Peter ever lifted a paintbrush. But her death, and his one-man show, were benchmarks of liberation for this son and erstwhile artist manqué.

Peter moved to the Village in 1913 after a fight with Kathryn and his sister Sarah over the Daugherty family. Until 1912 the Daughertys had lived in the house next door to the Phelan homestead on Colonie Street; but that year the Daugherty house burned and its only occupant of the moment, Katrina Daugherty, died on the sidewalk in her husband's arms, victim of smoke, anguish, and a prolonged marital emptiness.

One year later, on the anniversary of Katrina's death, her husband, Edward, an established playwright, would celebrate her by staging the play in which their idyllic marriage and blatant infidelities were dissected. This play, *The Flaming Corsage,* would run for two nights on the stage of Albany's premier theater, Harmanus Bleecker Hall, and would be assaulted unto death by critics, and by civil and ecclesiastical authorities, as a menace to the purity of the community. During this fated year the playwright would thus not only lose his wife, and see his lifetime accumulation of papers and unpublished plays incinerated, but would also find his career halted, and his voice silenced at the peak of its eloquence.

Edward Daugherty would recover from this assault, but my father would not, quite. Exposed for a decade and a half to the chorale of vitriol directed against Edward and Katrina Daugherty by his mother and sister—"a family of filth . . . an evil man . . . a low woman . . . a vile slut . . . a corrupter of innocents"—Peter at long last counterattacked, defending Katrina, whom he had coveted as long as he could remember, as a splendid woman, whatever her peccadilloes, and the exemplary mother of his closest friend, Martin Daugherty; also defending Edward as a genuine artist and the only real writer Albany had produced in the new century, this latter defense being as much an expression of the passion for art that lay within Peter's own heart as it was empathy for a friend. Peter stood up from the dining-room table, which gave a view onto the ashes and embers of the Daugherty house, and told his sister she would shrivel from the vinegar in her veins, told his mother she was a wicked-tongued bigot whose poisoned thought came up from the cellars of hell, and told both that he would listen to them not a minute longer.

He climbed the stairs to his bedroom, pulled his steamer trunk out from the attic crawlspace, packed it (as he had planned to do five years earlier, when a similar impulse to escape was on him), filled it with art implements, shirts, socks, and umbrage, hoisted the trunk onto his shoulder, and then in the midst of a rainstorm that would not only drench him to his underwear and the brink of pneumonia, but would precipitate the worst flood in Albany's modern history, walked twelve blocks to Keeler's Hotel for Men Only, at Maiden Lane and Broadway, and there slept his first night of freedom from the matriarchal whipsong.

The next morning his brother Francis, with his son, Billy, came for Peter in a rowboat, and they rowed up the two-foot-deep river that Broadway had become, to Union Station, where Peter boarded the New York train. By prearrangement he settled in at the apartment of Edward Daugherty on MacDougal Street in Greenwich Village, those quarters not used by Edward during the year that he had stayed in Albany to stage his play, and now the temporary home of Edward's son, Martin. It was Martin who had convinced Peter that his future lay here among the artists, writers, political rebels, free-thinkers, unshockable women, and assorted social misfits and fugitives who were amorphously shaping Manhattan's new bohemian order.

Peter found work illustrating reprints of children's editions of James Fenimore Cooper, Jack London, and Mark Twain novels, and used a corner of the Daugherty kitchen to set up his easel to begin anew the work of his life. But it would be a year before he was able to think of himself as a genuine member of the bohemian brigade; for he was incapable of fully representing himself, even to himself, as an artist, that word too imperious for his provincially crippled soul. And so he ate, drank, and worshipped with the Village's Irish working class, into whose midst the bohemians were relentlessly intruding.

These Irish, who looked so very like his neighbors on Arbor Hill in Albany, but were so very unlike them in speech, formed the core of subjects for Peter's early paintings. He sketched people, if they'd let him, then grew brassy enough to carry his sketch pad to the saloon or the park and sketched what he saw, whether the subjects liked it or not. From hundreds of sketches his imagination would let one, then another, single themselves out for delineation in oil, his theme always being: this is evidence that yesterday did exist; this is what yesterday looked like.

One early choice was the face of Claire Purcell, a nineteen-year-old beauty from Brooklyn with a cascade of dark red hair, brown eyes, and milk-white skin, who resembled he knew not whom, but someone; and her curiosity about his sketch of her feeding pigeons in Washington Square on a spring morning in 1914 began the relationship that would dominate both their lives and lead to the erratic romance that would be interrupted first by the Great War (Peter enlisted in 1917, became a wagoner with the 304th Ammunition Train, ferried shells and bullets to troops in the Argonne, was hit at St.-Mihiel by shrapnel which dislodged his helmet, ripped his gas mask in two, and knocked him into a shell hole from which he was eventually carried to the hospital and evacuated back to New York, the episode earning him a disability pension, two medals, and frontal semi-baldness from the gas), and interrupted the second time by my birth out of wedlock in 1924. Claire gave me her own name, Purcell, first name Orson, for Peter would neither marry her nor allow his own name to be given to me, uncertain as he was of the source of my conception.

The man Peter suspected of siring me was Rico Luca, a vaudeville magician known to audiences as Manfredo the Magnificent, who had hired Claire to be his assistant (known to audiences as The Beautiful Belinda) in 1923, two years after Peter moved into the boarding house on Waverly Place run by Claire's widowed mother. Peter and Claire pursued their romance in separate bedrooms until Claire's mother died and they then moved in together, marriage always a subject only for future discussion; for would not marriage negate the freedom that Peter had come to the city to find?

A decade of life amid the pagan romps of *la vie bohème* had conditioned him to think of fidelity as an abstraction out of his past, and yet he practiced it, and expected it from Claire without ever speaking of it. Then, when travel to the vaudeville houses of the eastern seaboard became part of Claire's life as well as the means of support for the boarding house that no longer accepted boarders, and whose upkeep and mortgage were beyond Peter's income, Peter entered into fits of jealousy. He was certain that a woman as comely as Claire, whose body clad in tights was a cause for whistles and hoots from any audience, would be unable to fend off forever the advances of the handsome Manfredo and the stage-door lotharios Peter imagined waiting for her at every whistle stop.

When she announced her pregnancy, Peter broke silence on fidelity and suggested Manfredo as just as likely a parent as himself. Claire first wept at the accusation, then grew furious when Peter persisted, and at last retreated into silence and a separate bedroom; and so the subject was tabled. Jealousy only fattened Peter's passion for Claire, and after some days she acceded to it. In this way they continued their lives until my birth, the cloud of bastardy always hovering even after I grew to resemble childhood tintypes of Peter (and even of his brother Francis), and even though Martin Daugherty insisted Peter had no worries, for clearly I had been made in the Phelan image. Without legal or moral ties, without faith in itself, this anomalous, double-named family persisted, jealousy, wounded love, and fear of error (in Peter) being the bonding elements of a tie that would not break.

Kathryn Phelan died in her sleep, presumably of a stroke, this, her second shock, coming on opening-night-minus-two of Peter's one-man show. For the next several days The Beautiful Belinda would be prancing on the boards somewhere in Boston, and therefore it was decided that I should stay in New York rather than travel with my mother, artistic revelation being more valuable to my young life than backstage privilege. But then arose Peter's dilemma: since the one-man show and its opening could not be canceled on behalf of a corpse, so long-standing had its planning been, would the artist, then, present himself among his works and bask in whatever glory accrues to such presence, or would he return to

Colonie Street to bask in the cold exudation of a dead mother?

Several months after his breach with Kathryn and Sarah in 1913, Peter had returned to the house for fortnightly overnight visits, and also contributed to the support of the family with pittances that increased as his ability to sell paintings improved. The healing of the breach with the family had come so soon after the separation that Peter perceived that rancor was never the cause of the break, but merely the ruse by which he had gained momentum to pursue his art; and in perceiving this he understood that, even in aspiration, art is a way of gaining some measure of control over life.

And so, really, the dilemma's solution was foregone; for kinship maintained the major share of control over Peter's life, and his art, in the end, could only bear witness to this. He would go home.

2

Because of the pre-sale of two of his paintings Peter left Manhattan with four hundred dollars in his pocket, the most money he had ever held in his hand. The dawning of this realization spurred him to show the money to me when we settled into our seats on the Lake Shore Limited out of Grand Central Station.

"Four hundred dollars there, boy," he said. "Feast your eyes. The sky's the limit on this trip."

I took the money into my own hand, counted it (fifties and twenties), tapped it on my knee to even its edges as I would a pack of cards, folded it, felt its thickness and heft.

"It's nice," I said. "What are you going to buy with it?"

"I'm going to buy the light of the world and bring it home," Peter said.

"Where's the light of the world?" I asked.

"I'm not sure," Peter said, "we'll have to go shopping."

I smelled the money, then gave it back to Peter, and we watched the streets of New York whiz by our window.

Peter had small alternative to bringing me with him to the wake, for my mother would be away through the weekend, and there was no one to leave me with (I was ten) except an untrustworthy neighbor. And though the poison thought of bastardy never stopped giving pain to Peter's gizzard, he was also coming to the conclusion that he really might, after all, be my father; and what sort of father would that be if he kept me apart from the blood kin I had never met, especially if he allowed me to miss out on the ultimate silencing of the whipsong?

And so he had packed my bag, and we rode in a taxi from the Village to Grand Central Station, my first taxi, and walked across the heavenly vaulted concourse of the station with its luminous artificial sky that bathed me in awe and wonder. We rode the train north out of the city and along the banks of the great Hudson, monitored the grandness of its waters and natural wonders, and emerged into another vast and dwarfing room, Albany's Union Station, this entire experience creating in my mind a vision of the American way that I would carry throughout my life: capitalism as a room full of rivers and mountains through which you rode in great comfort in the vehicle of your choice, your pockets bulging with money: an acute form of happiness.

Peter, holding me by the hand, walked out of the station and with evident purpose strode two blocks down Broadway from Union Station to the Van Heusen, Charles store (next door to where Keeler's Hotel for Men Only had been until it burned in 1919), the store a source of elegance and social amenity for many years, the place you went when you didn't know the difference between a butter knife and a fish knife (and you had better learn if you wanted your marriage to remain socially solvent), and where Peter suspected he would find the light he meant to bring home to Colonie Street.

He found the familiar face of Rance Redmond, who had been selling silver and china and vases and linens in this store for thirty years, and Peter told him precisely what he wanted: three chandeliers of similar, non-matching styles, plus sufficient wiring to bring power to them from the street; and an electrician to install them.

Rance Redmond, his pince-nez spectacles pressed into use to guide Peter's glance aloft to the broad display of suspended chandeliers, ceiling fixtures, and wall sconces, pointed out the new designs: chrome and milky glass globes of the Art Deco mode; clear glass etched with roses in the Art Nouveau mode; one-time gas chandeliers with a hanging bowl, pendant gasoliers transformed to electroliers.

"No, no gas, not even a memory of gas," Peter said. "We're finished with gas." And he chose the milky Art Deco because it seemed the most modern and also reminded him of Claire's skin in the sunlight, and chose two others that seemed compatible with the first: the Claire fixture to give light in the front parlor, the second for the back parlor, the third for the dining room.

Jotting down their prices in his sales book, Rance Redmond spoke without raising his glance. "I can have these delivered by the middle of next week."

"No, I need them today or it's no sale," Peter said.

"Today?" said Rance, his pince-nez falling to the end of their ribbon. "That's not possible."

"How long would it take to put them in a box?" Peter asked.

"Ten, fifteen minutes, I suppose," said Rance.

"How long would it take to put them in the back of one of your trucks?"

"But that's it, the trucks are busy."

"Then put them in a taxi," Peter said. "I'll pay the fare."

"Well, I suppose we could do . . ."

"And an electrician. There's no power in the house. It's still lit by gaslight."

"Is that right?"

"No, it's not right, but that's how it is, and that's why I want an electrician. Have you got one?"

"I don't know. And there's the power company. You can't just . . ."

"I'll pay the electrician extra. I'll call the power company myself."

Rance's pince-nez had gone on, off, and on again, a manic

measure of his fluster at such impetuousity in these sedate show-rooms, but he handed Peter the telephone and then, clutching the sales slip that totaled more than one hundred and ninety dollars for the three fixtures, the largest sale he had made all week, Rance retreated to the store's artisan quarters to search out an electrician, and found one who approved of extra money; found also a taxi, into whose trunk and front seat two chandelier boxes were placed while Peter and I clambered into the rear seat with the third box. The taxi then led the way to Colonie Street, the electrician fol-lowing in his truck with as much wire as any imagination could reasonably measure, and the two vehicles parked in front of the Phelan house. The power company's man would arrive within two hours.

Only with the death of his mother was Peter now able to challenge the light on Colonie Street. It was fitting that she died in early December, for on these days the exterior world matched the pale gray and sunless interior of the house, night coming on almost as a relief from the daytime sky that hovered over the city like a shroud. Peter remembered his own mood always being depressingly bleak during this time of year, days getting shorter, and darker; and not until January's false spring would the season of desperation begin to fade with the fading of this miasmic light.

He had not known he would buy the chandeliers until he showed me the money on the train; but he knew then that he could buy them and would, for at long last it was time. He knew also that Sarah would fight him on the matter and that Molly and Chick would join him in overriding her objections. But Mama's grip on the past had been released finally, she having been as dark-willed as the biddy of story who refused an indoor, running-water toilet saying, I wouldn't have one of them filthy things in the house, and equally adamantly Kathryn refused electric current as being dia-bolical; and so the children rarely brought visitors home, so shamed were they that their house, its clutter, its mood, even the odor of its air, had slowly become a museum of everybody else's rejected past.

With my help, Peter carried the Claire chandelier up the front stoop, opened the door with his key, and entered with the call, "Peter is here." He and I then carried the boxes into the front parlor as the electrician hauled his gear and wire into the house. Chairs and side tables, including Peter's leather armchair, footstool, pipe stand, and ash tray, had been moved from in front of the parlor's bay window, the designated area for coffin and corpse, though no corpse had occupied it for thirty-nine years, not since Peter's father waked here after stepping backward into the path of a slow-moving locomotive in 1895. Peter cut the twine on one box, put his hand inside, then turned to see his sisters, Sarah and Molly, in the doorway watching him.

"What are you doing?" Sarah asked. "What is that box? Who is this boy, and that man there?"

"The man is our electrician. The boy is my landlady's son, Orson. Orson Purcell. Say hello to Sarah and Molly, Orson. My sisters."

I saw two women who seemed at first to be twins, so alike was their dress: long-sleeved, high-necked white blouses, full dark skirts well below the knee, hair done in the same style: upswept into a soft crown, pinned in a bun at the back of the neck. But in glancing from one to the other I saw nothing else in their faces that matched: Sarah, with dark hair going gray, small round spectacles, hazel eyes very close together, long nose, pursed mouth, cheeks on the verge of sinking: here was plainness; and Molly, the same hazel eyes, but a longer, more finely pointed nose, finer symmetry and greater breadth to the eyes and mouth, and a fullness to the lips, and her hair still a pure, burnished yellow: here was beauty.

"How do you do," I said. "I'm pleased to meet you."

"And we you," said Molly.

"He speaks well," said Sarah.

"His mother is very bright," Peter said, "and he and I do our share of talking, don't we, Orson?"

I nodded and smiled and looked at my father, who seemed so utterly unlike his sisters. There he stood, hand inside the chandelier box, still in his slouch hat and all-weather raincoat, his hair halfway down his neck and as unkempt as his handlebar mustache, his black corduroy shirt and twisted brown tie hanging like the end of a noose, the totality of his clothing, seen in the context of this house, a uniform of rebellion.

Everything I remember from this room on the day the light of the world arrived, had a fragility to it, the Queen Anne table, the china tea set, the French Antique sofa and love seat, the dragonfly lamps, the Louis Quinze chairs that seemed incapable of supporting adults. And the room was dustless: wood and vases and figurines and even the white marble bust of a beautiful woman on her five-foot pedestal (Peter had given it to Julia on her eighteenth birthday) scrubbed and shining, all tables oiled, all brass polished, all floors waxed, all things gleaming, even in that rationed fragment of gray December light that was allowed entry past the mauve drapes.

"What is in that box?" Sarah asked.

Peter, squatting, his right hand still in the box's mysterious interior, suddenly lifted the chandelier into freedom (like a magician, I could say), and with his other hand pulled away the tissue paper that surrounded it, then held it aloft. Presto!

"*Fiat lux!*" Peter said.

"What?"

"Light," said Peter. "Electric light. To replace that monstrosity." And he gestured toward the pendant gasolier on the parlor ceiling. "That ugly thing's been here since before Cleveland was President. Light. New light in this house, Sarah."

"We don't want it," said Sarah.

"How well I know *that,* dear sister. But we *shall* have light on the corpse of our mother, light unlike any that ever found its way into this arcane cave of gloom."

"I love it," said Molly. "It's so pretty. Look at it, Sarah, look how it shines."

"Wait till you see it lit," Peter said.

"If you put it up I'll have it taken down as soon as you leave," Sarah said.

"And if you do that," said Peter, "I shall come home with a club and break every piece of your beloved pottery, glassware, and bric-a-brac. Believe me, Sarah, I am serious."

"You're a villain," she said, and she walked into the hallway and up the front stairs.

"Don't mind," Molly said. "I'll take care of her." And she walked to Peter and kissed his cheek, studied the chandelier which with his right arm Peter still held half aloft. She touched the shining chrome rims around the bottom of the globes, touched the ball-shaped switches under each globe.

"Isn't it beautiful," said Molly.

"It's all of that," Peter said. "It will give us pleasure. It will banish our shame at being the leftover household. It will put a sheen on your beautiful hair, my sweet sister, and it will satisfy my craving to be done with gloom and come home to respectable radiance."

I looked at the light around me for the first time in my life. Never had I considered it a topic worth conflict, or enthusiasm. Light was; and that was that. What more could you ask of it? It was bright or it was dim. You saw in it or you didn't see. If you didn't then it was dark. But now came revelation: that there were gradations, brightness to be measured not only in volume but in value. More brightness was better. Amazing.

The doorbell sounded, a pull-bell ding-dong. Molly answered the bell and accepted from the delivery man a small basket of white and purple flowers, brought them to the back parlor, and set them atop the player piano (which had replaced the Chickering upright that Julia Phelan played until she died; and music in this house died with her until Peter exchanged the Chickering for the player and bought piano rolls of the same songs Julia had played since they were children together).

"I know they're from Mame Bayly," Molly said. "She's always the first flowers at every wake, always a day early. By the time we get to the cemetery they'll be brown and wilted."

The electrician had decided that the emergency installation of the chandeliers could be done only by running wire along the ceiling and through the outer wall to the nearest power pole and Peter said fine, run it anyplace you like, just get the power in here; and took off his coat and hat at last, and with his own tool chest began undoing the gasolier and capping the pipe that carried its gas. Since the death of his father Peter had been the master mechanic of the family, even in absentia, consulted via telephone on every plumbing and structural crisis, consulted when the back porch railing fell off, consulted on retarring the roof and on installing storm windows when the price of gas escalated in 1921.

I explored the downstairs rooms, finding photographs of my father when he was a youth (wearing a high collar and a short tie; he never dressed like that any more), and photos of the women I'd just seen, but as girls in bathing suits (with their mother, was it? mother in black long-sleeved high-necked beachwear that came to her shoetop), and I saw a cut-glass dish full of apples and oranges and grapes on the dining-room table and a photo of twenty men posing beside a locomotive, and over the piano a photo of a woman who looked like the beautiful Molly but more beautiful still, and younger, with her hair parted in the middle, and when Peter saw me looking at it he said, "That's my sister Julia, Orse," and he whispered in my ear, "Don't tell anybody, but she was my love, my favorite," and he said Julia had played the piano. He opened the seat of the piano bench and took out a scroll of paper titled "In the Shade of the Old Apple Tree."

"She played this one all the time. We both loved it."

He opened a sliding door on the piano's upright front and inserted the roll, then sat at the piano and pumped its two pedals with his feet, and the roll moved as I watched with wonderment. Paper that makes music? Then Peter stood up and sat me in his place and told me to put my feet on the pedals and press, first left, then right, and I did and saw the paper move, and then I heard music, saw the keys on the piano depress themselves, and I said, "It's magic!"

"Not quite," said Peter, and I kept pumping and then my feet weakened, as did the song, and Peter said, "Faster, kid, keep a steady rhythm," and after a while the jerkiness went out of the song and out of my feet and the piano made beautiful music again and Peter sang along.

> I can hear the dull buzz of the bee
> In the blossom that you gave to me,
> With a heart that is true,
> I'll be waiting for you
> In the shade of the old apple tree.

"Are you insane? Are you out of your mind?"

It was Sarah, back with her black mood, black skirt, fierce voice, and I stopped my feet and Peter said, "For chrissake, Sarah, I'm invoking Julia. Don't you think she has a right to be here today? Are you going to keep this wake all to yourself?" And Sarah again could not answer, and fled to the kitchen, slamming the door behind her.

"Continue, Orse," Peter said, and, as I moved my feet, music again rose in the rooms where light and death were on the way.

.   .   .

The phone rang in the back parlor and Molly came down the stairs two at a time to answer it, then reported to all auditors that it was Ben Owens, the undertaker, and that he'd be here within the hour; which meant that Mama Kathryn would be returning to the front parlor to be observed in her death rigors, powdered and coiffed as she rarely had been in life; and to me it meant a question mark, for this was my entrance into the world of death.

Again the doorbell sounded and I placed myself in the angular hallway that ran from front door to back parlor, hiding behind wicker filigree decked with clusters of china, people in breeches and wigs and hoopskirts, and dogs and cats with flat bottoms, and then I saw a man with a happy and perfectly round face beneath a bald dome take a cigar out of his mouth and say to Peter, "I got your mother here."

And Peter said, "Bring her in, she's welcome," and from the smiles that followed this exchange and from all the smiles and music and ongoing electrification, I would take home from this day my first impression of death: that it was an occasion for music, levity, light, and love.

"How've you been, Ben?" Peter asked.

"If I was any better," said Ben, looking for a place to rid himself of the half-inch ash on his cigar, "I'd call the doctor to find out what ailed me."

"In the window," Peter said. And Ben swung his portly self toward the street and motioned to the four men standing at the back end of the hearse, and home came Kathryn Phelan, her last visitation in the flesh. Just ahead of her came another man with the catafalque, a four-wheeled accordionesque platform which stretched to meet the space, and upon which Kathryn and her mahogany coffin came to rest, the coffin's closed cover gleaming in the sunlight (no electricity yet).

The onlookers now included Ben Owens, Molly, Sarah, Peter,

me, and the electrician, who was on a ladder in the middle of the room installing the Claire chandelier, and who said, "Do you want this thing workin' tonight?" and Peter said, "We do," and the electrician said, "Well, then, I ain't movin' offa here," and Peter said, "There's no reason you should. Make yourself at home up there," and so they moved the coffin around his ladder and the advent of the light proceeded as planned.

The family then retreated to the back parlor as Peter closed the sliding doors between the two parlors and waved a go-ahead sign to Ben Owens. And then the tableau that I would carry with me created itself: Peter sitting at the piano, Sarah standing by the kitchen door off the back parlor with folded arms, Molly settling into the armless horsehair ladies' chair beside the piano and staring at Peter as he pumped up the music. I, sensing tension and trying desperately to make myself disappear, retreated to a far corner of the back parlor where I could observe the expanse of tradition and sibling relationships manifested in objects and body postures, and listen to love manifested in music, and perceive, I knew not how, the ineffable element that seeped under the closed parlor doors when the coffin was opened; all this fixing forever in me the image of life extended beyond death, and fixing too the precise moment of the advent of the light.

The electricity would insinuate itself from the power line on the outside pole, through the front wall, across the ceiling, and into the chandelier at the electrician's touch, and the onset of the light would startle Ben Owens so that the comb he was using to touch up Kathryn Phelan's hair would fly out of his hand and into a shadowy area behind the coffin, and Ben would say, "Cripes, what was that?"

And light would seep under the sliding doors to be greeted by Peter's remark: "It's here," and the apple-tree song would end as light began.

William Kennedy

The sliding doors would open onto the new tableau of under-taker, electrician, siblings, and myself, all of us staring at the corpse that was so regally resplendent in high-necked magenta burial gown and pink-taffeta-lined coffin, and Mame Bayly's flowers would give sweet fragrance to Kathryn Phelan's final performance—her first under the bright lights—on this very old stage.

3

Chick Phelan took a half-day off from his job as a linotypist in the *Times-Union*'s composing room for this first night of the wake, the night the family and a few select friends would have the corpse all to themselves. He brought home four bottles of Schenley's whiskey and a box of White Owl cigars for the wakegoers, and announced his partial list of bearers for the funeral: the McIlhenny brothers, Dave and Gerry, nephews of Kathryn recently off the boat from County Monaghan; Martin Daugherty, Barney Dillon from across the street, and two more to be recruited at the wake.

Food began to arrive. Betty Simmons sent her teenage son over with a turkey and stuffing; the Ryan sisters baked a ham and made their famous potato salad and delivered it themselves but didn't come in, would wait for the wake's second night, when friends called. Flowers came: six baskets at once, one from George and Peg Quinn and family, plus the pillow of red roses from the Phelan children, with the word "Mama" in gold letters on a ribbon. When the deliveryman handed Peter the last basket of flowers and went back down the stoop to his truck, a figure came limping across the street and stood at the bottom step, hands in pockets, fedora at a rakish tilt, clothes old and grimed, and this man looked upward into Peter's eyes.

"I'll be a son of a bitch," Peter said.

"Ya always have been," the man said with a small smile.

Peter put the flowers aside and extended his hand. "Come on in," he said, and the man came up the three steps, wiped the soles of his shoes on the doormat, and stepped inside, gripping Peter in a strong handshake. Peter closed the door, holding the man's shoulder, and walked him down the hallway to the back parlor where Molly was giving a last-minute dusting to the furniture.

"Say hello to your brother, Moll," Peter said, and she turned and looked and gaped and dropped the feather duster, and then ran four steps and threw her arms around the man and said "Fran," and looked at him again and cried and kissed him and cried some more. "Fran, Fran. We thought you were dead."

"Maybe I am," Francis Phelan said.

He looked toward the front parlor and saw the corpse of his mother in her final silence. He stared at her.

"Go on in," Molly said. "Go in and see her."

"I'll get to it," Francis said, and he continued to stare.

"I'll tell the others you're here," Molly said and she went toward the back stairs.

"How'd you find out?" Peter asked.

Francis broke his stare and looked at Peter. "I was in a lunchroom down in Hudson. Been stayin' down there all fall, pickin' apples, fixin' up trucks for the owner, and this fella next to me gets up and leaves the Albany newspaper. I never do read a damn newspaper, but I pick this one up and turn the page and there's the obit. I look at it and I figure right off this fella left that paper so's I could see that, and I say to myself, Francis, maybe it's time to go back and see people, and I took the next train that come by."

Francis turned back toward the coffin and Peter read the look on his face: The bitch is dead . . . lower away. Francis's honesty in the teeth of unpleasant truth was galling to Peter; always had been.

Hypocrisy is a sometime virtue, but then again fraudulence can stifle, even smother. Hadn't Peter's stifling of his own anger cost him years of bondage to this woman, this house?

"What's goin' through your head?" Peter asked.

"I was just thinkin' how much she missed by bein' the way she was," Francis said. "She didn't really know nothin' about how to live."

"Of course you're the expert on that," Peter said. "You're a walking example."

Francis nodded, looked down at his ragged attire, his shoes with even the uppers falling apart.

"Ain't sayin' I ever figured out how it was done, but I still know more'n she did. I got nothin' against her any more. She done what she hadda do all her life, and somethin' gotta be said for that. I just never bought it, and neither did you."

"Things got better when I moved to New York," Peter said.

"That's what I mean," Francis said. He looked again at his mother, nodded once, that's that, then turned his back to her.

Molly came in carrying two of the six flower baskets from the front hall. She set them on the floor near the head of the coffin.

"Everybody'll be right down," Molly said.

"Who's everybody?" said Francis.

"Sarah and Tommy and Chick. They're all home. Tommy's a bit confused."

"That figures," said Francis.

Francis saw me edge into the room and sit in an empty chair. "Who's the kid?" he asked.

"That's the boy," said Peter. "I mean the son of my landlady. Orson, say hello to a brother of mine, Francis."

"How do you do, sir," I said.

"I don't know how I do sometimes, kid. Nice t' meet ya." And

Francis shook my hand. He looked at his own hands then. "Can I wash up a bit?" he said, and he rubbed his palms together. "Kitchen'd be fine. Still where it used to be?"

"Go upstairs, use the bathroom," Molly said.

"No need," said Francis, and he moved to the kitchen, shoved his coat sleeves upward and soaped his hands with a bar of tan common soap. Molly watched him from the kitchen doorway, handed him a towel.

"Have you had lunch?" she asked.

" 'bout a week ago," Francis said.

"I'll set the table," she said. "There's cold chicken, and Sarah's biscuits."

"Sounds mighty good," Francis said.

He walked to the dining room to take his old place, his back to the famous china closet, facing the window on the yard where Katrina's house had stood before it burned. Now only tall brown stickweeds inhabited the vacant lot where the house had been.

"You're limping," Molly said.

"Bumped my leg a few days ago, but it's gettin' better."

"Let me look at it."

"Nah, it's fine. Nothin' to see, just a black-and-blue mark."

But the leg was more than black and blue. It was a massive infection whose pain had grown, subsided, grown again. Francis had bathed and bandaged it when he could, but the last bandage had come off during his climb onto the train up from Hudson, and he threw the soiled cloth out the freight-car door after he'd settled in. The wound was a legacy from being hit with a club by a flophouse bouncer, and what seemed like a trivial gash turned into an ulceration six inches in length with a purplish center, a gouge from which pus oozed, scaly white skin flaked and peeled, and flesh vanished. Francis now saw the wound as an insurance policy against life. When times got worse, as they seemed to be doing, he would cultivate the pus, the pain, the purplish-white crust of poison. What's a little pain when it leads to the significant exit?

He heard steps on the back stairs, turned to see the feet of his brother Tommy, unmistakable canal boats in soiled white work socks, and behind him brother Chick, wearing galluses on a collarless shirt, a mile-wide smile on his face as he ogled Francis from midstairs.

"Hey, you old bastard," Chick said. "How you doin'?" Chick came down the final two steps, pushed Tommy aside, grabbed Francis's hand, threw an arm around his shoulder, slapped his back. "You old bastard," Chick said. "Where you been?"

"How you, old Chickie pie? You're fat as a pregged-up porker."

"I can't believe this, Francis, I can't believe it. We give up on you years ago. Never thought I'd see your mug in this house again."

"I thought the same thing."

"Franny? Franny?" Tommy stood at Francis's elbow, squinting, focusing. "Franny?"

"Tommy. Howsa boy? Eh? Howsa boy, old Tom-Tom?"

"Franny?"

"It's me, Tom. It's me. You remember me?"

"Sure I remember, Franny. How's things, Franny?"

"Things is like they are, Tom boy." Francis stood and wrapped his arms around Tommy's shoulders, then kissed him on the cheek. "You old horse's ass."

Tommy smiled.

"Horse's ass. Franny. You shouldn't call me a horse's ass."

"Why not?" Francis said. "Where'd a horse be without his ass? Think about it."

"Horse's ass," said Tommy in a whisper to Molly. "Franny called me a horse's ass."

Francis patted Tommy's right cheek and the room glowed with laughter, and the generosity of abuse.

Peter Phelan looked at his brother and saw himself as he wished he'd been but could never be. He saw a man who pursued his own direction freely, even if it led to the gutter and the grave. Francis was a wreck of a man, a lost soul on a dead-end street, yet in him was no deference to the awful finality of his condition. He did not seem to notice it. Nor did he defer to anything else, not the dead mother, or the need to spruce up for the family, or Tommy's softness. And not Peter. Especially not Peter.

"So what's with you, Fran?" Chick asked. "You gonna hang around or are you gonna disappear again?"

"Couldn't quite say," Francis said. "Just came to see the family."

"Will you see Annie and the children?" Molly asked. "Peg sent flowers, you know. I'm sure she and George and Annie will be coming."

"Don't know about that," Francis said. "Don't know what tomorrow'll bring. If I'm here and they come I guess I'll see them."

Francis had been gone from Albany since 1916, a fugitive from wife and children after his infant son, Gerald, fell and died while Francis was changing his diaper. But Francis had been gone from *this* family long before that: from the early days of his marriage to Annie Farrell. No, even before that.

Peter watched Francis chew a chicken leg, saw the lineaments of face, the geometry of gesture that had not significantly changed since childhood. The way he wiped his mouth with his knuckle was the same as when he'd sat in that seat and eaten cold chicken fifty years ago. Nobody ever changes: a truth Peter had embraced with reluctance. Did anybody really *progress,* or was it illusory? (Wasn't the illusion of change another opiate of believers? Carrot and stick, keep 'em movin'.) Certainly it was illusory in art. After twenty-one years Peter has a one-man show whose meaning he fails to comprehend. Perhaps, he concedes, it has no meaning, and I'll always be viewed as a pygmy among men.

But he can claim credit for having brought the light to Colonie Street. Top that, brother. There is serious merit in bringing the light. The better to see you with, *mon frère*. Peter: the voyeur still, where Francis is concerned; and then Peter called up Francis's last days as an intimate member of this household. That was in '98, and Francis was eighteen. They were at the table, Mama and all the children sitting then where they are now (Mama's chair empty now), Sarah then sitting where Papa had sat, for she had become Little Mother, that status her legacy from Papa, who, on his deathbed after the train accident in '95, grasped her hand and said to all in the room, "I don't care who gets married as long as Sarah stays home with her mother." Sarah was twelve then. And hadn't she done admirably well what her father asked in the thirty-nine years since his death? Oh hadn't she?

They were finishing supper that night in '98 when Francis carried his plate to the kitchen and announced that he had to go over and work for Mrs. Daugherty, painting all her interior doors, windows, woodwork, two weeks of evening work at least. Francis then went out the back door and over the fence into the Daugherty back yard. Peter remembered the look on his face as he went: nothing betrayed, no hint that he was off on another mortally sinful expedition into the house of lust.

Lust thrives in the summertime. "Outdoor fucking weather," is how Peter heard Francis phrase it one day in front of Lenahan's grocery with half a dozen other boys, all Peter's elders. Peter did not think Francis had ever experienced any full-scale fucking, outdoors or in. Francis wouldn't risk that, Peter reasoned, wouldn't chance the damnation of his immortal soul for all eternity for the sake of "getting his end wet," another indelible phrase out of Francis. But Peter had gone through his childhood underestimating

105

Francis, misjudging what he would and wouldn't do. Also Peter perceived in Katrina Daugherty a sensual streak possessed by no other woman he had ever known, loved her face and her hair and her body (body so perfectly designed with the proper arcs and upheavals, body he tried to imagine naked so he could draw it and possess its replica long before he'd ever given a thought to a career as an artist).

And so he waited until summer darkness enveloped Colonie Street, then left the baseball field, where after-supper sport was winding down, and fled across gulley and yard to the apple tree whose upper branches gave sanctuary and vantage to a voyeur seeking to verify the secrets of life and lust among the Daughertys. He had once watched Katrina and her husband, who were unaware that the trees had eyes, half disrobe each other, then walk all but naked up the stairs and out of his sight.

For the past three nights he had watched Katrina alone, or Katrina following Francis around the house, sitting by him while he painted, talking, always talking, never touching or kissing or disrobing, nothing, in sum, that would hold truly serious interest for a spy. But his reading of Francis—that this formidable brother would not be spending his nights painting if all that it availed him was money; that he had to have another motive to keep him from the baseball games that went on three blocks away every night of the summer that was not ruined by rain—kept the spy twined among the branches of the apple tree, waiting for the inevitable.

When it came Peter was not expecting its suddenness, even less so what came with it. His eye found Francis on a ladder, painting the window molding in an upstairs bedroom, saw Katrina's silhouette in the next room, visible through translucent curtains and moving with a purpose he could not define, saw her then with full clarity when she entered the room where Francis was, this room curtainless to receive the new paint.

Peter was close enough to throw an apple and hit Francis on the ladder, yet was certain he was concealed by the lush leafing of the tree, certain also that on this moonless night his profound purpose was served: the cultivation of an internal excitement like nothing he had ever known. The excitement came not only when he saw Francis and Katrina together (even if they only talked), but more so when she was wandering through the house and talking to herself, or reading a book as she walked, which, irrationally, excited him most: knowing she was oblivious of him and even of her present moment, seeing her transported as much by a book as he was by her solitary grace.

She came to the window, wrapped in a yellow robe, and with a matching ribbon holding her hair at the back of her neck, and looked out at the night, at Peter, seeing only shadows, and the lights next door, seeing nowhere near as much as Peter could see with his night eyes. She stood by the window and spoke (to him, he tried to believe), said clearly, "For thou alone, like virtue and truth, art best in nakedness . . .

"Francis," she then said.

"Yes, Katrina."

"Thy virgin's girdle now untie . . ."

"What's that, ma'am?"

And she undid the cloth rope that bound her robe about her waist, opened the robe and then let it fall, then undid her ribbon so that her hair fell loose on her shoulders, and Peter for the first time saw her perfect nakedness, thinking: this can't be a dream, this must not be a dream, and then she turned her back to him and presented herself to Francis. The branches of the tree moved and Peter looked down in a fit of fright to see Sarah climbing toward him.

"I've been watching you," she whispered. "What are you looking at?"

"Shhhhh," said Peter, for Sarah's whisper rang through the night like the bells of St. Joseph's Church, and he was sure the naked woman had heard.

But she had not. Katrina pursued her plan, embracing Francis about the knees as he stood on the ladder. Sarah, agile as a monkey, was now beside Peter in the crotch of a branch, and so he could not look at what his eyes wanted so desperately to see. But Sarah could look, staring with her usual inquisition at her brother and the naked Katrina, and so Peter rejoined the vision, watching her take her arms from around Francis's legs and stare up at him as he came down the ladder, then (Sarah unable to restrain a gasp) seeing him kiss her and embrace her naked body. Sarah climbed down the tree then with greater speed than she had climbed up it. She ran off, not toward home but rather, Peter would later learn, toward the church, to seek out the priest and confess in the parish house what she had seen, confessing not her own sin but Francis's, as if his sin were *her* damnation as well as his own.

Peter did not leave the tree and knew Sarah would fault him for this; but he was fearful that this might be his only chance for years to come to witness what it was that people did to each other when they were naked. He saw Katrina unbutton Francis's shirt, then unbuckle his belt, saw her walk again to the window to show her full self to Peter, lean over and pick up her robe and then spread it on the floor, lie on it on her back as Francis, now naked, stood over her, then knelt astraddle her, then finally leaned his full self forward and on top of her into a prolonged kiss.

And thus did Peter Phelan, age eleven, witness with the eye of an artist-to-be the rubrics of profane love. He knew too, for the first time, a nocturnal emission that was not the involuntary product of his dreams; and when that happened to him he began the careful, soundless climb down from the tree, shamed by his spying and the wetness of his underwear (more afraid now of having to explain that wetness than of having to give good reason for peering at people from a tree), and regretting even as his feet touched the ground that he had not continued to watch until there was nothing more to see. He thought of his brother as a figure of awesome courage and achievement—courting damnation by conquering the body of the most beautiful woman in the world—but he also sensed, even in the callowness of his newborn pubescence, that, however much he admired Francis, he would never be able to forgive him for doing this before his eyes. Never.

Sarah had been watching Peter for two days before she decided to follow him to the apple tree. She had seen the oddness of his behavior, erratic, skulking in places he had no reason to be (such as the back yard, looking over the Daugherty fence), and in time she put it together as Peter's secret mission. He was, after all, only a child. But what the child led her to was the shock of her life.

In the infinite judicial wisdom of her Little Motherhood, Sarah, now fifteen, called a meeting of the witnesses and the accused in order to define the future. Clearly capital punishment for Francis was what the heavens screamed aloud for; but Sarah was no vessel for that. All she could do was elevate sin to communal knowledge, spoken of openly in the presence of the sinner (sinners, to be sure, for Peter was not without culpability). So she summoned them to the front steps of St. Joseph's and, wearing the mantilla that the old Spanish nun had given her in school as a prize for her essay on chastity ("the virtue without which even good works are dead"), Sarah defined the terms under which she would allow her brothers to continue living in the same house with her and her mother, and the sainted moron Tommy, and the hapless Chick, and the good sisters, Molly and Julia (who, Sarah knew, had chastity problems of their own, but she chose not to raise them here), and the terms were these: That Francis would confess that he had been living in the occasion of sin by working for Mrs. Daugherty, whose behavior we must somehow reveal without being vulgar. We can never tell our mother that you put your hands on her naked body, how could you do such an awful thing?

"Listen," Francis said, "don't knock it till you tried it," whereupon Sarah ran up the stairs into the church and did not talk to either brother for three days, after which time she raised the issue at the dinner table.

"Mama," Sarah said to all assembled siblings, "Francis has something to tell you."

"No I don't," Francis said.

"You'll tell her or I will," Sarah said.

"I got nothin' to say," Francis said.

"Then Peter will tell," Sarah said.

"Not me," Peter said.

"Will somebody tell me what this is about?" Kathryn Phelan asked. Her other children, Chick, Julia, Molly, and Tommy, looked bewildered at their mother's question.

"It's what Francis is doing," Sarah said. But she could say no more.

"Sarah doesn't think I oughta work for Katrina," Francis said. "I think Sarah oughta mind her own business."

"Why *not* work for her?" Kathryn asked.

"There's more than work going on over there," Sarah said.

"And what might that mean?"

"Are you going to tell her?" Sarah asked Francis.

Francis stared into Sarah's eyes, his face crimson, his mouth a line of rage.

"Well?" said Kathryn.

"She put her arms around him," Sarah said.

"What does that mean?"

"It doesn't mean anything," Francis said.

"Why did she do that?"

"She likes the way I work," Francis said.

"He's lying," Sarah said.

"How do you know?" Kathryn asked. "Did you see her do this?"

"Yes, and so did Peter."

"I don't know what I saw," Peter said.

"Don't lie," Sarah said.

"Everybody's a liar but Sarah," Peter said.

"What were you doing watching over there?" Kathryn asked Sarah.

"I followed Peter. He's the one who was watching."

"You're a lousy rat, Sarah," Peter said. "A real lousy rat."

"Never mind name-calling. I want to know what went on. What is she talking about, Francis?"

"Nothin'. I work for her, that's all. She's a nice person."

"She was naked," Sarah said.

"Naked!" Kathryn said, and she stood up and grabbed Francis by the ear. "What've you been doing, young man?"

Francis stood and jerked his head out of his mother's grip. "I walked into her room when she was dressin'," he said. "It was a mistake."

"He's lying again," Sarah said. "He was painting and she took her robe off and was naked and then she threw her arms around him and he did the same thing to her."

"Is that true?" Kathryn asked, her face inches from Francis.

"She's a little crazy sometimes," Francis said. "She does funny things."

"Taking her clothes off in front of you? You consider that funny?"

"She doesn't know what she's doin' sometimes. But she's really all right."

"He put his arms around her and they kissed for a long time," Sarah said.

"You bitch," Francis said. "You stinkin' little sister bitch."

Kathryn swung her left hand upward and caught Francis under the jaw. The blow knocked him off balance and he fell into the china closet, smashing its glass door, shattering plates, cups, glasses, then falling in a bleeding heap on the floor.

Thirty-six years gone and here he is back again, Peter thought, and there is the china closet, and here we all are (Sarah will come down from her room eventually; she will have to face the reality of his return), and here minus Julia are the non-conspirators, Molly, Chick, Tom-Tom, Orson, the added starter, about the same age I was when all this happened, and Francis, who is no more repentant today of whatever sin than he was when Mama knocked him down with her left hook.

"I thought Sarah was comin' down," Francis said.

"She'll be down," Molly said. "She's getting dressed for tonight."

"You look pretty, Moll. Real, real pretty. You got a beau? Somebody sweet on you?"

Molly put her eyes down to her plate. "Not really," she said.

"How about Sarah? She didn't marry, did she?"

"No," said Molly.

"I ran into Floyd Wagner down in Baltimore. I'm on my way to Georgia and old Floyd, he's a cop now, was gonna arrest me. Then he seen who I was and instead of arrestin' me he bought me a beer and we cut it up about the old days. He said he went out a few times with Sarah."

"That's so," said Molly. "Sarah broke it off."

"So Floyd said."

"Never mind about Floyd Wagner," said Sarah, descending
the back stairs into the room. She was in total mourning, even to
the black combs that held her hair, her dress a high-necked, ankle-
length replica of the recurring dress that Kathryn Phelan had worn
most of her life, always made by the perfect, homemade dressmaker,
Sarah. It was less a mourning garment than a maternal uniform—
black cotton in the summer, black wool in winter—that asserted
that unbelievable resistance to anything that smacked of vanity,
though not even that: of lightness, of elevation. Her children and
relatives had tried to sway her with gifts of floral-patterned dresses,
colored skirts and blouses, but the gifts remained in boxes for years
until finally Kathryn gave them to the Little Sisters of the Poor.

Francis looked at Sarah and retreated in time. Here was the
mother incarnate in Sarah, now fifty-one, a willful duplicate; and
Francis remembered that Sarah had even wanted to call herself Sate
when they were young, because people called their mother Kate;
but Mama would have none of that. Sarah would be Sarah, which
was no hindrance at all to emulation, as this presence now proved;
uncanny resemblance, even to the combing and parting of the hair
and the black-and-white cameo brooch that Kathryn always wore
at her throat.

"Hello, Sarah," Francis said. "How you been?"

"Fine, thank you."

"Good. That's good."

"Sarah looks like Mama," Tommy said.

"I noticed that," Francis said.

"So you're back," Sarah said to Francis. "You're looking well."

"Is that so?" Francis said. "I wouldn'ta said so."

"Francis can be a bearer," Chick said. "I just thought of that.
Then we only need one more."

"Francis won't be here," Sarah said. "Francis isn't staying."

"What?" said Peter.

114

"He's not staying," Sarah said. "He's not a part of this family and hasn't been for over thirty years. Feed him if you like, but that's all he gets out of us."

"Sarah," Molly said, "that's wrong."

"No," said Sarah, "nothing wrong except that he's back among us and I won't have it. Not on the day my mother is waking."

"Right," Francis said. "I seen her wakin'. I seen her dead, and now I see her again, not dead at all. Nothin' changed here since I left the first time, and now I remember why I left. Sarah's got a way of joggin' your memory."

"Sarah doesn't run this house," Peter said.

"Right," Chick said. "Absolutely right. Sarah don't run nobody."

"It's okay," Francis said. "Not a thing anybody's gotta worry about. I'm a travelin' man, and that's all I am. Never counted on anything more than seein' she was really dead. I figure, she's dead, I'm free. Know what I mean, Chickie pie?"

"No."

"What's gone's gone, and I figure, good riddance. She wanted *me* dead is the way I figure it. Ain't that right, Sarah?"

"You were dead for years. You're dead now. Why don't you go live in the cemetery?"

"You know, you turned out just right, Sarah," Francis said. "Just like I knew you would. You ain't got a speck o' the real goods in you. You ain't got one little bit of Papa. You got it all from the other side of the family, all from that Malachi crowd. You're somebody they oughta cut up and figure out, 'cause you ain't hardly human, Sarah."

"You're a tramp, Francis. You were a tramp when you were a child. You and your Katrina."

Francis turned his eyes from Sarah and faced Peter, who could not take his eyes from Francis. Francis smiled, a man in control of his life. Oh yes.

"She remembers Katrina, Pete. Got a memory like a elephant, this sister of ours. You remember Katrina too?"

"Everybody remembers Katrina," Peter said.

"Unforgettable lady," Francis said.

"Don't bring that old filth back in here," Sarah said.

"Filth," Francis said, "that's Sarah's favorite word. Where you'd be without filth I can't even figure, Sarah. You and filth— some double play. Old Floyd Wagner told me how you and him talked about filth all them years ago."

"Make him leave," Sarah said to the entire table.

"Floyd said the last time he saw Sarah . . ."

"Never mind anything Floyd Wagner said," Sarah said.

"Sarah, let him talk," Peter said.

"What about Floyd Wagner?" Chick asked.

"Old Floyd. He came to see Sarah one night and she threatened to stab him with a pair of scissors."

"What?" Molly said.

"It's a lie," Sarah said.

"Floyd said she was afraid he might kiss her and start doin' other filthy stuff, so she snatched up the scissors and told him to keep his distance or she'd stab him in the belly."

"Oh, you foul thing," Sarah said, and she pushed her chair back and walked to the living room.

"Floyd swears it," Francis said (and in the front parlor Sarah, standing beside the corpse of her mother, covered her ears with both hands to fend off Francis's words).

"Floyd said he never did get to kiss Sarah, and after the scissors business he sorta lost interest."

"I think we can change the subject," Peter said.

"Suits me," Francis said.

All eating, all talk at the table stopped. The front door bell changed the mood and, as Molly went to answer it, Chick said,

"That's probably Joe Mahar. He said he'd come early." And Chick too left the table.

Francis drank the last of his tea, popped his last crust of bread into his mouth, and smiled at Peter. "Always great to come back home," he said.

"I got to go to the bathroom," Tommy said, and he went up the back stairs.

"Just you and me, Pete," Francis said, ignoring my presence.

Francis saw Molly, Sarah, and Chick talking to a priest in the living room and he could recognize Joe Mahar, whose name he could never have brought to mind if Chick hadn't mentioned it, but he knew he was the boy who had gone into the seminary with Chick out of high school. Joe had obviously carried it off, but poor Chickie pie came home after three years (the first year Francis played for Chattanooga, blessin' himself every time he came to bat, and them rednecks yellin', "Kill the Irishman," but he kept on blessin' even though he didn't buy that holy stuff no more), and Chick's return plunged Mama into the weeping depths of secularity. No priests in the Phelan family, alas. Mama never to know the glory of having mothered a vicar of Christ.

"I see you got a new ceilin' light," Francis said, looking at the new fixture.

"Installed this afternoon," Peter said. "How do you like it?"

"Nice and ritzy. Who picked it out, you?"

"Orson and I did, didn't we, Orse?" And I nodded.

"You still doin' newspaper work?"

"No, I make my living as an artist, such as it is."

"Artist. By God that's a new one. Artist. What kind of artist?"

"A painter."

"That's good," Francis said. "I like paintin's. My most favorite saloon had a paintin' back of the bar. Only reason I hung out there was to look at it. Eased my mind, you know what I mean?"

"What was it?"

"Birds, mostly," Francis said. "Birds and a naked woman. Reminded me of Katrina." Francis winked at Peter.

Peter laughed, shook his head at Francis's philistinism. But it
was an involuntary and unjustified response, and he knew it; knew
that if Francis had set his mind to it he could have been an artist,
or a writer, or a master mechanic. Anything Francis wanted he could
have had. But of course he never wanted anything. Artist of the
open road. Hero of Whitmanesque America: I hear America
singing—about naked ladies.

"Peter," Molly called, "Father Joe wants to know about the
funeral mass. Just for a minute. He'll be right back, Fran."

Francis nodded at Molly, sweet sister, as Peter went to the
front parlor. Francis looked at me and smiled. Alone at the table
of his youth, made a hemispheric sweep of the room. No need to
look behind him at the china closet. He knew what that looked like.
He saw only one thing in the room that surprised him: the picture
of the family taken at Papa's forty-fifth birthday party at Saratoga
Lake, where they had a camp that summer, the summer of the year
Papa died. There was Francis at fifteen and Tommy as a baby.
Francis would not approach it, not look closely at what was then;
better off without any vision of a past that had led to these days of
isolation from both past and future. Gone. Stay gone. Die. Go live
in the cemetery.

Francis got up and saw that only I was looking at him. He
made a silent shushing motion to me, then found his hat and coat
on the hallway wall hooks, where Molly had hung them. He went
through the kitchen and out the back door into the yard, and I
followed him. We both looked at the dead automobile in the carriage
barn, a 1923 Essex, up on blocks.

"That your car, kid?" he asked me.

"No sir. I'm not old enough to own a car."

"Good," he said. "No point in ownin' that one anyway. Ain't worth nothin'."

Then he smiled, threw me a so-long wave, and walked out of the alley and down Colonie Street, heading toward the railroad tracks, his home away from home.

I watched him limp toward the street and knew he was going away, perhaps forever, which was precocious of me to think that, and which saddened me. He was an imposing figure of a man, even with his dirty clothes. His heavy-duty smile made you like his looks, and like him, even though he was beat up, and kind of old.

Now, reconstituting that moment twenty-four years later, I remember that my sadness at the loss of his presence was the first time I was certain that my father really was Peter, and that I really did belong in this family. I had seen something in the man's face that resembled what I saw in my own face in the mirror: a kindred intangible, something lurking in the eyes, and in that smile, and in the tilt of the head—nothing you could say was genetic, but something you knew you wanted to acknowledge because it was valuable when you saw it, even though you couldn't say what it was. And you didn't want to lose it.

Francis turned at the front of the house and walked out of my sight, and so I then went and sat in the old car. As if to fill the void, a girl my own age entered the alley with a small black mongrel at her heel and came toward the carriage barn. She looked up into the car's front window and saw me pretending to drive.

"Do you know how to make that thing go?" the girl asked.

"I'm not sure," I said.

"Then you shouldn't be up there. You could have an accident."

"This car can't move," I said. "It's on blocks."

The girl looked at the blocks and said, "Oh, I see." And then she opened the door and slid in alongside me. She was obviously a waif, her hair a stringy mess, her plaid jacket held at the throat with a safety pin, her feet in buttonless high-button shoes long out of fashion. But what overrode all things forlorn about her was her eyes: large and black beneath black brows and focused on me with an intensity that I now know was in excess of what her years should allow. This made me uneasy.

"Is that your dog?" I asked.

"He belongs to all of us."

"All of who? Who are you? What are you doing here?"

"I was sent here," she said.

"Who sent you?"

"My people. They want me to find something valuable and bring it back."

"Valuable how?"

"I don't know yet. They didn't tell me."

"Then how do you know where to look?"

"I don't know where to look. I don't know anything about this place. Would you like to help me?"

"Help you look for something you don't know what it is or where it might be?"

"Yes."

I was befuddled, and while I thought about how ridiculous this girl was I saw Molly come out the back door.

"Orson," she called out, "did you see Francis?"

"Yes, ma'am," I said, sticking my head out the car window. "He went out the alley and down the street."

Peter came out then, shoving his arms into his coat, and, when Molly told him what I had said, he too went toward the street.

"I have to go now," I said to the girl.

"I'll go with you," she said, and she left the Essex and followed me, as I was following Peter, the mongrel keeping pace behind us. When I reached the street I saw Peter already at the corner, looking in all directions, then heading toward Downtown on the run. I jogged and the girl jogged beside me.

"Are you looking for the man in the hat and the old clothes?" the girl asked.

"Yes, how did you know?"

"He didn't go that way," she said, pointing toward Peter. "He went straight ahead." And she gestured toward the river.

I stopped and wondered whether the girl was lying, or knew something.

"He was limping," she said.

"All right," I said and I resumed jogging toward the river, wondering what I would do or say if I found Francis when Peter was not around. At least I could say Peter was looking for him, and Molly too.

We ran past an old hospital, empty now, with posters pasted haphazardly on its walls advertising the O. C. Tucker Shows, a carnival with high divers, games, rides, a fortune-teller, a freak show, dancers galore. On another wall I saw a minstrel-show poster of a man in blackface, and yet another of Fredric March in *Death Takes a Holiday*.

"That's where I live," the dark-eyed girl said.

"In that empty building?"

"No, in the carnival."

"Where is it now, around here?"

"Down that street," the girl said, but she did not change her direction to go toward the carnival, if it was there, which I doubted, for this wasn't the right weather for carnivals or circuses. It was too cold for outdoor shows, and it was probably going to snow. I was not cold, because I was running. But I knew when I stopped I would feel chilled beneath my sweat.

"I think he went down there," the girl said, and she ran ahead of me and down a dead-end street, beyond which lay the river flats at the edge of the old Lumber District. To this day I cannot give a cogent reason why I followed this girl, trusted her to lead me to a stranger she had seen only once, if that. But I felt that the child should not be resisted if I wanted to find Francis.

"How do you know he came this way?" I asked.

"I saw him," the girl said.

"You couldn't have seen him down here."

"That's what you say," the girl said.

"I think you're a little crazy," I said, to which the girl did not reply.

We left the paved streets of the city and ran on a dirt path toward the railroad tracks, across fields of weeds and trash, and I saw in the distance half a dozen shacks that hoboes had built, saw people moving near them. Then I saw eight freight cars on a siding, with more people sitting by fires, cooking something.

"That's where I live," the girl said, and Orson saw the lettering painted on the cars: O. C. Tucker Shows.

"You live on the tracks?"

"We're waiting for a steam engine to take us south," the girl said. "We have to bribe the railroad men."

I understood nothing about this girl. We ran in silence and then I saw Francis, walking on the flats with his limp. And how he had gotten this far walking at that speed was a mystery. Perhaps the girl and I had run in a roundabout circle to get here, though I doubted it.

"There he is," I said, and I stopped running.

"You see?" the girl said.

We were uphill from Francis, fifty feet from him, on a slope covered with trees and high weeds, and I then chose to hide myself and watch Francis as he walked north along the tracks, his limp worse than when I last observed him. I felt myself in the presence of hidden meaning (was that what the dark-eyed girl was looking for?) both in my decision to hide, and in the vision that lay before me; and I shivered with the chill of comprehension that something woeful could happen that would mark me. In the presence of malevolence I understood that this is what you feel like before the woeful thing happens. I turned to the girl and saw her petting a kitten, stroking its head with her long, dirty fingernails. Her dog was nowhere to be seen. From the pocket of her jacket a naked doll with only one leg protruded.

"Where did the cat come from?" I asked, and I realized I was whispering.

"He found me," the girl said.

"And the doll?"

"It was in the car that's up on blocks."

"Then it doesn't belong to you."

"No, it's yours," she said.

"I don't own any dolls," I said.

"It's yours because I give it to you," the girl said, and she handed me the one-legged doll, which I assumed had belonged to Molly, or Sarah, or maybe the long-gone Julia. I put the doll on the ground and looked at Francis, who had stopped walking and was staring up the empty track, nothing to be seen. I felt the chill I knew would come. I heard noise to my right, someone walking, and turned to see Peter not thirty feet away, standing still and mostly concealed by bushes, looking toward Francis, who was standing beside the tracks. Peter, the dark-eyed child, and I now formed Francis's silent audience in the weeds.

Francis is a peasant, Peter thought. He is a polar bear. He can live in the snow. He is a walker, look at him walk with that game leg. What did you do to your leg, Francis? Francis is a buzzard, feeding on the dead. Francis is a man who never lost his looks, though he is in terrible condition. You cannot lose the shape of your face unless you lose all your flesh, or stretch it with fat, like Chick. Look at the way Francis wears his hat. In destitution he exudes style. He walks along the gray gravel of the track bed. He casts his shadow on the silverbrown tracks. He walks past a track signal light whose

William Kennedy

color I cannot see. The weeds where he walks are dun, are fawn, are raw umber, khaki, walnut, bronze, and copper. The sky is the color of lead, soon to be the color of mice. Bosch, *The Landloper*. Look, he sits on the switch box. He raises the leg of his trousers that are the color of lampblack gone to smoke, and he studies the wound that makes him limp. Not in my line of sight. He nods and decides that his leg has improved, though it pains him. He wipes sweat from his forehead, or is it an itch? He puts his hat on again, stands and walks, stops. Why walk? He will have to run when the train comes. I can see him running with his gimp gait, clever enough to grab the step-iron of the ladder and hoist himself aloft with arm strength alone, perhaps help from a push with the good leg, and up he goes, off he goes to the future in the noplace village of his nowhere world. Away we go, Francis, away we go, swinging from the rope on the hill, flying down into the mud pond. Do not miss the water or you will break your bones. I never missed. Francis taught me how not to miss. Can he see me now? He cannot, yet he can teach me still. The tracks converge in a distant fusion I cannot see from here, but I see them narrowing, darkening as they go, see the yellow lights of a lumber yard still busy, lights of a house so solitary, lights of a burnt-ocher fire (other fires toward the city, carny fire probably fake like everything about carnies), and I see you, Francis, in your termination, the end of family tie, the beginning of nothing. You will carry on, Francis. You will find a way not to die in the midst of your nothingness. You will feel the triumph of the spirit as you leave us in the dust of your memory, obliterating us as you go toward oblivion and the bottom of the jug. Be of good cheer, Francis. Wondrous drunkenness lurks in your future. You will recover from the awfulness of your finality and you will go on to the heights of the degraded imagination, always conjuring yet another rung on which to hoist yourself to new depths. Francis, in your suite of mice and dun, in the majority of your umberness, in the psychotic melancholy of your spirit, I salute you as my brother

in the death of our history. You more than I knew how to murder
it. You more than I knew how to arrive at the future. In solitude
you are victorious, you son of a bitch, you son of a bitch, will
you never give me peace? Son-of-a-bitch brother, why is it you do
not die?

Francis put his foot on the track and felt the train before he could
see it, or hear it. You goddamn leg, you rotted on me. Let *them*
rot. Why'd it have to be me? Why not? Not a time to go for the
religion. Sin and punishment, all that shit. Don't clutter your head,
Francis. This is tricky. You don't want to miss. One time and we're
on the way. Hey, boys, I'm goin' for a ride. You'd think a guy'd
get an invite to at least sleep over after how the fuck many years.
Too many to count. Don't bother. But they give you a chicken leg,
and don't let the door hit you in the ass on the way out. Woulda
seen Annie if this'd worked, if there was a place to stay and go
slow, do a visit and get the lay of the land, don't push it too fast,
but you can't goddamn go home lookin' like this, goddamn bum
and filthy, got a chicken leg in his belly and that's all he's got. And
lookin' out the window at Katrina. Jesus, lady, you don't go away
easy, do you? Like a life you lived afore you was alive. A way of
lookin' at women that keeps you on the edge of the goddamn
furnace, dangerous, them women, God bless all of 'em, and I don't
leave out none, all welcome here. Welcome, ladies, welcome. Anything I can do for you while you wait? Spurt up a couple of kids?
How'd ya like that, Helen? You can't have no kids. And Bessie,
you were some bundle, I'll tell the world, wouldn't of been the same
world without that month, or was it a week? Who gives a barrel of
shit? Not Francis. Francis knows there's no . . . I see it. I got a
minute. A minute? Less? Step lively, Mr. Francis, 'cause the time
is now. Chicken leg here you go wherever the hell you're goin',
chicken leg step lively step

·   ·   ·

When Papa died, Peter thought, there was Francis with him. Francis had everything.

When Papa died he stepped onto the track backwards and didn't know the engine

When Papa died he took my hand and said to me, "Fear Christ."

When Papa died

Francis is stepping onto the track

I scream.

Peter heard Orson yell and saw him running toward the track yelling a scream that had no words and he saw Francis turn and look not toward him not seeing him running toward the train and saw Francis stop look toward the train as if he and it were making no sound as if he were a figure in a dream where nobody hears what you most desperately want to say as if you were a nonexistent nothing nowhere and he even so steps off the track bed and looks toward you with a surprise in his eye and the train goes by and you can stop all that yelling now, Orson.

Not dead yet, Francis said silently, and he stepped off the track bed and out of the path of the fast freight, and said aloud, "Fuck that nonsense," and heard the screaming then and turned to it, saw the boy and Peter both coming toward him, both. They been watchin', the two of them, that's a pair, the boy can't even talk, just there.

"Are you all right?" Peter asked.

"I ain't been all right in ten years," Francis said. "Whatcha doin' down here, keepin' an eye on me?"

"You left."

"You figured that out."

"You left the house."

"You been watchin'. You both been watchin'."

"No," I said.

"No," Peter said.

"Did ya have a good time?" Francis asked. "How'd I do?"

Only now has it begun to snow

Only now

I remember backing away mumbling scream, I did scream as soon as, and I saw the cat with its front left leg bleeding and the naked doll with both its legs gone now and the dark-eyed child gone

snow now

now snow

BOOK THREE

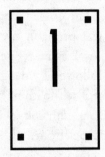

The solidification of my father's reputation prior to this present hour, the summer of 1958, followed the exhibition of the six canvases and many sketches he made during the years 1936–1939, the ostensible subject of these works being the near suicide of Francis as witnessed by the artist, by the cruel waif from the carnival, and by myself.

In the wake of the aborted suicide, Peter fell into an artistic silence that persisted for much of 1935. I judge it to have been induced by his guilt over not confronting Francis when he first saw him beside the tracks, but instead waiting for the train he thought would carry the man away—and thus would Peter have been done with a pesky brother.

But again Francis confounded his sibling, stepped onto the track bed, then stepped off again, a game of perilous hopscotch if there ever was one. And what this did was derange Peter for more than a year, the greatest thing that had happened to him as an artist up to that time.

Artists, of course, use their guilt, their madness, their sexual energy, and anything else that comes their way, to advance the creation of new art. Peter had fared modestly in his one-man show in that winter of 1934, realizing some dollars, plus an enhanced (but still marginal) reputation, and proving to the gallery owners that, although he was perhaps not Matisse, he was worth wall space. But Peter, given this green light, immediately stopped painting, and no one could get him to say why. It all looks crystalline now in retrospect, but it was probably mysterious even to him for a time. His artistic cycle, as I came to perceive it, was this: profound guilt and remorse, followed by delight with the remorse, for it created the mood for art; self-loathing that followed being delighted by remorse; boredom with self-loathing; rumination about self-destruction as an escape from self-loathing; resurgence of boredom when self-destruction is rejected; and resumption of art to be done with boredom, art again being the doorway into the emotional life, the only life that mattered to him as an artist.

He began by objectifying, in segments, the scene as it had been, or as he had transformed it in his memory, revealing all that I saw, even to the cat, the legless doll, and especially the waif, which surprised me. She disappeared after I screamed at Francis, but Peter had already seen her in the weeds, and drew her peering out at the tracks like a vigilant demon, which is how I thought of her in subsequent years.

In one canvas he drew the scene from the perspective of Francis, leaving out the tracks, but including the lumber mill, the switch box, even the Phelan house, which he placed on a hill several blocks to the east and transformed into a place of dark and solitudinous dilapidation. He used the light of dusk, which was when the whole event took place, but he also painted Francis in bright sunlight, a way I never saw him. He painted the carnival boxcars in the background of one work, its people minimally developed, but busy with violence, copulation, voyeurism, and domestic acts around an open fire, none of which I had observed.

Peter learned about Francis's leg wound from me (it was years before we knew how he'd gotten it), for I had seen it at the house when, sitting alone at the table, he wrapped a napkin around it, then tied it with a piece of string he took from his pocket; and I saw it again clearly when he sat on the switch box and raised his pant leg to examine his lease on death, so to speak. Peter created one picture in which only that ghastly leg exists on a realistic plane (precisely the repulsive purplish-and-white scaliness as I had related it to him), vividly detailed in drybrush watercolor. The rest of the scene—the body of the leg's owner, the sky, the tracks—he rendered with a few pencil strokes and a smear of color. The leg in that drawing appeared to be a separate being, an autonomous entity. It did belong to a body, but further specifics of that body remained for other drawings to reveal.

I'm speaking now about the sketches Peter drew (he liked to quote Ingres that drawing included three-quarters of the content of a painting, that it contained everything but the hue), to some of which he added watercolor, most of them in pen or pencil or charcoal, depending on the tool at hand when the impulse came to conjure yet another response to the event. Peter did forty-nine sketches for the three paintings, which may seem sizable, but is really a parsimonious figure when one compares it to the hundreds of sketches he did for the Malachi paintings.

The Itinerant series, as the Francis paintings came to be called, was the realization of Peter's new artistic credo: profligacy in the service of certitude. He came to believe that he could and would paint for decades to come, and that there was no such thing as too much prefatory creation to any given work. But he did not behave in any way that supported his new flirtation with infinity. When he removed himself into silence he also began to ignore his personal life. He grew further estranged from Claire, remote from me (which I didn't understand; and I felt myself guilty for having done something I had perhaps not understood, or did not know I'd done; but I had *not* done anything except witness his fratricidal behavior), his personal hygiene deteriorated to the level of the most unwashed of those bohemians in whose midst he lived; his work as an illustrator, more in demand than ever, became loathsome to him, and he did less and less of it until his income was zero, and in this latter action he achieved a secondary goal: to so impoverish himself that he would henceforth be of no help whatever to Claire in supporting the house.

He was slowly converting himself into a replica of Francis at trackside: man without goal, home, family, or money, with only his wits to keep him alive. This was art imitating life, artist imitating man who lives or dies, who cares? Art be damned. Useless art. Pointless art. Now is the time to live or perish.

In this way Peter moved forward, trying to discover how the phantasm of death is visually framed in this life.

Peter concealed his *Itinerant* series for two years after he completed it, his first manifestation of that reclusive temperament that would continue for another two decades, and sold only three unrelated oil portraits (commissioned) to support himself. His year of silence had obviously fed his imagination, and led to the creative explosion he could no longer keep to himself. Critics who subsequently wrote about these paintings gave Peter his first leg up to fame, finding in them the originality he'd long sought, and either ignoring his earlier work or relegating it to the status of preparatory effort. They did not yet see that all six paintings had their subliminal inspiration in one late masterwork by Hieronymus Bosch, even to the name: *The Peddler,* or *The Tramp,* or *The Landloper,* or *The Prodigal Son,* as the Bosch work was variously called.

I doubt seriously Peter ever knew all the parallels the Bosch would have to his own work, his own family. He was not derivative, always argued against emulating the Impressionists who had so moved the American artistic world in the Armory Show in that year of his arrival in Greenwich Village, 1913. He resisted also the thrust of the Surrealists, who dominated the direction of art in the 1930s and 1940s. Peter used all these schools in his own way, never fitting any categories; yet the critics, after *The Itinerant* series, linked him to proletarian realists and Depression agitators, all of whom he might admire in principle, but would loathe in the particular for their politically partisan cheerleading.

An Interview with Peter Phelan

by Orson Purcell

O: These *Itinerant* paintings, they're all about your brother Francis, are they not?

P: No. They're not about anybody.

O: Who is the tramp figure in the paintings?

P: He's anybody, nobody.

O: How can you tell me this when you and I were watching as Francis stepped onto the tracks and then off?

P: Artistically I never saw that.

O: You're clearly lying, even to yourself.

P: All art is a lie.

O: Is your life a lie as well?

P: More often than not.

O: With the success of this art do you consider yourself an arrived man, a famous artist?

P: I will never arrive, but I'm famous with my friends.

O: Who would they be?

P: They're all dead. Their names no longer matter.

O: What motivated you to paint *The Itinerant* series?

P: The paintings, as they took shape.

O: The paintings inspired themselves?

P: That's how it happens. There is nothing and then there is a painting.

O: But things happen to make you arrive at a certain subject matter.

P: No. Nothing happens ever. There is no subject matter until the painting exists.

O: You are putting the egg before the chicken. What makes the egg?

P: The artist. He is an egg factory. He needs no chickens.

O: No guilt or envy or enmity or smoldering hatred or fratricidal impulse ever inspires art?

P: I know nothing of any of that.

O: You talk as if you have no internal life, as if only an empty canvas exists on which you, a mindless vessel, an automated brush, shape the present. This is the school of unconscious art, is it not?

P: You see this painting here? That's a shoulder bone. This is a chest bone.

O: Whose bones are they?

P: Anybody's. Nobody's.

O: Why did you paint them?

P: Because they emerged.

O: Then they are your bones.

P: Quite possibly.

O: Just as *The Itinerant,* if not Francis, is then you?

P: I wouldn't deny it.

O: What else wouldn't you deny? Paternity, perhaps?

P: What?

O: I say paternity?

P: What?

O: I suggest that all your work and hence all your life is a parody of that subconscious you so revere. I suggest you cannot even take that deepest part of yourself seriously, that you have trouble acknowledging your status as a human being, as well as the status of your son, whom you treat as one of your works of art, disclaiming responsibility for him, allowing him to float free in the universe, devoid even of the right to the intentional fallacy. Your stance suggests you did not even intend him as quantitatively as one of your paintings, and so he remains a happenstance of history. Tell me if I am close.

P: Art is the ideation of an emotion.

O: Do I qualify as a work of art?

P: Art is the ineffable quotient of the work, the element that emerges when the work is done, that does not itself exist in the spatial qualities of the finished painting. Art has no subject matter.

O: Then neither do I.

P: Art is a received conception.

O: I am here, therefore I was conceived.

P: The conception of art has no logic and means nothing.

O: What does mean anything?

P: Art, as it exists.

O: What does art do after it exists?

P: It represents, it symbolizes, it expresses. Art is impact.

O: On whom? On what?

P: On the universe.

O: I doubt it.

P: Doubt is an impaction.

O: As a work of art I doubt myself, my conception, my creation.

P: A theory and its opposite may coexist in the same mind. The unavowed is the companion of mystery.

O: And mystery is the secret of art and paternity.

P: As you like it. As you like it.

I was home from Germany five and a half months in March of 1953 when I visited with my mother for the first time in four years. We talked on the phone from time to time but she consistently put off any meeting. She was no longer Claire Purcell. She now called herself Belinda Love (not legally) and said at last she'd meet me, under the clock in the Biltmore Hotel, because she saw that happen once in a movie.

I arranged my one outing of the week for that day, a visit to the publishing house for which I was editing and tidying up the erotic memoirs of Meriwether Macbeth, an extroverted and pseudonymous bohemian writer and sometime actor who was having a renascent vogue as a result of having been murdered. This was an assignment that seemed doable to me, first because it was the story of a real life lived in Greenwich Village, my environment of the moment; and further because Peter had known Macbeth personally in the 1920s and loathed his acting, his writing, his ideas, his presence, and his odor.

I brought in the heavily edited and rewritten segments of Macbeth's manuscript to my editorial boss, then walked the several blocks to the Biltmore, where I settled onto a bench from which I could monitor all who organized their futures under the clock.

I spotted my mother as soon as she appeared in the lobby, and saw that she looked remarkably like herself of five years gone. She was fifty-eight, looked forty-five, and exuded (with long, scarlet fingernails, spike heels, pillbox hat, wasp waist that was visible beneath her open, form-fitting coat) the aura of World War Two, the era when her independence had reached its apogee, the time of her final separation from Peter, and of her entrance into a solo career as singer and mistress of ceremonies, first in local Albany nightclubs, then with traveling USO shows, and, after the war, in a 52nd Street jazz club where she sang with the resident Dixieland group, her looks and her legs equally as important as her voice, and, ultimately, more interesting. As she walked across the lobby she drew the stares of the bell captain and his minions, then turned the heads of two men waiting to check in. Nearing retirement age and still a dazzler. Mother.

"Hello, darling boy," she said when we embraced beneath the clock, "are you still my darling?"

"Of course, Mother."

"Are you well?"

"I wouldn't go that far."

"Your letters were dreadful. You sounded positively wretched. So discontented, so—what can I say?—scattered."

"Scattered is a good word. I'm nothing if not that."

"Whatever happened to you?"

"I went out of my mind."

"Just like your father."

She signaled to the maître d' of the Palm Court and we were seated under a chandelier, amid the potted plants, the tourists, and the cocktail-hour habitués. She ordered a Manhattan on the rocks, I an orange juice, my alcohol intake at zero level as a way of not compounding my confusion.

"When was Peter out of his mind?" Orson asked.

139

"Ever since I've known him. And I was out of my mind when I took up with the man. I thought he'd have committed suicide by this time. Miraculous he hasn't."

"Why would he commit suicide?"

"I certainly would have if I were him. The man is daft. Bats in his hat."

"He's painting well."

"Yes. He does that. Does he have any money?"

"Not really."

"Of course not. How are you living?"

"Frugally. I'm editing a book for a publisher, and my wife is working."

"Oh yes, and how is she? The dear thing, she couldn't bring herself to join us?"

"She's in Germany."

"There now, a wife who gets around. Something I always wanted to do."

"I remember you got around in vaudeville."

"The east coast. I never went to Europe until the war."

"What are you doing now, Mother? Are you singing?"

"Good Lord, no. I'm running a talent agency."

"For singers?"

"Singers, jugglers, magicians, dancers."

"Strippers?"

"One stripper."

"Tell me her name?"

"Why do you want to know?"

"So if I see her I'll think of you."

"I don't think I like that reason."

"She's your client."

"I was never a stripper."

"You came close with some of your costumes."

"If you're going to attack me I'll leave."

"I don't want you to leave. It's taken five months to get you here."

"I've been traveling."

"It's all right. We mustn't dwell on maternal neglect. Tell me something important. How sure are you that my father is really my father?"

"Absolutely sure."

"Manfredo had nothing to do with me?"

"Nothing."

"He had something to do with you."

"In a moment of weakness. You shouldn't have seen that."

"Where is he now? Do you still see him?"

"Not for fifteen years or more. He has palsy and can't do his stage act any more. He does card tricks at veterans' hospitals."

"Peter thinks Manfredo was the one. Nothing convinces him otherwise."

"It's his way, to be difficult."

"He really is consistent about it."

"I gave up trying to persuade him when you were a baby. Doesn't he see how much you look like him? It's quite uncanny, the resemblance."

"His sister Molly tells him the same thing, but he refuses to believe."

"It's rotten that he still does this to you. And you've grown so handsome since I saw you last. Has he told you about all his women, how he even brought them home? He thought every man I knew was my lover, so that's the way *he* behaved. A severe case of over-compensation if there ever was one. Is he still the king of tarts?"

"He sees several women. I don't think they're tarts."

"Take a closer look."

"It's difficult getting close to him. I never even know what to call him. I've spent my whole life not calling him Dad. I don't think he'd answer if I ever did call him that, or Pa, or Papa. I never call him anything."

"It's so depressing. The Phelans are crazed people. They always have been."

"No more so than the rest of the world."

"Oh yes. There's a history of madmen in their past."

"You're making that up."

"Get your father to tell you about his Uncle Malachi."

"I've heard him mentioned, but not with any specifics. They don't like to dredge him up."

"Of course not. He was certifiable."

"What did he do?"

"I'm not sure. But I know it wasn't good for anybody's health. Ask your father."

She finished her Manhattan and touched a napkin to her lips, and I saw in her face beauty in decline, the artful makeup not quite camouflaging the furrows in her cheeks that I couldn't remember seeing five years ago. She pushed her glass away and reached for her purse.

"I must dash, darling. I have a dinner party."

"You're such a butterfly, Mother. I didn't even get to ask what I wanted to ask you."

"Ask away."

"It's awkward."

"You can ask me anything."

"All right, anything. Can I move in with you? Temporarily. Peter works all hours of the day and night and I can't sleep. It's rather a small apartment."

"Yes it is."

"It truly is cramped."

"I'm sure."

"What do you think?"

"Oh darling, I don't think so. I have any number of people coming through all the time. Friends, clients. You'd hate it."

"Probably so."

"You're far better off with your father."

"Perhaps that's true."

"Do you have money?"

"I can cover the drinks."

She placed on the table, in front of me, a folded one-hundred-dollar bill she had been holding in her hand.

"Buy yourself a shirt. Something stylish."

She stood up, leaned over, and kissed me on the cheek.

"And do get some rest," she said. "You look worn out. Call me some night and we'll have dinner."

Dearest Moonflake,

I write you from the dregs of my father's teapot. We live together in an armed camp, tea leaves and silence being our weapons of choice. Neither of us drink any more, he out of fear that the rivers of hooch he has already drunk have given his muse cirrhosis, I because the jigsaw puzzle that is my life becomes increasingly difficult to solve when several pieces of the puzzle are invisible. You, for instance. It is coming onto six months, your contract is up, and when are you coming back?

I cheer your early photographic success from this remote bleacher seat, slowly gnawing away my own pericardium. I miss you with every inch of that bloody sack and all it contains. I live in a world without love, without affection, without joy. I have taken to sleeping for twenty-four-hour stretches whenever I can manage it, so as to lose a day and bring the time of your arrival closer. The job affords me small pleasure, but it does fill the hours with reading that does not remind me of my own inability to write. The author I'm editing is a micturator of language, a thirsty, leaky puppy whose saving quality is his cautionary, unstated message to me never to write out of the ego; in exalting himself he wets the bed, the floor, the ceiling below.

I finally visited with Mother Belinda this week. We met for a drink and I examined her being and found her in full, late-blooming flower, not that she hadn't bloomed in earlier seasons, but now she has the advantage of looking as young as she was in the previous blossom, quite an achievement for the old girl. She is utterly without guilt concerning her abandoned child and husband. She thinks him mad, and though I would also like to judge him so, I cannot; and she thinks me "scattered," which I suppose is how I appear to those unable to perceive any purpose in my chaos. There is purpose, of course . . .

It was at this point, while pacing the room and considering how to value my chaos on paper, that I went downstairs to the mailbox and found Giselle's letter. It was brief: "Dearest Orson, I'm arriving at Idlewild Tuesday at 3 p.m. on Air France. Please meet me with love. *Life* magazine wants me to work for them. Thrilling?"

The letter was six days in arriving, and so I had only one day to make the apartment livable. My stomach was suddenly full of acid, my head ached, I was weary to the point of collapse, and relentlessly sleepy.

I began moving things, carrying a three-foot standing file of Peter's finished and unfinished canvases out of my bedroom and into his studio, which may once have been a living room. Tubes of paint, boxes of tubes, jars of old brushes, boxes of jars, table sculptures, easels, palettes, rolls of canvas, and half-made frames had also spilled into my room from the studio. Whatever the artist used or created eventually found its way into every corner and closet, onto every table and shelf in the four-room apartment. He threw away nothing.

I swept the floor, washed dirty dishes, hid dirty laundry, stacked my scatter of books and manuscripts, made up the sofa bed on which I slept and which I would give to Giselle for sleeping. I would sleep on the floor, use the throw rug and two blankets as a mattress, it'll be fine; and Giselle and I would reconsummate our marriage on the sofa bed, wide enough for one-on-one, wide enough for love. We'd often done it in more cramped accommodations.

"What the hell happened here?" Peter asked when he entered the apartment, finding his studio devoid of disorder and dustballs, his own bed in the corner of the studio made with fresh pillowcase, clean sheet turned down with precision, blanket tucked army style.

"My wife is coming home," I said.

"Home? You call this home?"

"What else would I call it?"

"Anything but home."

"It's not your home?"

"Colonie Street is my home. This is my studio."

"Your studio is my home. I have no other."

"But it's not your wife's home."

"Home is where I hang my hat and my wife," I said.

"That remains to be seen," Peter said. "You know she can't live here."

"Why not? There's plenty of room."

"There isn't even any room for mice."

"Are you saying she can't come here?"

"No, I'm telling you it won't work. She wouldn't stay here with me hanging around the place all day long. Don't you know anything about women?"

"I like to think I'm an expert on the subject."

"I once thought I knew all about the art world, but I didn't know my ass from third base, as your Uncle Francis used to tell me as often as possible."

"My Uncle Francis?"

"You know who I mean."

"Is he really my uncle?"

"He said I was born innocent and would grow old that way. I believed him for years, but I've outgrown his prophecy. Now I'm beginning to wonder whether I've passed my old condition on to you."

I looked at Peter and saw myself as I might be in thirty-seven years, when I too would be sixty-six. It could be worse. I knew men of fifty-five who seemed decrepit, ready to roll obligingly down that beckoning slope. Peter was still a vigorous figure, grizzled of mien, with his voluminous gray mustache all but minimalizing the crop of gray hair that sat in wavy rumples behind his half-naked forehead; robust of torso, a man who professed no interest in clothing, but who in public wore the uniform of creaseless trousers, formless coats, always with leather elbows (where did he find them?), each coat a perfect fit; an open-collared shirt to which he added a neck scarf for dress occasions; the jaunty fedora which, no matter how many times it wore out from fingering and grease, was always replaceable by a twin from the new age; and two pairs of shoes, one for work, one for walking through the world, the latter less speckled with the artist's paint. In short, the man presented himself as a visual work of art: casual self-portrait achieved without paint or brush.

"She might not stay, but I want to bring her here."

"Bring her, bring her," Peter said. "I'd like to see the look of anybody who'd marry you."

Peter smiled. I examined the smile to evaluate its meaning. Was it a real smile? It looked like a real smile. I decided to return it with a smile of my own.

Son?

Dad?

The bright light of the day had cheered me all the way to Idlewild Airport, spring only a day old but the brilliant white clouds racing ahead of my step, even so. I felt the fire of the equinox in my chest, a sign of certainty: Orson Purcell, no longer an equivocator. I saw Giselle coming toward me from a distance, hatless in her beige suit, frilly white blouse, and high heels designed in heaven, and I quick-stepped toward her, stopped her with an embrace, kissed her with my deprived mouth that was suddenly and ecstatically open and wet. Even when I broke from her I said nothing, only studied all that I had missed for so long, reinventing for future memory her yellow hair, the throne of her eyes, the grand verve of her mouth and smile; and I felt the fire broiling my heart with love and love and love. Love is the goddamnedest thing, isn't it? The oil of all human machinery. And I owned an oil well, didn't I? Separation would be bearable if it always ended with rapture of this order.

I retrieved her one suitcase (the rest of her baggage would arrive later) while she went to the ladies' room; then we quickly reunited and resumed our exotic obeisance to unspoken love. So much to say, no need to say it. In the taxi I stopped staring at her only long enough to kiss her, and then I realized she was naked beneath her skirt, which buttoned down the front. I stared at the gap between two buttons that offered me a fragmented vision of her not-very-secret hair, reached over and undid the button that allowed expanded vision, and I put my hand on her.

"Did you travel from Europe this way?"

"Only from the ladies' room." She kissed me and whispered into my ear: "I've been with you for twenty minutes. When are you going to fuck me?"

I immediately undid more of her buttons and parted her skirt to each side: curtain going up at the majestic theater of lust. I loosened my own clothing, shifted and slid her lengthwise on the seat and maneuvered myself between her open and upraised legs. The cab driver screeched his brakes, pulled off into the breakdown lane of Grand Central Parkway.

"That's enough of that," the driver said. "You wanna behave like a couple of dogs, get out on the highway and do it, but not in my cab."

I saw a crucified Jesus dangling from the driver's rearview mirror, and a statue of the virgin glued to the top of the dashboard. The first time in my life I try to make love in a taxi, and the driver turns out to be a secret agent for the pope.

"This is my wife," I said. "I haven't seen her in six months. It's her first time in this country."

"I don't care if she's your long-lost mother. Not in my cab."

Giselle was sitting up, buttoning up, and I tucked in my shirt. The driver pulled back onto the parkway and turned on the radio. Bing Crosby came through singing "Bewitched, Bothered and Bewildered."

"I'm overcome by irony and chagrin," I told the driver. "If I were you, I wouldn't expect a big tip."

"Just what's on the meter, buddy. I don't take tips from creeps like you."

Condemned by taxi drivers. A new low in moral history. I took Giselle's hand in mine and put them both between the opening in her skirt, then covered her lap with my topcoat. Clandestinely, I found the passage to the Indies, stroked it as passionately as a digit would allow, and made my wife sigh with some pleasure. Life has never been easy for immigrants.

I directed the cab to my father's apartment, and Giselle was barely inside when she told Peter Phelan, "I must photograph you."

"What for?" asked Peter.

"Because you cry out to be photographed. Has anybody ever done a portrait of you in this studio?"

"Never."

"I'm surprised."

"You're naïve. I'm not important enough to be photographed."

"I disagree," said Giselle. "I love the paintings of yours I've seen. I like them better than some of Matisse. I took photos of him a month ago in Paris. He was a charmer."

"Orson," said Peter, "I know why you like this girl. Her lies are as beautiful as she is. How did you convince her to marry you?"

"He didn't convince me," Giselle said. "He *wooed* me, and carried me away to Never-Never Land."

"You still hang out there?" Peter asked.

Giselle looked at me. "I don't know, do we? Don't answer that."

"Why not answer?" Peter asked.

"I want to talk about Matisse," Giselle said. She opened her camera bag, took out her Rolleiflex, and looped its strap around her neck.

"I'm struck that you know Matisse," Peter said.

"When I went to see him he was in his pajamas. I fell in love with his beard."

"He says light is the future of all art," Peter said. "I thought that was pretty obvious, but he must understand darkness in some new way or he wouldn't think that was an original idea."

"The only thing I understand is photographic light. I once heard a lecturer say that without light there is no photography. How's that for obvious?"

"I avoid lectures on art," Peter said. "It's like trying to ice-skate in warm mud."

"Orson," Giselle said, "I'm falling in love with your father."

"Gee," I said, "that's swell."

Peter leaned on the table and stared at Giselle. She focused her camera, snapped his picture.

"Orson," she said, "stand alongside your father."

"Father in a manner of speaking," I said.

"However," said Giselle. "Just move in closer."

I so moved, and there then came into being the first photograph ever taken of Peter Phelan and Orson Purcell together. In the photo, it was later said by some who saw it, the two men bear a family resemblance, though Peter's mustache destroys any possibility of establishing a definitive visual link. My full head of dark brown hair has a torsion comparable to Peter's, and our eyes both shine with the dark brown pupils of the Phelan line. By our clothing we separate themselves: Peter, in his bohemian uniform, I a spruced dude in double-breasted, gold-buttoned black blazer, gray slacks (retrieved that morning from the cleaners) with razor-edge creases, black wing-tips burnished bright, black-and-white-striped shirt with winedark four-in-hand perfectly knotted, and red-and-black silk handkerchief roiled to a perfect breast-pocket flourish as the finishing touch.

I had not groomed myself so well since I'd arrived in New York as a basket case. This was a gift to Giselle: a vision of myself in meticulous sartorial health: no longer the manic, self-biting spiritual minister to the rabble; now Orson Purcell, a man in command of his moves, a surefooted, impeccable presence ready to enter, at a highly civilized level, the great American future, with his beautiful wife beside him.

It had been my plan to use the one hundred dollars my mother gave me to pay for a weekend at the Biltmore with Giselle, maybe even ask for the room where Zelda and Scott Fitzgerald had spent their honeymoon. This was a harebrained idea, but I thought the ambience of that outlandish marriage might serve as a psychic prod to our own marital adventure, which seemed as blasted from the outset as the Fitzgeralds' most vulnerable union.

I broached the matter in the taxi back from the airport, but Giselle had scant memory of Scott or Zelda (though I had lectured her on both).

"Anyway," Giselle said, "we already have an apartment on the West Side. Twelfth floor, three bedrooms, view of the river. A *Life* editor I met in Paris offered it to us. He was doing a story on Matisse the same week I was there to photograph him. You know I knew Matisse when I was little, did I ever tell you that?"

"No," I said. "Lots of things you've never told me."

"The editor's in Japan for two months," Giselle said. "We can have his place for the whole time, if we want it."

Giselle's steamer trunk had arrived ahead of us, and was already inside the apartment. I wanted only to make love to her, immediately and fiercely, but she flew into instant ecstasy at seeing the place, which was a triumph of modern decor, full of paintings, photos, books, mirrors, bizarre masks, pipes, stuffed birds, shards and estrays from around the world, the collections of a cultured traveler, Picasso on one wall, a sketch by Goya on another.

"It's such a stroke of luck he and I were both in Paris at the same time," Giselle said.

"You're good friends, then," I said.

"Well, we're friends."

"He's most generous to you."

"He's like that."

"Are you lovers?"

"Orson, please."

She opened the steamer trunk and rummaged in it for a folder with several dozen photographs. She stood them on end, one by one, on the sofa and on chairs, laid them on the dining-room table for viewing.

"This is why they want me to work for *Life*," she said.

I looked through the photos Giselle had not put on exhibit and found more quality work; also two portraits of one Daniel Quinn, in uniform sitting on a pile of rubble, somewhere in Germany, and in mufti at a sidewalk café, somewhere in Paris? I then looked carefully at each of the photos Giselle had put on display, a photo of my sugar whore fellating the handless man; a photo of me biting myself; a group portrait of the rabble in the Garden of Eden; a photo of a smiling Henri Matisse in pajamas on his sofa, and on the wall above the sofa a painting of a cross-legged nude woman; industrial images—great gears and machines of unfathomable size and function in a German factory; a barge on a German river with a deckhand waving his hat and pissing toward the sky; a woman sitting in a *Bierstube* perhaps exposing herself to two American soldiers; two seated women in their seventies, elegantly garbed, aged beauties both, in tears.

"I can't imagine *Life* running most of these pictures," I said.

"What they like is that I seem to be present when strange things happen. Keep looking." She stood beside me as I looked.

A farmer was plowing his field behind an ox that had been branded with a swastika.

"When *Stars and Stripes* printed this one," Giselle said, "somebody went out to the farmer's place and killed the ox."

To my eye the photos all had quality. The woman had talent for capturing essential instants, for finding the precise moment when the light and the angle of vision allow an act or an object most fully to reveal its meaning or its essence. These pictures set themselves apart from routine photojournalism. Giselle, six months ago an amateur, was suddenly light-years ahead of so many of her peers. Obviously she had a future in photography. Her beauty would open every door of all those male bastions, and this artistic eye, perhaps developed in childhood in her mother's art gallery, would carry her forward from there.

"This looks familiar," I said, and I picked up a photo whose locale I recognized: the stage of the Folies Bergère. A dozen near-naked chorus girls and the beautiful Folies star, Yvonne Menard, were in seeming full-throated song, all watching, at center stage, an American-army corporal kneeling in front of a statuesque beauty in pasties and G-string, the corporal wearing a handlebar mustache for the occasion, his face only inches from the dancer's crotch.

"It looks sillier than I imagined," I said.

"It is quite humiliating," Giselle said.

"How did you arrange it? They never allow photos during the show."

"I told them I was on assignment for *Life,* and they let me do anything I wanted. I did get others but this is all I really was after."

On our first trip to Paris, before we married, I took Giselle to the Folies and, because I was in uniform, an easy object of derision, I was dragooned from the audience onto the stage by the beautiful Yvonne, put in the same situation as this kneeling corporal, then pulled to my feet, drawn to the abundant bosom of the dancer who had stuck the mustache on my lip, twirled about to a few bars of music, and then abandoned as the stage went black and the dancers ran into the wings. Like a blind man, I felt with my foot for the edge of the stage (a six- or eight-foot drop if I missed my footing), found the edge, sat on it with legs dangling, and slid sideways toward the stairs that led to the audience level. I was still sliding when the lights went up and I was discovered in yet another ridiculous position. I scrambled down the stairs and back to Giselle, who was so amused by it all that she kissed me.

"You were very funny," she had said then. "It was just as funny when I took this picture," she said now. "The poor boy didn't even know he was being humiliated. Neither did you, did you, my love?"

"If you have a mustache to put on me, I'll be delighted to be *your* fool and give a repeat performance," I said. "I'll even do it without the mustache. I'll even do it in public."

I embraced her and undid her blouse and knew that she and I would separate, that something fundamental had gone awry and very probably could not be fixed. With her every breath she revealed not only her restlessness but her faithlessness. I saw in her that surge of youth and beauty that was so in love with itself and its imagined possibilities (they must surely be infinite in her imagination now) that even the fetters of marriage were not only ineffectual, they were invisible to the logic of her private mystique.

Standing before me in her uniform of love, she was voluptuosity itself: books could be written about the significance of Giselle in her garments, and how, together, she and they communicated their meaning. The word "noble" came to mind. What could that possibly mean? I backed away and studied her.

"Do you think we married too soon?" I asked.

"I didn't," she said.

"You seem so certain."

"I never make a wrong decision on things like that."

"Are there any other things like that?"

"I know what I want," she said.

"And do you have it?"

"I have some things. I have you."

"Well, that's true enough."

"Why do you want to talk? Why don't you make love to me?"

"I'm discovering what a noble creature you are. I understood it at the baths in Wiesbaden but I didn't put the word to it until now. Noble. How you carried that remarkable body of yours, the way you sliced the water with your arms when you swam, the way you sat beside me on the bench in the steam room with all those other ignoble nudes, enveloped in clouds of love and heat, and you a presence as brilliant as the fire that heated the rocks. The way you looked when you lay on that cot behind the white curtain to take your nap, the erotic extreme of your arched back when I knelt by your cot and offered you worship."

"Nobody ever made me explode the way you did then. If I said skyrockets you'd scold me for using a cliché. How did you learn so much about women?"

"I've been a lifelong student."

"I wonder what will happen to us."

"Everything," I said.

"It must be valuable."

"Very true. If it isn't valuable it's a malaise."

"I don't ever want to do anything to hurt you."

"But you might."

"You really think I might?"

"Giselle is an undiscovered country."

"So is Orson."

"No, not any more."

And this was true. I knew what was in store for me, felt it coming. I decided to blot it out and I pulled Giselle toward me.

3

"I am desperately weary of contemplating the fact that I have nothing to contemplate except the weariness of having nothing to contemplate."

The sentence took form in my mind as I sat in the anteroom of the publishing house that had hired me to edit the pretentious subliterary drivel of Meriwether Macbeth. On the walls of the anteroom, whose floor was covered with a solid dark red carpet suitable for red-carpet authors, I looked up at the giant faces of writers whose work had been published by this house, and who had very probably trod this carpet, or these bare floorboards in pre-carpet days, hauling in their MSS. in briefcase, suitcase, steamer trunk, wheelbarrow, or perhaps only jacket pocket if the author was a poet. A pantheon is what one might call the epiphany on these walls: Dreiser, Dos Passos, Yeats, O'Casey, Wharton, Frost, Joyce, Steinbeck, Sherwood Anderson. We or our work have all passed through these hallowed halls, they say; and we are what hallowed them. Which boards, which carpet will Orson Purcell hallow in his future? None at all should my present frame of mind continue, for I knew that line of mine—I am desperately weary et cetera—was hardly the mind-set required of hallowed hangables.

My editor was in conference but would be available soon, the receptionist said. I waited, trying to conjure a way out of the conversational cul-de-sac any statement about literary weariness would lead me into, and returned always to the magnificence of my morning romp on Giselle's sacred playing fields. But it is written: one may not raise with one's editor such uxorious delight unless one's editor raises the subject first. Better to speak of the upcoming Hemingway, the Salinger phenomenon.

I walked to the rack of books on display for visitors, found the Cassirer, leafed in it, always wanted this. I'll ask Walker for it. I went back to my chair, opened the book randomly to an early page, and read: "No longer can man confront reality immediately; he cannot see it, as it were, face to face. Physical reality seems to recede in proportion as man's symbolic activity advances. Instead of dealing with the things themselves man is in a sense constantly conversing with himself."

A book about me, I thought, and I put it in my pocket. The use of the word "symbolic" brought Malachi to mind, and also what Peter had said when I asked if Malachi really was a madman, as Mother had suggested.

"The man had madness thrust upon him," Peter said. "The poor son of a bitch lost his cow to a Swedish cardsharp in a poker game and never got over it, blamed his wife, the devil, all Swedes, half his relatives. I never got the full story, just hand-me-down snatches from Sarah and what Molly got from Mama. As to madness in the family, Tommy's not all there, but that's not madness. And who's to say I'm not nuts? We're an odd lot, boy, we Phelans."

I wasn't sure whether I was included in that grouping; and I let it pass.

Walker Pettijohn, venerated editor, emerged from his inner sanctum with the durable particularities of his presence in place: the wild crown of the whitest of white hair, the face flushed not from booze but from the wrong shaving cream, the corporate stomach made round by the most exquisite restaurants in New York, the smile known round the world of international publishing, and the genuine glad hand that was as reassuring to me as the very light of day when I awoke at morning. The Pettijohn handshake drew me into the sanctum and toward the boar's nest of books and paper that was the workspace of this legendary discoverer and shaper of American literature.

"Did your wife arrive?" he asked me.

"She did. Indeed."

"And all is well?"

"Let's not get into wellness," I said. "She may go to work for *Life* magazine."

"How fine."

"Yes, perhaps."

"Ah, you're in your gloom still."

"It's gloomy, this life."

"Meriwether Macbeth had a good time all his life."

"All right, we're around to that."

"Are you ready to talk, or should we do this next week? I can wait."

"Now is the time."

"Then what I need is more of that wildness of Meriwether, that silliness, that absurd boyishness that kept him floating in that crazy, artistic, and erotic world of his. Peter Pan de Sade."

"He wasn't really erotic. He was just a satyr."

"Same thing in print."

"No. He's an asshole."

"Of course, that's his charm."

"Assholes are now bookishly charming?"

"This one is. He did whatever came into his head."

"Infantile behavior to be cherished."

"You know what I'm talking about, Orson. Don't get remote. Use that brilliant brain of yours."

"If I were brilliant I wouldn't be dealing with this fool."

"What I want is more of the stupidity of the man's life, the empty nonsense, the ridiculous logic, the romancing of worthless women, the publishing of rotten poetry. I think of that masterpiece you tossed out: 'Naked Titty Proves God Exists.'"

"My life is full of error," I said. "I stand corrected."

"We're not trying to be objective here about poetic values, we're revealing Macbeth for what he was, and if we do this book right the whole world will have a fine old time seeing through his façades."

"They're not worth seeing through."

"Orson, you're being difficult. You don't want to quit this, do you?"

"Of course not. It's my life blood."

"If you say you'll do it we'll move on to more serious matters, like your own work. Shall we do that?"

"Let's do that."

Pettijohn reached into a pile of manuscripts and pulled out one bound in a yellow cover (after Giselle's hair), and opened it, revealing handwritten notes clipped to the first page of the manuscript. He looked at me and I instantly understood that here would come a true judgment on my would-be work and my surrogate self. Now would come the revelation of my flawed brain, errant heart, rapscallion soul. The eradication of the future was at hand.

"This is absolutely brilliant," Pettijohn said. "I love it."

I was stunned.

"There's a very original voice in these pages," said Pettijohn, "and nobody writes dialogue better than you. You're the best since O'Hara."

I could not speak.

"There's a potentially great book here," said Pettijohn, "and I want you to know I'm behind it one thousand percent." He paused, stared me in the eye. "But I can't get anybody else in the house to back me up. Nobody sees what I see in it."

The iceman finally cometh.

"I've made notes on it, and I've included what others say about it, so you'll know the negatives."

"Then you're rejecting it."

"Not I," said Pettijohn, "not I. But I'm only one opinion here, and one opinion does not a novel publish."

"A rejection by any other name."

"Consider it temporary. Let me see it again when you've gone further with the story."

"What do people fault?"

Pettijohn cast his eyes toward the ceiling. I anticipated a rain of slush from anonymous editorial heights.

"People like the story up to a point, but they think the writing lacks the necessary poetry. And they say it lacks a verve for life, that it's life seen through a black veil of doom. The truth is, Orson, that people do occasionally laugh, even on the gallows. But this book is absolutely joyless all the way. This doesn't bother *me,* but others it does. To hear them talk you'd think nobody had ever written negatively about life before you. But my arguments convince nobody about this manuscript."

"No poetry, no verve for life, eh. They should've seen me in bed this morning. I was poetry in motion."

"A wonderful way to avenge yourself on your enemies. Fuck them all to death."

I stood up and so did Pettijohn, who picked up the manuscript.

"You want to take this?"

"I'll get it another time."

"What about these notes?"

"Their essence is enough for one day."

"You'll fatten up Meriwether's book, won't you?"

"I'll make it obscenely obese."

We nodded and shook hands across the desk and then I found my way out through the warren of corridors to the waiting room.

I kept my gaze level and steady, did not glance upward toward the epiphanic walls.

Lacking in my work, and perhaps in the deepest reaches of my person, the necessary poetry, the necessary verve for life, I decided to acquire some of each, or, that being impractical, to discover, at the very least, where, how, and from whom verve and poetry were dispensed to seekers.

When I came out of the lobby of my publisher's building and stepped onto Fifth Avenue I felt the pulsation of a new vibrancy, putting me at one with possibility in the land of opportunity. I knew this was a wholly unreasonable attitude in the face of what I had just gone through, but one must not look too closely at what liberates one into excitement. I assayed the sky and found it clear, blue, and glorious. I welcomed the snap in the early spring breeze, and I crossed to the sunny side of the avenue to confront the warmth and light of the noonday sun, which was just slightly past its zenith.

I was hungry and I envisioned food of delectable piquancy, served in luxurious surroundings by punctilious and servile waiters. I would order veal, possibly venison, perhaps duck. But I did not yet want to become stationary, however tempting and elegant the atmosphere. I would walk now, but where? I had almost three hours to spend before meeting Giselle. I'd told her to meet me about three o'clock in an Irish bar on Sixth Avenue, not far from her point of rendezvous with the editors of the greatest picture magazine in the world. Should I now walk north to Central Park, embrace the natural world of trees, of soft spring earth and new greenery, or weave my way among the sumptuous lobbies and cafés of the hotels on Central Park South? No, I longed for something grander and with more verve than those, something even more poetic than nature.

I strode southward on the avenue and knew the instant pleasure that came from the high elegance of the windows of the great stores. In Saks' window I saw a suit that I instantly coveted, a double-breasted gray glen plaid, one of the grandest-looking suits I'd ever seen. In the window of The Scribner Book Store I found two books that suited my mood: *Life Is Worth Living* by Fulton Sheen and *The Power of Positive Thinking* by Norman Vincent Peale, wise men both. I would buy both books when I had the money. I turned, decided to say hello to Jesus at St. Patrick's Cathedral; and I remembered the flustered Methodist cleric who protested to his Irish taxi driver that he had asked not for St. Patrick's, but for Christ's Church, and the driver advised him, "If you don't find him here he's not in town." There's verve.

I crossed the avenue at 49th Street and walked west between the British Empire building and La Maison Française toward the sunken plaza in Rockefeller Center. I stopped and read the credo of the great John D. Rockefeller, Jr., carved into a slab of polished black marble: "I believe in the sacredness of a promise, that a man's word should be as good as his bond; that character—not wealth or power or position—is of supreme worth." Wonderful. And more: "I believe that the rendering of useful service is the common duty of mankind and that only in the purifying fire of sacrifice is the dross of selfishness consumed and the greatness of the human soul set free . . . I believe that love is the greatest thing in the world . . ." And so do I, John, so do I.

I continued my walk through the Center, the greatest concentration of urban buildings in the world. I remembered coming here with Peter when I was a child to see the tallest Christmas tree in the world. I followed my shoes and found myself in the lobby of the Time-Life building, home to the greatest concentration of magazines in the world, and considered going up to the office where Giselle was being seduced away from me, but descended instead into the underground world of Rockefeller Center, the most labyrinthine subterranean city since the catacombs, passing stores and restaurants and murals and sculpture, far more exciting to a refined sensibility than any underground passageway anywhere, including Mammoth Cave, or the sewers of Paris. I took a stairway up into the RCA building, home to the greatest radio and television networks in the world (and next door the Associated Press building, home to the greatest news service in the world). Nothing in urban, suburban, or rural history could compare with this achievement, and as I moved through the magnificent corridors I noted shining brass everywhere: in the floors, the hand railings, the revolving doors; and the thought of the cost of such elegance exalted me.

The very idea of selfless munificence in the service of the architectural imagination was surely a pinnacle in the history of man's capacity to aspire. And aspire I did, assuming the poetry of all this grandeur into my eyes, my ears, my sense of smell, the poetry of man the master builder, the poetry of man who climbed to the skies with his own hands, the poetry of Babel refined into godly and humanistic opportunity and respect and mortar and stone and endeavor and joy and love and money and thickness and breadth and luxury and power and piety and wonder and French cuisine and the American novel and jazz music and (oh yes, Meriwether, oh yes) the naked titties of ten thousand women. Oh the immensity of it all!

I taxied back to the apartment where Giselle and I were staying and, from the desk where our host kept his financial records, expropriated two checkbooks, two dozen of the host's business cards, several letters that would verify my identity if the business cards and the checkbooks did not, assorted press credentials from the U.S., West Germany, the Soviet Union, Brazil, and an Arab nation whose name I did not immediately recognize, all identifying the owner as a writer for *Life* magazine. I folded these items into one of the host's several empty breast-pocket wallets, dialed the number at *Life* Giselle had given me, and left a message for her: "Meet me at either the Palm Court or the Oak Bar of the Plaza Hotel, the greatest hotel in America, when you are free," and I then set out in further quest of poetry and verve.

The first thing I did was register and establish my credit with the Plaza's front desk, then equip myself with ready cash. I engaged a corner suite that looked out on Fifth Avenue, Central Park, and the Grand Army Plaza, and then I descended to Fifth Avenue and on to Saks, where I bought three new shirts and ties, pocket handkerchiefs, shoes, belt, socks, and the gray glen plaid suit I'd seen in the window; but I would accept it all, I told the clerk, only if alterations were done within the hour (cost not an obstacle) and delivered to my suite at the Plaza, which they were.

I bought two pounds of Barricini chocolates for Giselle, and back at the suite ordered two dozen yellow roses from the hotel florist and four bottles of her favorite French wines from room service. I went back downstairs and explored the lobby, found the Palm Court too crowded, sought out an empty corner of the Oak Bar, and ordered my first drink in five and a half months, a Scotch on the rocks with water on the side. I sipped it with care, waiting for my system to feel the first alcoholic rush of the new year, and wondering if Dr. Tannen's prophecy would be correct: that, should I ever again drink alcohol, the flood controls of my brain would let the madness cascade back into my life.

I affirmed my disbelief in this diagnosis with another sip of whiskey, and only then did I look about me at this walnut-dark, wood-paneled male saloon, with its murals out of the storied past of the Plaza—a horse and carriage in a snowstorm in front of the old hotel, water spilling out of the fountain's dish while a full moon is all but covered by clouds. By the light from the room's wall sconces and copper windows this country's Presidents, giants of capital, movie stars, and great writers had drunk for half a century. I recognized no one. I took another sip and knew the ease that drink had always provided me, a flow of juices that wakened dormant spirits and improbable values. The first sips alone did this. Consider, then, the potential of an entire bottle.

For months I had not seen anybody through the auroral brilliance that those summoned juices could generate. My life had been repetitive ritual: rise from narrow bed, dress in sordid clothing, eat meagerly and without relish, go out into the world to edit a book you loathe, confront what you now knew to be an unpublishable novel of your own making, come home in darkness to reinhabit your father's bohemian gloom, and write your daily letter to Giselle.

I knew the danger of imposing too much trivia on my letters and so, one by one, I outlined the lives of my putative relatives to her, also wrote her short essays on the values assorted poets and writers imparted to the world, even if they never published a word. The task, of itself, I wrote her, was holy, the only task atheists could pursue that was buoyed by the divine afflatus. As for myself, the afflatus was flatulent.

I realized with each new sip of Scotch that Dr. Tannen was wrong. I had, since Germany, accepted the doctor's rules and entertained no temptation to suck on a whiskey bottle. But here again came that most wondrous potion into my life, already sending enriched phlogiston into my internal organs, upthrusting my spirit to an equivalency with Presidents, giants of capital, movie stars, and great writers, and providing me with all this not through fraudulence, bravado, delusion, or hallucination. None of that was on the table. This was real. I saw the future unrolling itself before me, knew phlogiston, fraudulence, badness, chocolates, yellow roses, and new neckties when I saw them, Mr. Plaza.

I ordered another Scotch.

A man of about forty years sat at the next table and placed his folded *New York Times* on an adjacent chair. I could read one headline: U.S.–South Korea Units Lash Foe; Jet Bombers Cut Routes Far North. The owner of the newspaper ordered a martini and I asked him, "Could I borrow your *Times* for a quick look?"

The man shrugged and nodded and I looked through the paper: Senate will confirm Chip Bohlen as ambassador to Moscow despite McCarthy attack. Alfred Hitchcock melodrama, *I Confess,* is panned by reviewer. Twenty-three killed, thirty wounded in Korea, says Defense Department. *Salome,* with Rita Hayworth, Stewart Granger, and Charles Laughton, opens at the Rivoli Wednesday.

It all served to incite informational depression in me, especially the opening of *Salome.* We all know what Salome does to John the Baptist, don't we, moviegoers? I folded the newspaper and returned it to my neighbor.

"The news is awful," I said.

"You mean out of Korea?" said the man, who had a look about him that Orson seemed to recognize.

"Everywhere. Even Alfred Hitchcock isn't safe."

"Who's Alfred Hitchcock?"

"He's a Senator. A Roman Senator. He looks like Charles Laughton."

"Oh."

"He's married to Rita Hayworth. You know her?"

"The name has a ring."

"I agree," I said. "Reeeeee-ta. A ring if there ever was one."

"I *beat* Korea," the man said.

I now realized that this man looked very like Archie Bell, the warrant officer I had served with at Frankfurt. It wasn't Archie, of course, but there was something about the mouth; and the eyes were similar. But the face, the hair—nothing like Archie.

"They sent me to Korea," Archie said, "and they thought they were givin' me tough duty. You know what I did? I beat the shit out of my knee with an entrenchin' tool and got a medical discharge. They thought I caught shrapnel. Got the pension, all the musterin'-out stuff, and right away I invested it in Jeeps. Willys, you know the company?"

"The name has a ring," I said. "Wil-yyyyyys."

"Today Kaiser-Frazer bought Willys for sixty-two mill. You know what that means?"

"Not a clue."

"That's major-league auto-making. My broker says I could double my money."

"Smart," I said. "Very smart. I had a pretty good afternoon too. I started out with a hundred, and it's ten times that now, maybe more."

"Hey, buddy, this is a good day for the race."

"The human race?"

"Nooooooo. The race race. We're beatin' the niggers."

"I noticed. They don't have any in here. But then again Lincoln used to drink here," I said.

"Izzat right?"

"Every President since Thomas Jefferson drank here."

"Izzat right? I didn't think the place was that old."

"Who's your broker?"

"Heh, heh. You think I'm gonna tell you?"

"You know who my broker is?"

"Enhhh."

"Thomas Jefferson."

"A two-dollar bill."

"My card, friend," I said, handing him the business card of the *Life* editor. "Call me anytime. Let's have lunch and plan some investments."

"Watch out for falling rocks," the man said.

"Here?"

"Everywhere," he said, and he smiled a smile that I recognized from the poker games in Frankfurt. This was the Captain, invested with Archie Bell's smile. I left the Oak Bar without looking back, knowing my past was not far behind. I took the elevator to the suite, put on my new clothes, opened a bottle of Le Montrachet to let it breathe, then descended to the Palm Court to meet the most beautiful, most sensual, most photographic, most photogenic wife in the history of the world.

"You look *merveilleux*," Giselle said, stroking the waves of my hair, feeling the silk of my pocket handkerchief between her thumb and forefinger. I had been sitting alone in the Palm Court, sipping whiskey, listening to the violin and piano playing Gershwin's "Summertime," when the livin' is easy, a perfect theme for this day. The song wafted over the potted palms, over the heads of the thinning, mid-afternoon crowd.

"I never expected this," Giselle said.

"I decided to reward myself," I said.

"Reward? What happened?"

"My editor loves my book. I asked him for an instant advance and got it."

"Oh, Orse, that's beautiful." She leaned over and kissed me, pulled away, then kissed me again.

"And what about *your* day?" I asked.

"They hired me. I go to work whenever I want. Tomorrow if I want. I told them I wanted to go to Korea and cover the war."

"I knew it would happen. Why *wouldn't* they hire you?"

"I thought they wanted more experience."

"They buy talent, not experience. Everybody buys talent."

"Isn't it nice we're both so talented?"

"It's absolutely indescribable," I said.

"I always knew you were going to be famous," she said. "My wonder boy. I knew it. That's one of the reasons I married you."

"*Merveilleuse*," I said.

"I was so surprised when you said to meet you here," Giselle said. "I thought we'd meet in some terrible Irish café."

"There are no Irish cafés, my love."

"I'm so happy," she said. "Order me something."

"Port. You love port in the afternoon."

"And Le Montrachet," she said.

"I know."

She looked at the wine list, found half a dozen port wines listed, their prices ranging from one dollar to eighteen dollars. She ordered the four-dollar item, and the waiter smiled.

"You know," said the waiter, "this is the wine Clark Gable ordered when he proposed to Carole Lombard. Right at that table over there." He pointed to an empty table.

"It's fated," said Giselle.

"You two seem to be very much in love," the waiter said. I looked up at him and saw a Valentino lookalike, a perfect waiter for the occasion.

"What's more," the waiter added, "the first day this hotel opened, a Prussian count proposed to his American bride in this room. So you see, this is where happy marriages begin."

"What a waiter!" I said. "I'm putting you in my will. What's your name."

"Rudolph Valentino," the waiter said.

"I thought so," I said. "Bring us the port. Two."

Giselle kissed me again. "My wonder boy," she said.

The light in the Palm Court was pale beige, my favorite color on Giselle. I looked at the display of desserts the Palm Court offered: raspberries and strawberries, supremely ripe and out of season, bananas, grapes, peaches, plums, pineapples, and fruit I could not call by name. This was the center of the fruitful universe. All things that happened within its confines were destined to change the world. Values would tumble. The rain of money and glory would fall on all significant consumers. There was no end to the sweetness of existence that was possible if you ordered a bowl of raspberries in the Palm Court.

"This is what your life is going to be like from now on," I said. "This is what success looks like. The absence of money will never again interfere with your happiness."

Giselle beamed at me the most extraordinary smile ever uttered by woman. I considered it for as long as it lasted, tucked it away in the archives of my soul, and raised my glass of port to hers. We clinked.

"May our love live forever," I said.

"Forever," said Giselle.

"And if it doesn't, the hell with it."

"The hell with it," said Giselle.

"There's Ava Gardner over there," I said, pointing to a woman in close conversation with a man whose back was to us.

"Really?" asked Giselle.

"Indubitably," I said, but then I looked again and corrected myself. "No, it's not her. I was mistaken. It's Alfred Hitchcock."

Giselle's laughter shattered chandeliers throughout the Palm Court.

I stood next to the yellow roses, staring out of a window of our suite at Fifth Avenue below. The fading light of this most significant day (such frequent confrontations with significance were a delight) was troublesome to my eyes, but I could see a roofless motorcar stop at the carriage entrance to the hotel, saw Henry James step down from it, adjust his soft hat, then extend his hand to Edith Wharton, the pair bound for dinner in the hotel's Fifth Avenue Café. Teddy Roosevelt struck a pose for photographers on the hotel steps, his first visit to the city since shooting his fifth elephant, and Mrs. John D. Rockefeller waded barefoot in the Plaza's fountain to raise money for widows and orphans spawned by the oil cartel. As I stared across the avenue at the Sherry Netherland, I saw Ernest Hemingway in the window of an upper floor, his arm around Marlene Dietrich. The great writer and great actress waved to me. I waved back.

At the sound of a door opening I turned to see Giselle, wrapped in the silk robe and negligee I'd bought her when she learned we were staying the night at the hotel. I poured the Montrachet and handed her the glass, then poured my own. Never had a married man been luckier than I at this moment. By virtue of the power vested in me I now pronounce you husband and traitor, traitor and wife. God must have loved betrayals, he made so many of them.

"I think you are probably at this moment," I said, "the most fucksome woman on this planet."

"What an exciting word," Giselle said.

I opened her robe and peeled it away from her shoulders. The perfection in the placement of a mole on her right breast all but moved me to tears. She stood before me in her nightgown, beige, the color of pleasure, and as I kissed her I eased her backward onto the sofa, and knelt beside her. I put my hands on the outside of her thighs and slid her nightgown upward. She raised her hips, an erotic elevation to ease my task, and revealed the bloom of a single yellow rose, rising in all its beauty from the depths of her secret garden.

"Are there thorns on this rose?" I asked.

"I eliminated them," Giselle said.

"You are the most resourceful woman on this planet."

"Am I?"

"You are. Did Quinn ever tell you you were resourceful?"

"Never. Say the word."

"Resourceful?"

"The other word."

"Ah, you mean fucksome."

"Yes. I like that word. Don't get any thorns in your mouth."

"I thought you said there were no thorns."

"I don't think I missed any."

"Did Quinn ever have to worry about thorns?"

"Never. Shhhhh."

Silence prevailed.

"Aaaahhhh."

"Was that the first?"

"Yes."

Silence prevailed again.

"Aaaahhhh."

"Was that the second?"

"Yes."

Silence prevailed yet again.

"Aaaahhhh. Aaaahhhh."

"Third and fourth?"

"Yes. Say the word."

"Fourth?"

"No. Fucksome. Say fucksome."

"I'd rather you say it."

"Does your stripper say it for you?"

"Never."

"Is your stripper fucksome?"

"Somewhat."

"Do you tell her she's somewhat fucksome?"

"Never."

"Why are you still wearing your suit?"

"It's my new glen plaid. I thought you liked it."

"I do, but you never wear a suit when you make love."

"This is the new Orson. Natty to a fault."

"I want to go onto the bed."

"A sensational idea. Then we can do something else."

"Exactly. Are you going to keep your glen plaid on?"

"Yes, it makes me feel fuckish."

"Another word."

"Do you like it?"

"Somewhat. I think I prefer fucksome."

"They have different meanings."

"Does your stripper make you feel fuckish?"

"Somewhat."

"Have you told her?"

"Never. What does Quinn say that you make him feel?"

"I couldn't say."

"I think I'll take my suit off."

"I prefer it that way. It makes me feel fucksome."

"You mean fuckish."

"I prefer fucksome."

"Language isn't a matter of preference."

"Mine is."

Silence prevailed again.

"Is this better?"

"Much better. And a better view."

"How would you describe the view?"

"Classic in shape."

"Classic. Now that's something."

"And larger than most."

"Larger than most. That's *really* something, coming from you."

"It also looks extremely useful."

"You are a very fucksome woman, Giselle."

"Fucksome is as fucksome does," Giselle said.

4

Giselle and I walked along 57th Street and down Broadway, a change of scenery, a move into the murderous light of eschatological love and sudden death. I had convinced her after five hours of lovemaking that the walking was necessary to rejuvenate our bodies for the next encounter. Master the hiatus, I said, and you will regain the season. I did not tell her where I was taking her. I told her the story of Meriwether Macbeth, protagonist of the memoir I was putting together from a chaotic lifetime of journals, notes, stories, poetry, letters, my task being to create the quotient of one man's verbal life.

"He lived with a woman who called herself Jezebel Jones, a name she adopted after meeting Meriwether," I said. "She was a slut of major calibration, but quite bright and extremely willful; and together she and Meriwether cut a minor public swath through Greenwich Village for the better part of a decade. She was known for bringing home strangers and creating yet another ménage for Meriwether, who had grown bored with Jezebel's solitary charms. She turned up one night with a hunchback who called himself Lon because his hump was said to look very like the hump Lon Chaney wore in *The Hunchback of Notre Dame,* and Jezebel found the deformed Lon enormously appealing. But it turned out Lon was a virgin, a neuter, who had never craved the sexual life, was content

174

to move through his days without expending sperm on other citizens. Jezebel tried to change this by teaching the game to Lon and his lollipop. She enlisted Meriwether's aid when Lon visited their apartment, and Meriwether, through deviousness, bound Lon's hands with twine, then tied Lon's legs to the bedposts as Jezebel, having unsuited the hunchback, aroused him to spire-like loftiness, and mounted him. Released from bondage, Lon fled into the night, returned the next day with his Doberman, and sicked the dog on Jezebel and Meriwether. As the dog bit repeatedly into various parts of Jezebel, Meriwether took refuge behind the sofa, his face buried in his arms. Lon moved the sofa and, with the hammer he had brought with him, crushed Meriwether's head with a dozen blows. Jezebel survived and provided enough detail of the attack to put Lon into the asylum for life, and Meriwether moved on to a posthumous realm that had eluded him all his life: fame."

"This is where I spend a bit of my social life when the world is too much with me," I said, pulling out bar stools for Giselle and myself.

We were in The Candy Box, a 52nd Street club that featured striptease dancers from 6:00 p.m. till 3:00 a.m. It was eight o'clock and the low-ceilinged room was already full of smoke that floated miasmically in the club's bluish light. Four young women in low-cut street dresses sat at the bar, two of them head-to-head with portly cigar smokers. The other two, on the alert for comparable attention, turned their eyes to us, recognized me, gave me greetings.

I called them by name and sat beside Giselle. On the dance floor, Consuela, a busty platinum blonde, awkwardly unhooked her skirt to the music of a four-piece band, while three other club girls cozied a table full of men, and another dozen solitary males watched the blonde with perfect attention.

"This is so depressing," Giselle said. "Do you come here to be depressed?"

"I know the bartender," I said.

"You know more than the bartender."

"He's a friend. He lost his leg at Iwo Jima. A colleague in war, so to speak."

"And your stripper, she works here?"

"Five nights a week."

"Are we in luck? Will we get to see her?"

"It turns out we will."

"Is that her trying to make herself naked up there?"

"No, that's Consuela, one of the new ones, still a bit of an amateur. My Brenda is a talented stripper."

"Your Brenda," said Giselle. "Your behavior is ridiculous, Orson. It's the way you were back in Germany. You seem to like living in the sewer."

"Orson the underground man."

"What'll you have, Orse old buddy?" the bartender asked. He was tall and muscular, with a space where his left canine tooth used to be, a casualty of a bar fight. But you should see the other guy's dental spaces.

"Port wine, Eddie," I said. "The best you have. Two."

"Port wine. Don't get too many calls for that."

"It's a romantic drink, Eddie. My wife and I are celebrating our reunion. I brought her in to meet Brenda."

"Yeah? Now that's a switch, bringin' the wife in here. You don't see much of that either."

"Wives have a right to know their husbands' friends," Giselle said.

"Not a whole lot of husbands buy that idea," Eddie said.

"It's trust, Eddie," I said. "There has to be more trust in this world. Shake hands with Giselle."

"A pleasure," Eddie said, taking Giselle's hand.

"When is Brenda on?" I asked.

"She's next."

176

"We *are* in luck," Giselle said.

"Eddie, would you ask her to come out and say hello before her act?"

"Right away, old buddy."

"Eddie is certainly a friendly bartender for a place like this," Giselle said.

"You should avoid categorical thinking, Giselle. There are no places like this."

"They're all over Europe."

"The Candy Box is different. Trust me."

"Why should I trust you?"

"Because basically I'm a good person," I said.

"That's another reason I married you, but I've decided that doesn't mean I should trust you."

"In God we trust. All others should be bullwhipped."

I saw Brenda walking toward us from the back of the club, wrapped in a black dressing gown that covered less than half of her upper significance. On the stage Consuela was removing, as a final gesture, her minimal loin string, revealing a shaded blur that vanished in the all-but-black light that went with that ultimate moment.

I stood to greet Brenda, her eyes heavily mascaraed, her red lipstick outlined in black, her shining black hair loose to her shoulders. I bussed her cheek, offered her my bar stool, then introduced her to Giselle as "my good friend Brenda, who has done everything a woman of her profession is ever asked to do by men."

"And what is your profession, Brenda?" Giselle asked.

"She's a dancer," I said.

"I didn't ask you, I asked Brenda."

"Is this really your wife, Orson?"

"She really is," I said. "Isn't she lovely?"

"I'm a dancer," Brenda said to Giselle. "What's your profession, honey?"

177

"Giselle is a photographer," I said.

"You take my picture," Brenda said, "I'll take yours," and she parted the skirt of her gown and spread her legs.

"Is that what you'd like me to photograph?" Giselle asked.

"No," said Brenda. "That's my camera."

"She has a sense of humor, your Brenda," Giselle said.

"She's had dinner with Juan Perón, she's stripped for the Prince of Wales. Is there anything you haven't experienced, Brenda?" I asked.

"True love," said Brenda. "Men only want my body."

"What a pity," said Giselle.

"It's good for business, is how I look at it," said Brenda. She stood up from the bar stool. "Business calls me."

"Happy business," Giselle said as Brenda left us.

"A lively mind, don't you think?" I said.

"I'd say her tits were her best feature," Giselle said.

On stage Brenda worked with a film of herself dancing, and a stage spotlight. The film and her live dance were the same but in the film she was seducing a shadowy male figure. As she removed a garment on stage the camera moved in for a close-up on the area about to be revealed, then cut away as the stage garment was tossed. The spotlight dimmed progressively as nudity impended, and then the camera focused in grainy close-up on the parts of Brenda that were illegal in the flesh.

"Clever juxtaposition, isn't it?" I said. "It was Brenda's own idea."

"Two Brendas for the price of one," Giselle said.

I turned my back to Brenda's performance and faced Giselle. "I have something I must tell you," I said.

"Don't you want to see how Brenda comes out?"

"I know how Brenda comes out. My editor didn't buy my book, he rejected it. The money I spent belonged to your friendly editor from *Life*. I took two of his checkbooks and his identification to cash them. It's really quite simple to assume a new identity."

Giselle stared and said nothing.

"The care and feeding of love and beauty should be a primary concern of the human race, but if I can't afford it at any given moment, it doesn't follow I should abandon my concern. Making love to you this afternoon, I argued with myself about confessing the deed, but confession would have destroyed the aura of love that we'd created. I also tried to understand whether my fraudulence was enhancing or diminishing my excitement, and decided it wasn't a factor, that I existed for you apart from my fraudulence. But I knew the confession would change *your* view of what was happening, and I didn't want that. I wanted you to see what lies in store for you in America, the future of your ambition, which we both know is formidable. You will have a successful career, I'm certain of that. Given our marriage and our love, I suspect you'd be inclined to tuck me in your pocket and carry me along with you, or park me in an apartment on the Upper East Side while you circle the globe with your camera. But I would rather have no Giselle than half of Giselle. I could never survive the madness that would follow such a raveled connection."

I knew that as I talked Giselle's vision was framed by the real and the filmic visions of Brenda's performance, naked on screen, all but naked on stage. I turned to see Brenda remove her G-string and, unlike Consuela, stand before the club crowd without a garment, letting all eyes find what they sought while she danced another sixteen bars, and then, lights out, she was gone.

"Brenda looks naked, doesn't she?" I said. "More fraudulence. She never lets herself be naked. She's wearing an all-but-invisible G-string she puts on with adhesive. It covers her opening, and has a bit of hair that matches her own. She provides the illusion of nudity while she retains the protective integrity of the larger G-string, and so the customers never see the complete Brenda. I find a fascination in this betrayal of the public trust, don't you? Most of the time in this life when you see a naked pussy you assume it truly is a naked pussy. Since we all live in the great whorehouse, and since we all give a fuck whenever we can, no matter what the cost, the discovery that even the most openhanded lewdness is only another act of cynicism seems just right, admirable even. Dr. Tannen used to chide me for my quest for innocence, or at least that's how he described it. He said my time underground, or in the sewer as you put it, was really a search for something that didn't exist in the world, not now, not ever. How far back in darkness do you want to go to find that innocence? he asked. The womb? Amniotic innocence? Do you really think the womb was such an innocent place? Maybe you'd like to go back beyond the womb to the soul's descent *into* the womb, or back even to the soul's creation. Personally, he said, I don't think you can get there from here."

Giselle put her hand on the right side of my head and held it. "Do you still get the headaches?" she asked.

"Once in a while," I said.

"How often do you see the doctor?"

"We're quits. I can't afford him. But I understand. He doesn't run a free lunch counter."

"It was beautiful, what you did for me," Giselle said.

"I'm glad you liked it," I said. "I'll pay your friend back when I get the advance on the Meriwether book."

"Don't worry about it. I'll take it out of my paycheck."

"You are a generous woman, Giselle."

"You're a loving husband, Orson."

"Yes. That's true. Isn't it a pity."

Giselle dropped her hand from my head, took my hand in hers, and was smiling her smile of rue when the shooting began in the street. One shot broke the window in the club's door, and Eddie the barman yelled, "Get down, folks, they're shootin' out there."

I could see someone huddled in the doorway until the lights

went out, heard a pistol fired twice, three times, four, heard a volley of return shots, and then the doorway went silent. Eddie switched the lights back on and when he opened the door a man in a light-gray overcoat rolled down from the two steps where he'd been huddling. Two uniformed policemen with drawn pistols stood on the sidewalk observing the situation. Both holstered their pistols and one went elsewhere.

"Who is he?" Eddie asked the policeman.

"He just held up the joint next door."

An Interview with the Corpse on 52d Street

by Orson Purcell

The interview took place on the threshold of The Candy Box, a Manhattan nightclub on 52nd Street, a crosstown artery that is home to two dozen jazz bars and exotic dance clubs along its neon way. The corpse was male, reasonably well dressed, without a necktie, but wearing a shirt with starched collar, double-breasted dark gray suit, gray overcoat, and a gray fedora that had fallen off when the man was shot. Two policemen had come upon him almost as soon as he emerged, gun in hand, from an adjacent nightclub, where he had stolen an unspecified amount of money.

The door of The Candy Box remained open throughout the interview at the suggestion of police, who were awaiting the homicide photographer. A woman customer in The Candy Box was actually the first to photograph the corpse, using a Leica thirty-five-millimeter and natural light. This dramatic photo received wide currency, appearing in *Life* magazine six days after the shooting.

The corpse lay on its right side during the interview, bullet holes in its head, neck, chest, and other parts of the upper torso. The eyes were open, and the expression on the face (which was free of blood) was one of inquiry, as if the man had died asking a question. This was the first interview the owner of the corpse had ever given, either in life or in death.

O: Is there any single reason why you are dead?

C: The cops shot me eight times.

O: Why did they do that?

C: I shot at them.

O: Isn't that a crazy thing to do?

C: You could say that.

O: Do all hoodlums behave this way?

C: Not everybody. It's somethin' you decide.

O: Was your decision prompted by the fact that you're suicidal?

C: Hey, whatayou sayin'? I was raised a Catholic.

O: Then maybe you were just stupid.

C: Nobody calls me stupid, buddy.

O: This is speculative conversation. Crime is often an aggressive form of stupidity. Don't be upset.

C: You think stupid guys get away doin' what I do? You think the boss'd trust me if I was stupid?

O: Maybe you were doing it to escape.

C: Now you're talkin'.

O: But you didn't escape.

C: I had a chance.

O: You gambled with your life. You're a gambler.

C: I never win nothin'.

O: Would you consider yourself an unlucky man?

C: Yeah, could be. But, shit, luck ain't everything. I know a lot of unlucky guys who got nothin' but money.

O: Perhaps it was madness.

C: I'm as sane as you are, friend.

O: That's not saying a whole lot, but we won't go into that

here. Perhaps it runs in your family. If your entire family was mad then possibly you are as well.

C: My old man wouldn't let any nuts run around in the family.

O: What about fear? People get their backs up when they're afraid, when they think something might destroy them, or what is most valuable to them.

C: Balls. I been in half a dozen shootouts. You want the rundown?

O: No need.Consider that you may have been foolhardy. More brave than smart, in other words. Is that why you did it?

C: We do what we do because we gotta do it. You don't like that reason I'll give you another one. We do it because it's gotta be done.

O: A compulsive, responsible hoodlum. That's rare indeed. But shooting it out with the police all but presumes a belief in your own unkillability.

C: Oh yeah?

O: One might describe it as hubris, which of course means challenging the gods to destroy you.

C: You're one of them smart bastards.

O: If I may sum up, you enter into this sort of contretemps with total awareness, and you do it because you decide it's the valorous thing to do, because it proves that at your center you are a courageous individual, because it is your obligation to a world you mistakenly believe you understand, and that, no matter what the odds against you or your ideas, you are the final arbiter of your own action. Captain of your soul, so to speak. Am I wrong?

C: What the fuck are you talkin' about?

O: It remains to be seen. One final question. Do you think it's possible that you're not really dead, that you have a chance at resurrection, I mean coming back to life.

C: Nah, I'm dead.

O: Thank you, Mr. C.

I decided that not only was I an eschatophiliac, but also an eschatophile. It seemed to be the healthiest of all possible conditions. In this most illuminating darkness of the city's night I could distinguish the last weakened light of end times, could see, with my heightened vision, that in The Candy Box's sign the ionized neon had grown sooty in its finality, a soiled and fading flickering of the city's last artificial light. Above my head the sky had turned increasingly frigid and black in a sunless world, and I knew that death was on the prowl. Could judgment, heaven, or hell be far behind? Even scavengers cringe in light such as this, for it destroys even the *appetite* to survive. Only solitude, and the contemplation of the ease of existence in the face of futility, are viable now. Suicide is pointless, for the entertainment value of terminal events exceeds that of the vapid flight to oblivion.

I now realized how much I loved to lose. Acquisition had invariably brought with it the anxiety of loss, and the settling in of that anxiety had always proved to be a prelude to harsh reality for me. This was how I had lived. I created the highs and lows of my life. I accumulated the Giselles and Les Montrachets of my days, and then I lost them. I would never again enumerate all that had been taken from me, and I blamed no one for this recurring phenomenon. I was beyond blame and had come to understand that this was the natural curve of life, especially for the Phelans. This knowledge elevated my spirit, for I knew I would live under no more delusions. I would be prepared for the worst that life could offer. Solitude, contemplation, and waiting for the finale: these were the meaningful pursuits. And also, oh yes, the elimination of the past. I would throw out all that I had written, all my letters (including those from Giselle; especially those from Giselle). I would throw out all books that did not enhance solitude. I would throw out memory. I would throw out the memory of Miss Nelson, in whose home I roomed when I first went to Albany to live. Demure, old, white-haired Miss Nelson, retired schoolteacher, had lost her connection to significance long ago. Where had it gone? There, under her canopy bed, I saw one day the bright light of yesterday's loss shining on forty empty bourbon bottles. Goodbye, memory of Miss Nelson. I would also throw out the memories of Quinn. That would take time, there were so many. I would begin with the night at the Grand View Lake House when I was with Joanie Mac in the boat house, my hand down at Joanie's place, when we saw Wanda, the new waitress, come back to the hotel's servants' quarters with Liver Mason, back from the movies in Saratoga. Let me kiss you, Liver said, and as he threw his arms around her, Wanda peck-pecked his liverly lips and pushed him away. Tomorrow again? pleaded Liver. Tomorrow maybe, said Wanda, and she ran up the stairs to bed. Getting some air, Quinn came out the back door of the hotel bar, whistling, searching in life for the elusive meaning of his solitude, and Wanda, after less than eight bars of the whistling, bounded down the stairs, took Quinn's arm, and—just as if it were planned—they came into the boat house, his hand already up at Wanda's, and he said later he never expected it to happen, didn't know she was there, hadn't been following her and Liver, was surprised out of his socks, was just out for a walk, and other genuinely true lies he told himself. Quinner the sinner. Quinner the winner. Goodbye, Quinner at the boat house. Goodbye, Quinner in Europe with Giselle. And I felt lightened already. It would be a pleasant thing to unmemorize my life. It would prove I was no longer afraid of time. I would sit in my window and watch the garbageman take away the evidence that Orson Purcell had ever existed.

And so I moved on, ever deeper, into the lovely, lovely darkness, thrilled by it all as only a true eschatophile can be.

BOOK
FOUR

BOOK
FOUR

In the early spring of 1953, and with blinding illumination on through the fall of 1954, Peter Phelan came to perceive this: that individuals, families, or societies that willfully suppress their history will face a season of reckoning, one certain to arrive obliquely, in a dark place, and at a hostile hour, with consequences for the innocent as well as for the conspirators. Peter saw this first in my collapse, and then in the rolling boil of divine vengeance visited upon his brothers and sisters in these years.

In much the way that he had left Colonie Street in 1913 to escape what he saw as the shallow morality of his mother, only to discover that a tissue of other reasons had contributed to his move (and her behavior), so in November, 1954, did he return home to cope yet again with the Phelan family shallows, again pushed to doing so by ancillary reasons: the death and departure of so many friends from his changing Greenwich Village neighborhood and his near isolation as a result of this, his diminishing bank account, deficient income, and the appealing prospect of free rent in Albany, his growing problem with arthritic hips, which prevented him from standing at his easel and had sat him prematurely in the novice invalid's chair, his unflagging love for his brothers and sisters, and, not least, his distance from me, about whom he had begun to fret in unreasonably paternal ways.

Peter's return home was brought on by a series of events that began with a modestly scandalous public moment; but also by the climax of long and bitter discord in the lives of Sarah, Tommy, and Chick Phelan, and finally by the death of Sarah. The return would also transform Peter's work radically and set him on a quest not only to understand the chain of causation that had led the family to a crisis of sanity and survival, but also to memorialize it in art.

For Chick the year 1954 was full of crisis, a climactic time in his life. A failed priest in Sarah's eyes, Chick had been introduced to Evelyn Hurley, a handsome cosmetics saleslady at the John G. Myers Department Store, during a New Year's Eve party at the Knights of Columbus in 1937, by the *Times-Union* newspaper columnist Martin Daugherty. The introduction was followed first by Chick's privileged glimpse of Evelyn Hurley eliminating a wrinkle in her silk stocking by the most modest elevation of her skirt, that elevation the equivalent to Chick of a wild aphrodisiac; and second, by Chick's intense and private conversation with Evelyn immediately thereafter, during which he became acutely aware of the audible friction created when she crossed her legs under the table, her silk stockings sliding one upon the other and creating, in Chick's heart and soul, the phenomenon of love at first sound.

Chick then pursued her with ardent respect and found his ardor reciprocated, but found also that Evelyn, a widow, was a woman of the world in ways that Chick only hoped to be a man of the world; and so for seventeen years the Chick-and-Evelyn courtship frequently approached, but never arrived at, ardor's ultimate destination. Chick was too loyal a Catholic to use prophylactics, Evelyn too alert to possibility to allow access to herself without them.

Marriage was, of course, the answer, but impediments prevailed, principally in Chick, who, even after he bought Evelyn an
engagement ring in the tenth year of their courtship, chose to believe
he was seeing her circumspectly. None in the city except himself
thought it much of a secret, not even his sister Sarah, the chief
impediment, who for years refused to acknowledge that Evelyn
existed on the planet, and announced often at dinner that the Phelan
credo, in the abstract, allowed no truck with widows, or divorcees,
or women of loose character. Sarah, at a neighbor's wake, overheard
a man describe someone she assumed to be Evelyn as "loose as
ashes and twice as dusty" and, understanding the import of the
statement without grasping its particulars, thereafter actively did all
she could to discourage Chick from his pursuit, never, for instance,
allowing him to bring Evelyn into the house during the seventeen-
year courtship.

It was during the very early twilight of a June evening in 1954
that Chick found himself in a duel of screams with Sarah, he reacting
to Evelyn's ultimatum that if he did not marry her she would leave
Albany and go alone to Miami Beach to take work as the hostess
of a luxurious new Collins Avenue delicatessen that was about to
be opened by a friend who had moved to Florida and, with prudent
investment, found himself with money to burn. And how better to
burn it than cooking corned beef and blintzes?

Sarah and Chick each lacked novelty in their arguments—the
much-discussed moral position on widows and designing women,
the depravity of men's desires, the holy priesthood ("Once a priest,
always a priest"), maternal wishes, Catholic antipathy to Florida and
especially Miami Beach, and, the ultimate appeal, family loyalty:
"What will become of us if you leave?"—being Sarah's enduring
salvos; and Chick's—his fury at being thought of as a priest ("I was
never a priest, only a seminarian"), the right of men, even Albany
Irishmen, to marry, the right not to be interfered with by sisters,

the love for Evelyn (newly announced within the past week), the last chance for happiness, the only love he'd ever known in this goddamned life ("Don't you swear at me over your concubine"), and the ultimate truth: that he was goddamn sick and tired of being a slave to this family, goddamn sick and tired of not being appreciated, goddamn sick and tired of this stinking town and this stinking street and . . . and there Chick's tirade was interrupted by the front door bell; and he opened it to see a policeman standing on the stoop holding Tommy by the arm.

"Mr. Phelan?"

"Yes."

"Is this man your brother?"

"He is. What's the problem?"

"Well, he's more or less under arrest. It'd be better to talk inside."

Chick saw another policeman sitting in the squad car parked in front of the house and recognized Eddie Huberty, who used to play left field for Arbor Hill in the Twilight League. Chick waved a small hello to Eddie and backed into the house to let Tommy and the policeman into the parlor.

Molly, who had been upstairs in her room trying to shield her ears against Sarah's and Chick's eternal arguing, came down the stairs at the sound of the doorbell, and stopped behind Sarah as the policeman entered and took off his hat. He stood beside Tommy, who could look only at the floor, while Chick, in his shirtsleeves and suspenders, commanded the moment.

"Has he done something, officer?" Chick asked.

"It seems he has. We had a complaint from a woman on Ten Broeck Street that he followed her home from Downtown."

"He always walks on Ten Broeck Street," Chick said. "All his life. Did he do anything to the woman?"

"It seems he did," the policeman said, and Chick detected a small smile on the man.

192

"It was Letty Buckley, wasn't it," Sarah said.

"Matter of fact it was," said the officer. "How'd you know?"

"I know that one," said Sarah. "She's a troublemaker."

"I don't know about that," said the officer. "She called us and said your brother followed her two days in a row, always walking behind her, so the third day we followed along and saw him behind her, sure enough, carrying a cane, and when she got to her front stoop he hooked the neck of the cane under her skirt and lifted it up, up to her hips, and she screamed. He tipped his hat to her and kind of twirled his cane, and then he walked away. That's when we picked him up."

"Did you do that?" Sarah asked Tommy, poking his shoulder with one finger.

Tommy made no acknowledgment, stared at the floor.

"Did you, brazen boy? Did you?" Sarah screamed, and Tommy, crying, nodded yes.

"Don't yell," Molly said, pushing past Sarah and taking Tommy by the arm. "Come and sit down, Tom," she said, and she led him to the love seat and sat beside him.

"Is he under arrest?" Chick asked.

"Not yet," the policeman said, and added in a whisper, "Mrs. Buckley hasn't filed a complaint, and I'm not sure she really wants to. Probably get in the papers, you know, if she does. She just thinks he oughta be kept under control."

"We can guarantee that, officer," Chick said.

"You bet your life we can," Sarah said.

Tommy whimpered.

The policeman offered a faint smile to Chick and Sarah. "More of a joke, really. He didn't hurt her, and nobody saw what he done except us. And, o' course, Miss Buckley. Quite a surprise to her, musta been." And he laughed. "Just keep him close to home."

Chick nodded and smiled, and as they walked out to the stoop the policeman said softly to Chick, "Really was funny. Her skirt went about as high as it could go. He's pretty clever with that cane."

"We'll see it doesn't happen again, officer. And you wanna bring over a coupla tickets to the Police Communion Breakfast I'll buy 'em from you."

"I'll do that," the policeman said, and he got back in the prowl car. Chick waved again to Eddie Huberty.

Tommy's head was still bowed, his sisters watching him in silence, when Chick reentered the parlor, feeling that the policeman's smile had broken the tension. Chick tried to convey that in his tone. "Tom, what the hell did you *do* that for?"

Tommy shook his head.

"You know Miss Buckley? You ever been in her house?"

"No," Tommy said.

"You just like her looks, is that it?"

Tommy nodded yes.

"Where'd you learn to do that business with the cane?"

"Charlie," Tommy said.

"Who?" said Sarah.

"I'll handle it," Chick said. "Charlie who?"

"Charlie, the movies."

"Charlie, Charlie. Charlie Ruggles? Charlie Chan?"

"No," said Tommy.

"Charlie Grapewin? Charlie McCarthy?"

"No, Charlie with the derby," Tommy said.

"Charlie Chaplin he means," Molly said.

"Right. Charlie Chaplin," Tommy said.

"You saw him do that with a cane?" Chick asked.

"People laughed when he did it. People liked what Charlie did," Tommy said.

"When'd you see him do that?"

"Saw it with you."

"Me?" Chick said. "I haven't seen Charlie Chaplin since the 1920s, silent movies."

"Down at the Capitol," Tommy said. "You and me, we saw Charlie, and everybody liked what he did. They laughed. We liked him, you and me did, Chick."

"Jesus," Chick said. "He sees somethin' in the movies and then imitates it twenty-five, thirty years later. I *do* remember Chaplin used to do that with his cane. Did it all the time. It *was* funny."

"It was not," Sarah said. "Don't you dare encourage him. It's a filthy thing he did to her, even if she isn't any good."

"There's nothing wrong with her," Molly said. "She's always pleasant to us."

"She has men in, what I hear."

"She's single, what's wrong with that?"

"I don't want to talk about it any longer," Sarah said. "You come upstairs with me, young man."

"What're you gonna do?" Chick said.

"I'm going to punish him."

"Let him alone, won't ya? He's scared to death already."

"You want him to do it again?"

"No, of course I don't."

"Then he has to be taught a lesson."

"He's scared," Molly said. "He wet his pants."

"Get off the love seat," Sarah said. "Go upstairs and change. You're a bad boy."

Tommy quickstepped through the back parlor and went up the back stairs. Chick and Molly exchanged smiles as Sarah went up the front stairs.

"Brazen boy," Molly said.

"Sixty-three-year-old brazen boy," Chick said.

There is a photograph taken of Molly by Giselle in early September, 1954, sitting on the porch of the Grand View Lake House on Saratoga Lake, cupping a bird in her hands. She is looking with an oblique glance at the camera, a small smile visible at the corners of her mouth but not in her eyes. The photo is black and white and arrests the viewer with its oddness and its mystery: first the bird, a cedar waxwing whose tan, yellow, and red colors are not discernible, but whose black facial mask is vivid; and then the puzzling expression on the face of this obviously once-beautiful woman in her sixty-fifth year.

A facile interpretation of the photo is that the woman is perhaps saddened by the fact that the bird is injured, for it must be injured or else it would fly away. But this interpretation is not accurate. The memories and secrets that the bird evoked in Molly were what put the smile on her lips and the solemnity in her eyes; and it was this contradiction that Giselle captured in the picture, again proving her talent for recognizing the moment of cryptic truth in people she chose to photograph. Molly had been declining into melancholia before the photo was taken, the onset of decline dating back to the day Tommy was arrested for imitating Charlie Chaplin.

On that day, after the policeman left the Phelan home, Tommy went up to his bedroom to remove the underpants that his terror had caused him to wet. In the front parlor, Chick, awash in anger, pity, frustration, anxiety, and other emotions too convoluted to define in a single word, straightened his necktie, snatched up his seersucker sports jacket, and announced to Molly that he was going to dinner and a movie with Evelyn, goddamn it, and maybe he'd be home later and maybe he wouldn't.

When Chick left, a sudden isolation enveloped Molly: alone again in the company of Sarah, who could raise at will the barricades between herself and the rest of the family: a perverse strength in the woman to do what no one else wanted done but was always done nevertheless. Sarah would spank Tommy, as her mother had spanked all the children for their transgressions of rule. Tommy would cry openly, would wail and sob in his imposed shame, imposed because he was incapable of generating shame in himself, was without the guile, or the moral imperatives that induced it in others, was, in fact, a whole and pure spirit who had had the Commandments, and the punishment for transgressing them, slapped into his buttocks for six decades, but who still had no more understanding of them than when he was an infant. All he knew was that he should avoid the prohibited deeds that provoked spankings. Raising a woman's skirt with a cane had never been prohibited, but now he would realize he could never do it again. Now, truly; for his crying had begun and Molly knew Sarah was at her work.

The situation was old, Molly's guilt was old, the themes that provided the skeleton of the events taking place this minute were older than Molly herself, and she was sick of them all, sick of her helplessness in the face of them. She heard the sobs and loathed them. It was like kicking a dog for chasing a bitch in heat. Tommy had instincts that no amount of punishment would turn aside; they would always find a new outlet. But what of *your* instincts, Molly? Did you ever find another outlet for *your* stunted passion? It seems you did not, alas. No future for it. Animal with instincts amputated. But no. They were still there. Orson had raised them again last year, had he not? Bright and loving young man, prodding your memory of pleasure, revisiting feelings long in their grave. Orson is Peter's. Even Chick said he probably was. "Orson," Chick said, "anytime you need a place to hang your hat you're welcome here." Chick so easygoing, the trouble she gives him. He said he was sick of this stinking street. I know he was going to say this stinking house too, and this stinking family. These stinking brothers and sisters. Chick doesn't mean it.

But he does.

We all do.

Molly laid her head back on the sofa and closed her eyes to shut out Tommy's sobbing and Sarah's screaming. She tried to replace those sounds with the face of Walter as he stood tall before her, waiting for her kiss, expecting it, inviting it. Walter loves Molly's kisses. Loved. Don't pity yourself, Molly. Remember poor Julia, dead at twenty-two, Julia who never knew passion, Julia who was kissed by boys twice in twenty-two years and neither kiss meant any more than a penny's worth of peppermints. I was truly kissed, Julia. Your sister knew kisses and love and more. Much more. Never again. Other things. Never again.

Molly plunged into the blackest part of her memory to hide, to shut out the thoughts that were coming back now. So much wrong. So many evil things the result of love. Why should it be that we are gifted with love and then the consequences are so . . .

Tommy squealed and Molly rose up from her black depths, sat upright on the sofa, heard the squeal a second time, a third, the squeal of an animal in agony, and she was racing up the stairs in seconds toward the wretched sounds. She saw Tommy face down on his bed, Sarah striking his naked buttocks—she had never hit him naked before, never; nobody was ever hit naked, ever—her hand coming down again and again with the two-foot rule (and Molly saw that Sarah was hitting him not with the rule's flatness but with its wide edge and screaming, "filthy boy, brazen boy, filthy boy, brazen boy"), the Tommy squeals and Sarah screams beyond Molly's endurance.

But as Molly moved toward Sarah to snatch away the ruler Tommy suddenly rolled onto his back and with both feet kicked Sarah in the stomach as she was raising the ruler yet again, and Sarah flew backward across the room, her back colliding with Tommy's three-drawer dresser, knocking his clown lamp to the floor and throwing the room into darkness. And Sarah sat suddenly on the floor, breathless, her glasses gone, her expression not pained as much as incredulous that such a thing could happen to her.

So began Sarah's awareness of her mortality.

In her rage, Sarah damaged Tommy's spine so severely that he could not walk, could not stand or lie straight, could not bend over, could only rest and sleep sitting on cushions. Dr. Lynch, the family physician for thirty years, prescribed pain pills, a wheelchair, and X-rays, and accepted without question the explanation that Tommy had been attacked on the street by wild kids who hit him with sticks. Tommy would not eat or drink, would accept nothing from Sarah, and so Molly assumed control of his life and convinced him to take some bread pudding and tea. She put whiskey in the tea to soothe this grown-up child who never drank whiskey, or even beer or wine, in a house where it went without saying that a drop of the creature improved every living thing, including dogs and fish.

Tommy calmed down and Molly busied herself so totally with him that she could, for hours at a time, forget how dreadfully hostile she was to this house, this family, especially to the absurd and brutal Sarah, who could not only do such a thing but who could stand for the doing for decades, Sarah who felt no remorse, only mortal pangs of ingratitude that she should be isolated by her family after giving her life over to its care and feeding, its salvation from damnation.

Chick was the first to isolate her. When he learned what she had done to Tommy he immediately picked up the telephone, called Evelyn, proposed to her and was accepted, told her he would give two weeks' notice at the *Times-Union* and take whatever severance pay he had coming, then they would go to Miami as she wanted, she could work at the deli, he'd get a job somewhere, and they'd start a new life and never look back.

He said all this in earshot of Sarah, who was sitting in front of the television watching "Death Valley Days," a western series to which she gave loyalty because it advertised 20 Mule Team Borax scouring powder, which Sarah used for cleaning, as had her mother before her. Sarah said nothing to Chick when he hung up, did not acknowledge that he was in the room. He walked in front of the television and said to her, "Sarah, you and your mad ways are out of my life. And Tommy's life too."

The latter threat was not to be carried out. Chick had concocted an instant pipe dream that he would take Tommy to Florida with him, care for him, let him grow old in the sun. But Tommy could not move, and would not; said he didn't want to leave Colonie Street in such nice weather. Tommy, in a week, seemed to have forgotten the beating Sarah gave him. He did not really remember why he couldn't walk right, yet he shunned Sarah even so, leaving the room when she entered. He did not talk to her about the beating, or about Letitia Buckley, and when Molly tested him and asked what happened to his back he thought a while and said some bad boys hit him with sticks down on Pearl Street.

After six weeks in the wheelchair and sleeping on the sofa in the back parlor to avoid going up and down stairs, Tommy began to improve. Despite this, Molly felt herself sliding back into the melancholy mood that had enveloped her after Walter's death. She barely talked to Sarah, who had withdrawn into her cocoon of injured merit, and nurtured herself with silence and television. Also, with Chick being gone, probably forever, the house never seemed emptier to Molly.

She took short walks in the neighborhood, visited with neighbors, Martha McCall across the street, who was supervising the movers who would take her and Patsy and their household of forty-four years out of the neighborhood and up to a new house on Whitehall Road, and Libby Dolan, who said she was selling her house to a Negro woman. Would Molly know anybody on the block in another year?

Molly also bumped into Letty Buckley, to whom she had apologized coming out of church the first Sunday after Tommy's cane trick, and found Letty sweet, even forgiving, knowing how simple Tommy was, a bit abashed it was a simpleton who had done that to her, and even worried for him. Will you have to put him away?

No, never, said Molly. And she came home in a fog of emptiness.

Coming into the house made it worse. Talk to Tommy? Talk to Sarah? Talk to the walls? She called her niece, Peg Quinn, just to hear a family voice, and Peg was strong, as always. Molly updated her, leaving out the cause of Tommy's injury, and Peg immediately offered to come down and visit, or take Molly to supper Downtown, or a movie maybe? But no, that wouldn't solve anything. And then, after a half-hour of speculating on what would become of Chick in Florida, and analyzing Sarah's sullen isolation, Peg said, "Why don't you go up to Saratoga and spend some time at the hotel? The weather's beautiful, and Orson's there, isn't he?"

"He is," said Molly.

"Then call him and tell him to get a room ready for you, and one for Tommy, and for Sarah if she wants to go. Get a change of scenery. Do it, Molly, do it."

Do it. Molly understood the advice. Do it, Molly, Walter told her, Chick told her, Peter told her. And did she do it? In her way. But she didn't weigh much. Ha-ha.

"Maybe I will," Molly said. The hotel, the lake, Orson. "But Tommy needs his wheelchair. I couldn't handle it alone."

"I'll send Billy down to give you a hand getting him and the chair into the car," Peg said. "And Orson can help you at the other end."

Molly called Austin McCarroll at the Texaco station and told him to come and take her car down off blocks and make it drivable. Walter had given her the car, a 1937 Dodge, and taught her to drive it. In seventeen years Molly had driven less than four thousand miles, drove it back and forth to Saratoga, took Sarah and Tommy for drives in the evening to get ice-cream cones, went riding Sundays after the war. This year she didn't even bother to take it off blocks when the good spring weather came. No place to go any more.

But now Molly could see herself again at the wheel, driving up Route 9, going up the hill into the Grand View driveway, a thrilling prospect, something she hadn't done as a vacationer in years. Even though so much time had passed, the Grand View had never been out of her mind for long, and whenever she did find herself turning into its driveway she knew that it would be like going home again, going home to love.

2

The Grand View Lake House: An Old Brochure

Situated on the eastern shore of Saratoga Lake, fifteen minute ride from railroad station, our car and porter meet your train; the hotel and cottages offer beautiful vista, eighty rods from and 110 feet above lakeshore, avoiding excessive dampness at night, free from miasma and malaria; convalescents accommodated, consumptives not entertained. Rolling lawns, shade trees, canoeing, boating, fishing, bathing, tennis court, croquet, clock golf, eighteen-hole golf course nearby, bird sanctuary in woods, small game and bird hunting in season, tents available for camping in nearby woods, thousands of flowers, garage on premises, motor parties welcome. Dining room screened, strictly home cooking, all eggs, milk, cream, poultry, and vegetables from our own farm. Wide, 200-foot long veranda, two fireplaces, casino for dancing, piano, phonograph, talking pictures every Sunday night, shower baths, inside toilets, long distance telephone connection, cars carry our guests to nearby Catholic and other churches. Proprietors Patrick and Nora Shugrue, William Shugrue full partner. Hotel open from June 1st to October, 105 rooms, three cottages, special rate by the week, write for terms.

Molly and Giselle: A Colloquy, September, 1954

"I must tell you about love," Molly said.

"I must tell you about marriage," Giselle said.

"You seem to know nothing about love."

"I know everything."

"It would not seem so."

"Peter loves you."

"And I him. But he loved Julia more. I wonder did he ever love Claire."

"And Orson loves you."

"And I him," said Molly.

"I haven't loved much in my life, but I know I love Orson with a full heart," Giselle said.

"It would not seem so."

"You should know me, should be in my head. Then you would understand."

"You left him alone last year."

"We'd been apart for six months, but even so we were always together."

"It would not seem so."

"You are old. You don't understand the young."

"You must never leave them alone for long if you love them," Molly said.

"Then you live for them, not yourself."

"You seem to know nothing about love."

"You should have seen us together."

"It looks alike sometimes. It looks alike."

"You should have seen us together at the Plaza."

"You were not together then."

"But we were," Giselle said. "Even there in The Candy Box with his stripper I felt no jealousy. There was a woman in Germany he went with one night, and he must have had others in New York, but I was never jealous of any of them. But this night I loved him and yet I was jealous of the vision he had of me, for it wasn't me. That loving, successful, talented, noble woman, that was his invention of me. Orson hallucinating again. Orson of the brilliant imagination. Orson the fabulous lover, like none of the others. Orson the marvelous, loyal dog of a man."

"And that is what you think love is?" Molly asked.

"I knew he might go away from me, but I also knew it wasn't me he was leaving but the idea of me. And when I looked at his face I wanted to photograph what I saw. There was an uncertainty in his eye, a calmness, with that old wildness banished. There was something in him I didn't understand."

"As he didn't understand you."

"When we left The Candy Box after the shooting we took a cab back to the Plaza. He saw me to the elevator, then went out for a walk, to clear his brain, he said. He didn't come back, and after an hour I feared he wouldn't, so I got dressed again and scoured the lobby and the hotel bars, because I couldn't believe he'd left me. I preferred the *Life* editor's apartment, where my things were, if I was going to spend the night alone, but I still thought there was a small chance Orson would return. And I knew he knew I'd wait for him in the hotel. And so I did. I phoned Peter and found Orson had neither been there nor called. Peter said he knew an all-night bar where Orson sometimes went and offered to go there alone, or with me if I wanted. He said he'd call Claire, but I knew that would achieve nothing, and it did."

"We were up at Saratoga Lake for three weeks. Mama was dead six months and it was a suffocating summer. We were sitting on the veranda talking about I don't know what, and I saw that a new arrival, a good-looking fellow who had struck up a conversation with Sarah yesterday, was talking with her again. Then I saw a bird fly into a tree on the lawn, and it must've hit something, because it fell to the ground. I ran out to get it and picked it up and started to cry. The newcomer squatted down beside me and said, 'May I see it?' And I showed him this beautiful creature that he said was a cedar waxwing. 'It seems to have an injured wing,' he said. 'We can help him.' I asked how that was possible and he said, 'We'll keep him alive while he gets well.' And that's what we did for the rest of the week. We fed him and made a nest for him in the birdcage the hotel gave us and he became the pet of the guests. I loved him so, that little creature. Everybody came to my room to see him. We took him out of the cage and he did fly a little inside the room at the end of the week, but not very well. On the tenth day he seemed ready and, when I carried him to the veranda, a dozen guests and waitresses came out to watch him go. I released him over the porch railing and he flew so well, right up into the same tree he'd fallen from. We were all so happy. He perched there in the tree for a minute and then he fell again, not injured, but dead."

"Orson was gone two more nights before we found him. Peter had the idea to call Walker Pettijohn, Orson's editor, who suggested looking in Meriwether Macbeth's apartment. He said Orson sometimes worked there among Macbeth's papers that Macbeth's widow still kept intact, though she no longer lived there. And Orson was there all right, and as close to death as he ever will be until his time comes. He was in an alcoholic coma, five whiskey bottles, all empty, strewn around the room. Peter lifted him up and slapped his face but he didn't come to, didn't react at all. Death in life. And if he did live he wouldn't remember anything of this moment. I went out to a pay phone and called the ambulance."

"It was sad that the bird died. I cried so hard. But I've been grateful to it ever since, because that's how I met Walter. The cedar waxwing introduced us. Walter picked the dead bird up and took it into the hotel and wrapped it in a handkerchief and put it on ice and we

called around till we found a place, down home in Albany, that
stuffed birds. We drove down together and gave the waxwing to
the little man, who said he'd never stuffed such a small bird before,
usually folks only stuff the big ones they shoot, owls and hawks, or
their pet parrots. I still have the bird. I always bring it when I come
up here."

"Who is Walter?"

"Walter Mangan, my husband. He taught Latin in a boys' high
school. He died in 1937."

"And you miss him still."

"We were so in love. Nobody loves you like an Irishman. He
read me poetry about the bird.

> " '. . . A sparrow is dead, my lady's sparrow,
> my own lady's delight, her sweetest plaything,
> dear to her as her eyes—and dearer even . . .
> I'll attend you, O evil gods of darkness.
> All things beautiful end in you forever.
> You have taken away my pretty sparrow,
> Shame upon you. And, pitiful poor sparrow,
> it is you that have set my lady weeping,
> Dear eyes, heavy with tears and red with sorrow.' "

"I went mad for Orson when we met. He wasn't like anybody
else I'd ever known. He made me laugh and he was smart and he
was crazy and I loved it."

"You sent him home alone."

"He was sick and I knew he'd get well in New York. I had a
chance at a career, and I knew if I had to nurse him and abandon
the career I'd hate him. And what kind of marriage would that turn
into?"

"Walter was never sick. You must never leave them alone for
long. You would've gotten your career."

"Did you ever leave Walter alone?"

"Did I ever leave Walter alone."

"Orson left me alone and then he went off to drink himself into oblivion. He stole the world for me, put himself in jeopardy, facing jail, really, and then he went off to die. I love him so for that."

"You love that he wanted to die for you?"

"He wanted to die for the *image* of me. He was too crazy to see I was only a bright, immature woman out to save herself, which is really all I knew how to do. He wanted to make me into a goddess and I helped him, because I loved the idea of such a man, and loved what his love did to me."

"But the love was a lie."

"You should have seen us in bed."

"But you didn't stay in his bed."

"No."

"Did he ever understand how you were leading him on?"

"I wasn't leading him on. I was trying to be equal to his dream. I'd deceive him again if it meant keeping that love alive."

"Are you brighter than Orson?"

"Would it make any difference if I was?"

"You know something, but love isn't what you know."

"I know everything about love."

"Walter and I made love in a tent the first time. He set up his pup tent in the woods one night after supper, and went out to stay in it as soon as it got dark. I went down the back stairs and met him in the spot where we watched the birds, and Walter had a flashlight. We went to his tent and he loved me and made my heart bleed with joy . . . like . . . holy and blessed Jesus . . . like nothing else. There was never *anything* like that, ever before, in anybody's life I'd ever heard about. Have you? I'd bleed every night if I knew we'd both feel like that when we were done. Wouldn't you?"

"Yes. Maybe."

"He never came right out and asked me to marry him. We were walking on Pearl Street one day and he says to me, 'How'd you like to be buried with my people?' I said I'd like that just fine. But we didn't marry then, because I couldn't. We married when I was able and we took a flat up in the Pine Hills, and I was never happier, ever. A year passed and Tommy fell crossing a street and broke his wrist, and Sarah got sick and couldn't cook for Chick and him, so I went back home and ran things till Sarah could get on her feet. But she couldn't. The doctor tried everything, but she was so weak she couldn't get out of bed, and she wouldn't go to the hospital. Walter got impatient with me after two months of it, me being with her more than I was with him. And we fought. He said Sarah was faking sickness to keep me there, that she never forgave me for taking his attention away from her that day on the porch. But I couldn't believe that. Why would she ever do such a thing? Walter never meant anything to her. There was no sense to it. Walter said I should hire a woman to cook and keep house for two weeks so we could drive to Virginia to see his brother, and also break in my new car. He'd bought it for me, but I hardly drove it. It just sat in the alley on Colonie Street while I took care of Sarah. Sarah wouldn't hear of hiring anybody, wouldn't allow a woman in the house that wasn't family, so I didn't go to Virginia. Walter went with one of his friends from the school, and the friend fell asleep at the wheel and went over a ravine and they were both killed."

"Orson didn't die."

"He might have."

"No. He has things to do. With or without me."

"I fell apart when I heard the news. I couldn't do anything. Walter's family took over and had his body shipped home. They were furious with me and none of his sisters even called me. They sent the undertaker to tell me where the wake would be."

"I wonder which of us will bury the other."

"I went in and sat for the last hour of the second night of the wake and never spoke to any of them. They were cool to me, nodded at me when I came in, and one came over and tried to talk, Lila, the youngest, who I always liked. But I didn't say much, even to her. I just watched, and then when the undertaker came in to tell us to say good night to Walter, that he had to close up, I went and told Walter this was not good night, that we were leaving this place. Then I told his sisters, 'I am the widow. He was my husband. I have my own undertaker, and he's right there in the hallway.' And there was Ben Owens, standing there with three helpers, waiting for me to tell him what to do, and I told the others, 'I'm taking him to our home, and he'll wake from there, and I hope none of you try to stop me, because I have a letter my lawyer got me from the courts'—I really didn't have a letter; I made that up—'and if you raise one finger against me I'll have the police on you. I don't know what you thought you were doing taking Walter, but a widow is not without her rights.' They couldn't believe it. They thought he was theirs. But he'd left them and married me, that's what marriage is. And so Ben Owens put him in the coffin I bought for him and carried him out to the hearse and we went to our house and had the second wake. They didn't come. They drove behind to make sure where we were going. They thought I was totally mad, but I was never saner in my life. And I sat up with him all night long and then at five in the morning I called Sarah to tell her what I was doing, that she could come to the church if she wanted, seven o'clock mass at St. Joseph's, where we were married. And we had the mass, and Sarah got out of her sickbed and never went back to it, and Chick and Tommy came with her, and Peter would have too, but it was too short notice. And then we went to the cemetery, with Father Mahar saying the prayers at the grave. Us and Billy and his mother, and all the Quinns, and a few neighbors who'd heard about it were all the ones that came, but then almost nobody knew what I'd done. His family came to the cemetery and stood off to one side and nobody talked to them. And then we buried Walter in the Phelan family plot, right next door to where I'll be buried, not with his people at all. We always had too many empty graves in our family. We always prepared for death, never for life. So I did that for him anyway."

Giselle focuses her camera, Molly framed in her lens, the now mythical cedar waxwing cupped in her hands. Molly sits in the first rocker in a line of thirty rockers on the Lake House veranda, the rocker in the same place as when Molly first saw the waxwing fall from the tree, injured but still alive. The tree is still giving shade to the lawn, although Molly says it has lost many branches since that day nineteen years ago. Part of the tree is visible in the background of the photo (what is not visible is Tommy in his wheelchair, under the tree) about to be taken by Giselle, who is trying to record some part of the secret being of this sixty-four-year-old woman her husband loves: his aunt, if you can believe that; and Giselle is looking for a clue to what has generated this love, and what sort of love it could be, and why she is profoundly jealous of it. After all, the woman is thirty-four years older than Orson, forty years older than Giselle, a fragile and fading page of history, a woman who purports to know everything knowable about love, although she has probably known only one man and was married to him less than two years, which isn't much more than Giselle has been married to Orson; and Giselle has known more than one man, to be sure. Not *so* many more, but more. Giselle sees the family resemblance between Molly and Orson and Peter and she knows that her jealousy is irrational and that Orson is not about to break any taboos, but on the matter of taboos she also knows that there is the possibility of her own dalliance with Orson's father. The man is strong-minded, knows who he is. He's a talent and Giselle respects that above much else. He's taken with her as well, which she saw during the hours they spent looking for Orson in the Village bars and coffeehouses and movie theaters. In a Bleecker Street movie he took her hand, held it, told her, "Don't worry, he can't hide forever, we'll find him," and kept holding the hand as they sat in the back row looking over the audience. She had sat in back rows before, holding hands, and it was just like this, and she did not take her hand away. You carry on with a thing like that and if you're not careful you'll cross the line. Sitting beside Peter, she felt she understood his life as a painter, as a bohemian, for in spite of her bourgeois life she was free in the world (working for *Life* was not working, it was soaring), and she was pursuing her photography the way he pursued his art. They were kindred, if not kin, as Orson may be with Molly. But there is more between those two than blood. Orson says to Molly from his vantage behind Giselle, "Look at me, Moll, this way," and Molly turns her head and when she sees him she looks again at the bird and then at the camera, and the smile is there now and Giselle captures it, that smile: the soft currency of Molly's soul.

The things we do when we're alone, without a perch or a perspective, and when there is no light in the corner where we've been put. The things we do.

When I left Giselle at the Plaza, I walked the streets until I came to Meriwether Macbeth's corner. Then I went upstairs and sat in Meriwether's darkness and drank myself to sleep with whiskey. I awoke to dismal day and assayed the work I had previously done on Meriwether's jottings and tittlings, then set about the task of concluding it as Walker Pettijohn had suggested: expanding the jots, fattening the tittles. I read and culled for two days and two nights, breaking stride only to forage for an editorial survival kit: two sandwiches and three more bottles of whiskey. I decided I was done with the editing when only half a bottle of whiskey remained, and I knew then I had an excellent chance of dying of malnutrition, darkness, and Macbethic bathos. I wrote Pettijohn a note, told him to give to Giselle all money due me for this editing, and also to give the manuscript of my novel to the Salvation Army for public auction, any money realized from its sale to be used to purchase ashes, those ashes to be given free of charge to unpublished authors, who will know how to use them. Then I drank myself quiet.

Giselle is jealous of Molly. The attention she shows me in Molly's presence is different from the attention she shows me when we are alone. Giselle is always smarter than I judge her to be, no matter how smart I judge her to be. It doesn't really matter that she is jealous of Molly, though it's a change for both of us. It truly does matter that I love Molly.

A full day had passed before I realized that it was Giselle and Peter who had found me in my alcoholic coma. I opened a sobering eye to see her standing over my hospital bed, a tube dripping unknown fluid into my arm, my body in original trouble: nothing like this sort of pain ever before.

"You're still alive, Orson," was her first sentence.

"That's not my fault," I said.

"You idiotic bastard," she said. "It's one thing to be crazy, but it's another thing to be dead."

"Don't call me a bastard," I said, and I lapsed willfully into a coma-like sleep for two more hours. Giselle was still there when I again surfaced.

"You're getting better," she told me. "We're taking you to Albany. You obviously can't live in this city."

William Kennedy

"Are you coming with me?"

"Yes," said Giselle.

And I slept then, sweetly, ignorantly.

I put undeservedly great faith in hollow objects. What is the purpose of this?

I thought of the Grand View Lake House, which was at the edge of hollowness; all but empty of significance; "dead" would soon be another viable adjective. But it would not *really* die as long as the Shugrues stayed alive, and the loyal handfuls kept coming in season in enough numbers to cover expenses; and it would not die as long as I moved through its hollowness as helpful artisan, woodcutter, sweeper of leaves and dead rats, scraper of paint, mower of lawns, outwitter of raccoons, magus of empty rooms.

The Phelans had been coming to the Grand View for more than half a century. Pat Shugrue had worked with Michael Phelan on the New York Central, but quit in '91 to build three cottages on the shore of Saratoga Lake. Michael took his brood of seven (Tommy, the youngest, was one; Francis, the eldest, was twelve) to one of the cottages (three bedrooms) for a week the following summer, the first annual Phelan Saratoga vacation. When Shugrue upgraded the cottages to a Lake House, the Phelans were there for that first season.

The Phelan boys grew up with Pat Shugrue's son, Willie, who inherited the hotel and added two wings when Pat and Nora phased themselves out; grew up also with Willie's wife, Alice, who at first supervised the cooking at the Lake House in the late 1930s, but by the early '40s was the organized brain behind the business. Alice was also Molly's closest friend, ever since their days at St. Joseph's Industrial School, where Catholic girls from Arbor Hill learned cookery and needlework.

Giselle brought me to Albany in early April, 1953, stayed two nights with me in the Phelan house, and in that time revealed such

214

a restlessness that I insisted she go back to her career. "You weren't put here on earth to be a nurse," I told her, "nor could I abide watching you try to become one against your will."

It fell to Molly to oversee my reentry into the human race. An instrument of angelical mercy, she soothed my psychic wounds with gentleness, brought me food and the newspapers, told me stories of her life, convinced me I could trust her with my troubles.

But Molly perceived, as others in the family did not, that my recovery was static; that to recover fully I needed more than this household could offer; and it was she who in the late summer of that year called Alice Shugrue and asked whether she could use me at the hotel, provided I worked for my keep. She said I'd been raised by Peter (the Phelan handyman) and could do carpentry, plumbing, electrical work, and more; that I needed no wages, only a place to stay and something to do with my hands.

And so now, October, 1954, a year and months after that salvational intercession by Molly, something new can begin. The nights are beyond autumn, and beyond even that by the woods on the lake- shore, cold into the marrow, the morrow, reading *Finnegan,* yes, *carry me along, taddy, like you done through the toy fair!* And then doesn't the kerosene for the heater vanish entirely from the world? It does. Himself alone with that book and his own book, a writer and a woodsbee, a man in a manner of wondering, what manner of wondering man is this? A man in love with his wife and his-aunt- your-sister, tadomine. Of all love there is, this has been the most strange, leaving nothing undesired, nothing sired, the lover bald to the world, no heir. Was ever a family so sonless, so cold, dark, and bereft of a future as these fallow Phelan *fils?*

I was used to being alone here in the cottage, relieved to dis- cover that one did not wither in such solitude; that it really could be a nurturing force. What I did not expect was this onset of winterish night without heat. I put on my overcoat, muffler, hat, and one glove, the other hand free to turn the pages, and I kept reading, ranging now through the book's final pages, the glorious monologue of Anna Livia Plurabelle: *Why I'm all these years within years in soffran, allbeleaved. To hide away the tear, the parted. It's thinking of all. The brave that gave their. The fair that wore. All them that's gunne. I'll begin again in a jiffey. The nik of a nad. How glad you'll be I waked you! My! How well you'll feel! For ever after.*

Words alone, language alone, not always penetrable (like women with their mysteries; and how they do fill this life with spectacle and wonder), now filling the reader-and-writer with infeasible particulars, always the great challenge, is it not, to fease the particules and not malfease? Giselle was gone again, yet again, but in transition to something other than what she once was; and who knew how that would come out?

"I'll be up next weekend," she told me.

"That soon?"

"I like it up here."

"Not much action."

"I'm saturated with action," she said. "I like the calm of this place. I want to photograph it, and Saratoga too."

So, you see, that's a change in Giselle. I make no plans on the basis of it, however. Giselle is as mercurial as the early autumn in Saratoga: sunlit day become gelid night. Apart, we move together slowly into the future. But since coming here I do perceive a future, with or without the woman. Molly did this; brought me to see Alice and Willie Shugrue, Alice a tightly wrapped Irish whirlwind who holds the hotel together by dint of will and want: wanting nothing but this place now, living in the South Cottage with the rheumatoid Willie, a waning wisp of a fellow who can no longer afford artisans to stave off the decay of the buildings, can no longer climb a ladder himself. And all the while your man lives in the North Cottage, reading, learning to write, learning how to be alone. And out our windows we all watch the Lake House begin its struggle through

216

yet another winter, and we wonder: Is this the year it collapses of its own hollowness?

When I first came to live at the Lake House in 1953, Molly drove me with my baggage, helped settle me into the cottage, helped Alice Shugrue cook dinner for us all, and when Molly was leaving to go home she presented me with forty ten-dollar gold pieces to help finance my life while I waited for my survival advance from Walker Pettijohn. My manipulation of the Meriwether papers had pleased Pettijohn so much that when he learned I was neither dead nor dying he turned me loose to edit the fustian out of a pop-scholarly study of the love theories of Lucretius, Ovid, and Henry Miller.

The gift of gold from Molly was a stunning surprise, not least because it was gold, but also, as I would discover, because she had been hoarding it for two and a half decades, giving it away, five dollars at a time, to relatives and select friends on special occasions.

The August racing meet had ended at the Saratoga track, and most of the Lake House's last guests had gone home, except for a few couples who would stay through Labor Day; and so Molly really didn't go home that night. She decided to stay overnight when the Shugrues and I suggested it. This was when I first heard the story of the cedar waxwing, and Walter's sudden courtship of Molly on that late-summer day in 1935.

I'd been here once before, in the early 1940s, on a long weekend with Peter and Danny Quinn, and knew the place somewhat. But Molly now gave me her own private tour of the grounds and buildings, each weighted with memory.

"Right here," she said of an area now grown over, "was the clock golf that Walter and I had played every day. Here's where we played croquet and once I beat him. Here's the path into the bird sanctuary where we used to meet. There's the boat house where he first kissed me, and there's the barn that was our dance hall, isn't it wonderful? And because it's so away from the hotel we could play our music all night long if we wanted to, and nobody would yell at us for keeping them awake."

The barn had been a cow barn, sturdily converted to a weatherproof building in the early 1930s. It was a cavernous place with exposed beams, its never-painted dance floor now a challenge because of warped boards. The barn was redolent of raw wood and of the pine groves that bordered it outside, and Molly said it was the purest odor she ever knew, that it always turned her memory to those summer days with Walter; that in eighteen years this perfume of love never changed. The place is really just like it always was, she said, the phonograph still there on its table, and the old records (hundreds loose on shelves and in albums), some so old even I remember playing them on the wind-up Victrola. Some were cracked from careless use, but the Shugrues never threw any away, for this music was as much a part of the history of the place as their guest register. You expected the same records to be there, year after year, even the cracked ones.

Molly took down a pile of them, all scratched, no envelopes to protect them, shuffled through them, and found one. "Here," she said, and gave it to me to put on the turntable: "When I Grow Too Old to Dream," by Ray Noble and his orchestra, a waltz. And we sat then in two of the chairs that lined the barn's walls, and we listened to it all through. Then Molly said, "Put it on again and we'll waltz," and so we did. Step, slide, pivot, reverse.

"It was like this," she said. "Even when others were here watching, it didn't matter. We were alone in each other's arms and just with the holding we made our pact of love."

Step, slide, pivot, reverse, my hand on Molly's back, her full breasts against me, our thighs touching through her dress and my trousers as we spun around the floor, she so young, and I so beyond age of any number, just keepers of love in our arms, we creating love with our presence, my cheek against hers, her hair touching my eyes. When the music stopped I started it again, and we heard

the scratchings and skips of the song and we danced to that too,
and then I replayed it again, yet again, and neither of us said anything, nor did we fully let go of one another while I moved the
needle back to the beginning. Her hair, its yellow all but gone into
gray, was what Giselle's would be like years from now, her body in
its age fuller than Giselle's.

"Do you love her very much still?" Molly asked.

"I do. As you still love Walter."

"We are serious people about our love."

"We love. It's what we do."

And then I kissed her as one kisses one's love, a long kiss, and
then I stopped and we held each other, neither of us there, of course,
both of us looking at love, of course. And it looks alike sometimes.

I turn the page and I find: *But you're changing, acoolsha, you're
changing from me, I can feel . . . Yes, you're changing, sonhusband,
and you're turning, I can feel you, for a daughterwife from the hills
again . . . I pity your oldself I was used to. Now a younger's there.
Try not to part! . . . For she'll be sweet for you as I was sweet when
I came down out of me mother. My great blue bedroom, the air so
quiet, scarce a cloud. In peace and silence. I could have stayed up
there for always only. It's something fails us. First we feel. Then we
fall.*

"We'll go make a fire," Molly said, "and I'll tell you."

"Tell me what?"

"I'll tell you about me."

I shut off the phonograph and Molly took my arm and we
walked to the main entrance of the hotel, up the stairs, and into
the main parlor with yesterday's rustic furniture and scatter rugs
and shelves of forgotten books and the great stone fireplace and its
stack of wood and old newspapers, and no people but us two, the
other guests all in bed. I moved the screen of the fireplace and built

the fire. Molly knew where to find the matches and then we sat on the sofa and watched the fire grow, me keeping my distance from her, yet close, close, and we looked at one another and we smiled at what we saw. I had to touch her face, and then her hair, and then her neck, and I had to let my hand move down to her breast and I touched that, and she said, "Yes, do that," and I felt the softness and the fullness with just that one hand. She touched my face and ran her fingers through my hair, kissed me with the fullness of her mouth, then took my hand and put it back in my lap.

"We must find a way not to be naughty," she said.

And I read this: *I'll close me eyes. So not to see. Or see only a youth in his florizel, a boy in innocence, peeling a twig, a child beside a weenywhite steed. The child we all love to place our hope in for ever.*

"Walter and I made love every day for a week, sometimes twice a day," Molly said. "The family hardly saw me and they knew, though they didn't know exactly what they knew. Sarah hated it, scolded me every day, warned me, 'You'll be sorry,' but I didn't care. Then we all went home and love was over for the time being, though I found ways to meet him. And I did get in the family way. It'd have been a holy miracle if I hadn't. Me forty-five and him a year older, latecomers both of us to this, but I never told him. He died without ever knowing. When I was two months in I found ways to stay home, said I was sick and I was. We talked often on the phone and he couldn't understand why I wouldn't see him, and I always told him, 'I will see you, I will when I can.' I stopped eating so the weight wouldn't show, had a ketchup sandwich once in a while, and tea, and I was weak. Very. Nobody knew. I never let Sarah or my brothers know anything, didn't even let them see me unless I had a big robe on. And I could never in a million years tell Sarah. She always said after Tommy was born simple that there shouldn't be any more Phelan children. That was Mama's idea, of course.

Mama stopped sleeping with Papa after Tommy. No more, no more, it's a sign, I know it. We all heard them fighting about it. Did I want the baby? No. Not for Mama's reason but because I wouldn't want any man marrying me for that, could never raise a child alone, and couldn't ask for help. And so I started to take things to force the birth: medicines, potions, what I'd heard about through the years, pills I saw advertised once, and I knew I could hurt myself. I knew a girl once took a douche of gin and naphtha to get rid of it and she screamed for two hours, all by herself, until they heard her, and she kept screaming until she died. I wouldn't be that foolish. I tightened my corset as much as it went, but I kept growing. And then I called Mrs. Watson, the midwife, and asked her what a woman had to do if she was alone and the baby came, and she told me. 'But don't stay alone,' she said. 'Come and see me.' I doubted I'd be able. I always thought I'd have it alone. Not a soul in the world I could ask for help. Not a soul. *First we feel. Then we fall.* It was past four months when it came on its own, a boy, and dead. I cut the cord and mopped the blood when I could, never a scream or a moan out of me, can you believe that? In the night it was. No light till it was over with and I wrapped up the blanket and sheet and the towels and all, and put the baby in the steel box from the closet shelf, where I kept some valuables, and went down the cellar and buried it. I don't know where I got the strength to dig the hole. We don't know how strong we are, do we? I called the baby Walter Phelan and baptized him with water from the sink in a teacup and he's down there still, in a far corner of the cellar, with boxes of horseshoes and jam jars on top of him all these years, God forgive me. You're the only person in the world knows this. God was with the Phelans, don't you think? He took the baby but saved us from scandal and he let me have my love back. I was well in a week and Walter came and took me down to Keeler's for dinner and I remember he ordered a half-dozen clams and when they came he started to eat one and at the same time asked me would I marry him right away, not waste another day, and I said I would before the clam got to his mouth. I will marry you a hundred times, a thousand. And I did." *I done me best when I was let. Thinking always if I go all goes. A hundred cares, a tithe of troubles and is there one who understands me?*

One.

I turned the page.

The things we do when we're alone.

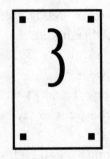

In the year after Molly and I fell in love with each other's failed love, I could at last say without equivocation that I had acquired a family, although a failing one. Sarah and Tommy passed on, Molly fell into her melancholy, and my father, mad with art, and obsessed with his imagery of pernicious life—this rage of creative excess being the condition to which he had aspired all his artistic career—nearly died of a heart attack. That attack reduced him to part-time mad-man, immobilized and weak, but insistent on working an hour a day, at least. It was because of his condition, and Molly's, that I eventually moved down from Saratoga to become magister of the Phelan house on Colonie Street.

Sarah died first. Molly encountered the beginnings of her sis-ter's decline upon her return from her and Tommy's Labor Day visit with Giselle and me at the Grand View. She found the interior of the Colonie Street house in total darkness at late afternoon, every window barricaded against the light by black drapes Sarah had nailed to the walls. Sarah had also unplugged all lamps, and removed all bulbs from the ceiling fixtures Peter had installed twenty years earlier. Molly found her in her room, sitting in her chair reading, by the light of a solitary candle, an old yellowed newspaper. Sarah seemed not to hear Molly enter the bedroom, but when she saw her she folded the newspaper and put it in the drawer of her bedside table. Then she blew out the candle, moved onto the bed, and pulled the covers up to her chin.

"What happened, Sarah?" Molly asked. "Are you sick?"

"You left me alone," Sarah said.

"I asked you to come with us. We went to Saratoga."

"I know where you went."

"Billy helped me bring Tommy's wheelchair into the house. He's downstairs. Don't you want to say hello? Don't you want to see Tommy?"

"No. You left me alone," Sarah said, and that's all she said for two days.

Billy and Molly plugged in the lamps, put the bulbs back in the chandeliers, pulled the nails out of the drapes and woodwork, some of which had splintered, the first serious damage to it since the house was built seventy-five years earlier. As Molly was trying to understand what could have possessed Sarah to do such a thing, she realized that being left by herself was reason enough; for it came to Molly that never in her life had Sarah spent one night alone in this house. Molly knew that she herself could be alone forever, *would be* alone forever, with or without other people, and that it wouldn't kill her; intensify the sadness she was never without, yes; but I am not going to die from such a thing, is how she put it when we talked about Sarah.

The decline of Sarah seemed uncharacteristically abrupt. We all thought she would struggle more vigorously against the cabal of forces that had beset her, but we misread her plan. All her strength and will centered on the downward rush to death, and she clenched her jaws against even minimal nourishment, ripping out of her arms the tubes that carried the life-sustaining fluids Dr. Lynch had ordered for her. She had a deadline for her death. She calculated her weakness until it was the equivalent of a newborn: helpless, pulled into a realm not of its own choosing, the newborn and the imminently moribund bound for an encounter at the symbiotic boundary of life and death. And she died two hours into November 17, 1954, her mother's ninety-fourth birthday.

Sarah left explicit instructions for her wake. She was to be laid out in the same style dress that Kathryn Phelan wore to her grave, and in the same style coffin, which was to be placed in the same position in the front parlor. A solemn high funeral mass should be said for her, as with Kathryn Phelan, and with Father Mahar, the pastor, to be the celebrant. She left the bankbook of the family savings account in the drawer of her bedside table, and it revealed a balance of $840.22. Sarah had no bank account of her own. What little money she earned sewing she always deposited to the family account.

Molly did not find the newspaper Sarah had put in the bedside drawer, nor had it been thrown away. Molly resolved to search for it when the funeral was over. She also chose to countermand Sarah's request for the ancestral dress.

"She'll wear her good Sunday dress," Molly said. "I won't have us a laughingstock, people thinking we're old-fashioned."

Tommy saw Ben Owens and another man carrying Sarah's body down the front stairs and out to the waiting hearse.

"What're they doing, Molly?" Tommy asked.

"They're taking Sarah," Molly said.

"Where they taking her?"

"To the funeral home," Molly said, and she sat down beside Tommy on the sofa. "Sarah died, Tom."

"She did?"

"She died this morning."

"Will they bury her?"

"Yes, they will."

"Why'd she die?"

"She was sad," Molly said.

"What was she sad about?"

"Oh a lot of things, Tom."

"Is she dead? Really, really dead?"

"Yes."

"I didn't think she'd die."

"Neither did I."

"Will you die, Moll?"

"Some day."

"How about me? Will I die?"

"I hope not."

"Me too," Tommy said. "I don't think I wanna die."

Molly called Peter and he said he'd be up the next day. When she called Peg to tell her the news Peg immediately came down and helped clean the house. I also came down after Molly called me, and made plans to stay over through the funeral.

Ben Owens brought Sarah home at early evening. There would only be one night of waking, the two-night wake going the way of gaslight and woodstoves. Molly had ordered two pieces of flowers and had them delivered immediately, which I found odd, for surely they'd look fresher if they were delivered the day of the wake. We imposed order and polish on the house, then ate the turkey sandwiches Peg brought for us. When Peg went home Molly put Tommy to bed, and then she and I sat alone in the back parlor, I expecting the full story behind Sarah's death. But Molly only sat with her hands folded in her lap, still wearing her kitchen apron, staring at the coffin in the front parlor.

"I should do it now," she said. "I may not have another chance after Peter gets here."

"Chance for what? What should you do now?"

"Bury my baby," she said. "Put him in hallowed ground."

"Jesus, Moll, are you sure? You want to go back and relive that whole thing?"

"I relive it every day of my life," she said.

"You mean you want Ben Owens to go down cellar and dig

up the bones and buy a grave and have a mass and all that? It could turn into a police matter. Can you seriously want that?"

"That's not what I want. Do you love me the way you did the night we danced?"

"I do, Moll," I said, "I think it's a permanent condition."

"I thought so. That's why I want you to dig up the baby for me."

Access to the cellar was through a trapdoor in the kitchen floor. The stairway was of narrow, warped boards, without a banister, and one achieved the bottom either in darkness or with a flashlight. The place had obviously been designed by a lunatic, the foundation a crazy collage of brick and fieldstone, the dirt floor never leveled, the place never wired for electricity, despite the former need for access to the now defunct coal furnace (oil now heated the house). The cellar gave off the cloistered odor of coal dust, dry earth, and crumbling mortar from the foundation walls, which were in a decrepitude parallel to that of the denizens of this house. Dozens of empty jelly and Ball jars lay in boxes on shelves, and beside them dusty rows of pickled cauliflower, tomatoes, onions, preserved fruit and jellies, and I wondered were these still edible, and how long had they survived in this dismal grotto?

Molly followed me down the steps, more surefooted than I, more used to the stairs' rickety incline. Some light from the kitchen shone through the open trapdoor, and so we could see each other dimly. She looked back up to the light.

"Imagine me holding the box with the baby, and finding my way with a flashlight because I didn't dare put on the kitchen light, and then coming down those stairs in my condition. I don't know how I did it."

"You're a strong-minded woman."

"Not strong-minded enough."

She took the flashlight from me and shone its beam into the area behind the stairs. Three more boxes of jars, a box of tools, a crank for an old automobile, a box of horseshoes, a few lengths of pipe, rusty plumbing fixtures, and a backless chair occupied the space. Molly shone the light onto the horseshoes.

"That's the spot," she said, and she reached into the coal bin, lifted a spade off a nail, and handed it to me. I moved the horseshoes and began to dig. It was a shallow grave. I struck the box on the spade's third thrust.

"Is it just one box, nothing else?"

"It was wrapped in a towel."

I scraped dirt away, exposing the box and small, decayed fragments of cloth no longer recognizable as anything in particular.

"No towel here any more," I said.

The light disappeared from the grave and I turned and saw Molly facing away, shining the light on a far wall.

"I need the light, Moll," I said.

She focused it on the dig but again looked away.

"I don't want to see it," she said.

"You won't have to."

I raised the box with one end of the spade, then lifted it out with my hand. Only with its touch did the next question arise: What do we do with it? Hallowed ground where? And how? Climb the cemetery fence at night, babe in hand and the spade strapped to my back? But Molly had already thought it through.

"We'll put the baby in the coffin with Sarah," she said.

I could only whistle my admiration at the tidiness of this.

"Put the box on her chest and fold her hands over it," I said, brushing dirt from the box.

Molly took off her apron and handed it to me.

"Wrap the baby in this, and then put the box back in the ground," she said. "I can't watch. Bring it up to the kitchen when you finish." And up the stairs she went.

I spread her apron on the lowest empty shelf and set the box beside it. In close light I saw the box was of a type that locked with a key, and it *was* locked, or sealed by rust under its eighteen-year-old layer of silt. I found a hammer and chisel in the tool box, easily broke the lock, and raised the top to see the remnants of a cloth of indeterminate type: a muslin pillowcase? a linen blouse? I tipped the box upside down to empty its contents onto the apron, but it would not release, the remains wedded to the interior rust. I did not want to touch anything, more out of sacredness than revulsion or fear of corruption. I nudged the edges of the cloth with the chisel and, as gently as the task demanded that I do this, scraped the swaddling cloth out of its coffin. It was far more intact than the towel, its underside discernible as linen, tanned by time and stained by blood and afterbirth. There was almost no shape to the remains of the child: no torso, no shoulders or rib cage, no limbs, no bones at all that I could see except the half-curve of the tiny skull that raised a doll-like protuberance under the cloth. I would make no inspection of what lay beneath the linen. I folded the apron around it and the odor that arose from the closure was neither of blood nor decayed flesh, but rather a singular emanation more powerful than the fused odors of earth and disintegrating metal: a pungent assault on the senses by the mortal remains of love.

In the kitchen Molly had prepared the burial packaging: a length of brown wrapping paper, a roll of Scotch tape and another of adhesive tape, and a white linen napkin with the scrolled letter P on one corner. I took the remains out of the apron and put them in the wrapping paper, this movement revealing that there remained nothing but human dust and the fraction of skull, and I wrapped and sealed this completely with the tape. I wrapped it then within the napkin, exposing the letter P, and wrapped that twice around with adhesive tape. The entire package was about the size of a poppy-seed roll from the Grand Lunch, and when I finished with it Molly took a small purse from the top of the refrigerator, put the remains inside it, and handed it to me.

"You decide where to put it," she said.

The logical place was under Sarah's head. I raised the head cushion, and Sarah as well, and fitted the purse snugly into the space. The change in Sarah's angle of supinity was negligible.

"Do you think people will be able to smell anything?" Molly asked.

"Your flowers should take care of that. Isn't that why you ordered them?"

"It is."

"You've thought about this a long time."

"For years. I knew I'd send Walter along with whoever went next in the family. I prayed I wouldn't go first."

"What do you think Sarah would say if she knew she was having company in her coffin?"

"She'd find fault. She found fault with everything."

"It gives a new meaning to 'virgin with child.' "

"We all would've been happier if Sarah wasn't a virgin."

"You really think that would have made a difference?"

"Virgins think about heaven," Molly said. "They don't care about what goes on down here."

Our neighborhood was in a stage of vanishing tradition, dying to its old self, an influx of Negroes creating a new world order, displacing the old Irish and Germans in the same way those two groups had displaced the Dutch and English gentry who so shortsightedly thought that bucolic Arbor Hill was to be their private garden forever. And so for this reason, and also because of the all-but-cloistered life Sarah had led, fewer people came to her wake than were expected, the most notable absence being Chick, who did not even telephone after he received Molly's telegram, but merely sent a modest basket of flowers, the card with them bearing nothing

other than the names *Chick and Evelyn Phelan,* the first announce-
ment to the family that Chick had married, and simultaneously an
act of distancing Molly took to be spiteful.

"Chick will regret this to his dying day," Peter said when he
read the card, "not because of Sarah, but because he'll eventually
realize what we think of his gesture. Anger makes people stupid."

Anger did not make Peter stupid. And surely it was at least
anger, perhaps even rage at the power of an abstraction as cruel,
remote, and inviolate as God, but not God, that propelled Peter
toward his masterworks. He saw, in the story of Malachi and Lizzie,
and then in the way that Kathryn and Sarah had nursed that story
and secretly kept it alive, a pattern that need not have been—a
wrong to two generations that might have been preventable, if
only . . .

I've generalized about cause and effect in this family, but one prox-
imate cause of what made Kathryn, Sarah, Peter, and the rest of us
behave in such diverse but consistent ways was chronicled in that
newspaper story Molly saw Sarah reading by candlelight. Molly
found the cache of old papers in a crawlspace that opened off the
closet of Sarah's room (Kathryn's and Michael's room before Sarah
took it over) into an unusable area of the attic. As children, Molly
and Julia had discovered the crawlspace and hidden in it to elude
Sarah, or merely to exist in a secret place no one else could enter;
but Sarah caught them coming out of it one day and the secret place
lost all value.

Molly found the papers in the small brown leather suitcase
Michael Phelan had used when his work on the railroad required
him to stay overnight in another city. There were a dozen newspapers
in all, telling day by day the story of Malachi and Lizzie, the marriage
destined for enshrinement in a lower circle of hell.

"So this," Molly said to me when she showed me the papers,
"is what she was reading at the last. Gone back to the first."

231

What happened with Malachi was hardly the first, but I do believe that that's how Molly and others in the family thought of it. Molly wasn't even born when it happened, nor were Julia and Tommy. Francis was seven, Sarah four, Chick one. Also Kathryn was pregnant with Peter when she went through the Malachi ordeal in 1887.

In the 1930s Peter had found his artistic vision in *The Itinerant* series, but then in subsequent years he foundered badly, dabbling in cityscapes, portraits, and in the new non-figurative, non-representational abstract mode, whose exercises in symbolic color and form, devoid of the human being, he could admire when done by others, but only loathe as pretentious failures when he created them himself.

In the weeks after Molly and I showed him the Malachi newspapers, Peter returned to figurative drawing, sketches of people closest to him, and felt instant strength, saw the abstract elements of these lives not as layers of scumbled space and violated line, but as the cruel specifics of eyes and jaw, the mournful declension of a lip line, the jaunty elevation of a leg. For years he had sketched the family, either from photographs or memory, or by cajoling his siblings (even Sarah one afternoon) into modeling for him. He never showed any of these works publicly, though he completed a dozen or more paintings from four or five score of sketches. Perhaps he was waiting for the moment when the visual reunion of his kin would make exhibitional sense.

That came to pass when the family, as he saw it, osmosed its way into his *Malachi Suite,* that manic outpouring of genius (I give him no less) that eventually drew me, and even Giselle, into its remarkable vortex. He sketched with a passion and painted with a fury that bespoke his fear of time, his full awareness that he had so little of it left in which to complete this now obsessive work. But he also painted with a sure hand, all errors deemed fortuitous and made part of the painting. His brush never wavered, these works of pain and poignancy stroked into existence with swiftness, certainty, and a realism that arrested the eyes of the beholder, held them fast.

In early childhood Peter had heard the Malachi events spoken of in cryptic bits by his mother, later heard more from Francis, who was seven when it happened, and in time heard it garbled by street-corner wags who repeated the mocking rhyme:

> If you happen to be a Neighbor,
> If you happen to be a witch,
> Stay the hell away from Malachi,
> That loony son of a bitch.

When the story took him over, Peter moved out of portrait sketching into scenes of dynamic action and surreal drama that in their early stages emerged as homage to Goya's *Caprichos, Disparates,* and *Desastres de Guerra.* But in his extended revelation of the Malachi-and-Lizzie tragedy (and mindful of Goya's credo that the painter selected from the universe whatever seemed appropriate, that he chose features from many individuals and their acts, and combined them so ingeniously that he earned the title of inventor and not servile copyist), Peter imposed his own original vision on scandalous history, creating a body of work that owed only an invisible inspiration to Goya.

He reconstituted the faces and corpora of Lizzie and Malachi and others, the principal room and hearth of the McIlhenny three-room cottage, the rushing waters of the Staatskill that flowed past it, the dark foreboding of the sycamore grove where dwelled the Good Neighbors, as Crip Devlin arcanely called those binate creatures whose diabolical myths brought on that terrible night in June of 1887.

His first completed painting, *The Dance,* was of Lizzie by the sycamores, her bare legs and feet visible to mid-thigh in a forward step, or leap, or kick, her left hand hiking the hem of her skirt to free her legs for the dance. But is it a dance? In the background of the painting is the stand of trees that played such a major role in Lizzie's life, and to the left of her looms a shadow of a man or perhaps it is a half-visible tree, in the dusky light. If it is a tree it is beckoning to Lizzie. If it is a man perhaps he is about to dance with her.

But is that a dance she is doing, or is it, as one who saw her there said of it, an invitation to her thighs?

In the painting it is a dance, and it is an invitation.

Why would Lizzie McIlhenny, a plain beauty of divine form and pale brown hair to the middle of her back, choose to dance with a tree, or a shadow, or a man (if man it ever was or could be) at the edge of a meadow, just as a summer night began its starry course? Aged twenty-six, married five years to Malachi McIlhenny, a man of formidable girth whose chief skill was his strength, a man of ill luck and no prospects, Lizzie (née Elizabeth Cronin) had within her the spirit of a sensuous bird.

Malachi imposed no limits of space on their marriage, and so she came and went like a woman without a husband, dutiful to their childless home, ever faithful to Malachi and, when the bad luck came to him, his canny helpmate: first trapping yellow birds in the meadow and selling them to friends for fifty cents each, but leaving that when she found that fashioning rag birds out of colored cloth, yarn, thread, feathers, and quills was far more profitable; that she could sell them for a dollar, or two, depending on their size and beauty, to the John G. Myers Dry-Goods and Fancy-Goods Store, which, in turn, would sell them for four and five dollars as fast as Lizzie could make them.

At the end of a week in early June she made and sold sixteen birds, each of a different hue, and earned twenty-seven dollars, more money than Malachi had ever earned from wages in any two weeks, sometimes three. The money so excited Lizzie that when crossing the meadow on her way home from the store she kicked off her shoes, threw herself into the air, and into the wind, danced until breath left her, and then collapsed into the tall grass at the edge of the sycamore grove, a breathless victim of jubilation.

When she regained her breath and sat up, brushing bits of grass from her eyelashes, she thought she saw a man's form in the shadowy interior of the grove, saw him reach his hand toward her, as if to help her stand. Perhaps it was only the rustling of the leaves, or the sibilance of the night wind, but Lizzie thought she heard the words "the force of a gray horse," or so it was later said of her. Then, when she pulled herself erect, she was gripping not the hand of a man but the low-growing branch of a sycamore.

Malachi's troubles crystallized in a new way when he lost his only cow to a Swedish cardsharp named Lindqvist, a recently arrived lumber handler who joined the regular stud-poker game at Black Jack McCall's Lumber District Saloon, and who bested Malachi in a game that saw jacks fall before kings. Lindqvist came to the cow shed behind Malachi's cottage and, with notable lack of regret, led Malachi's only cow into a territorial future beyond the reach of all McIlhennys.

The lost cow seemed to confirm to Malachi that his life would always be a tissue of misfortune. At the urgings of his older brother, Matty, who had come to Albany in 1868 and found work on a lumber barge, Malachi, age seventeen, had sold all that the family owned and left Ireland in 1870 with his ten-year-old sister, Kathryn, and their ailing father, Eamon, who anticipated good health and prosperity in the New World. In Albany the three penniless greenhorns settled in with Matty at his Tivoli Hollow shanty on the edge of Arbor Hill. Within six months Matty was in jail on a seven-year sentence for beating a man to death in a saloon fight, within a year he was dead himself, cause officially unknown, the unofficial word being that a guard, brother of the man Matty killed, broke Matty's head with an iron pipe when opportunity arose; and then, within two years, Eamon McIlhenny was dead at fifty-nine of ruined lungs. These dreadful events, coming so soon after the family's arrival in the land of promise and plenty, seemed to forebode a dark baggage, a burden as fateful as the one the McIlhennys had tried to leave behind in County Monaghan.

Malachi did not yield to any fate. He labored ferociously and saved his money. And as he approached marriage he bought a small plot of country land on Staats Lane, a narrow and little-used road that formed a northern boundary of the vast Fitzgibbon (formerly Staats) estate, and built on it, with his own hands, the three-room cottage that measured seven long paces deep by nine long paces wide, the size of a devil's matchbox. In 1882 Malachi moved into the cottage with his bride, the sweet and fair Lizzie Cronin, a first-generational child of Albany.

After five years the marriage was still childless, and Lizzie slowly taught herself to be a seamstress as a way of occupying her time, making clothing for herself and Malachi. But with so few neighbors she found other sewing work scarce, and her days remained half empty, with Malachi working long and erratic hours. And so Lizzie looked to the birds, the trees, the meadows of the Fitzgibbon estate, and the Staatskill, a creek with a panoramic cascade, churning waters, and placid pools, for her pleasure. Malachi saw his wife developing into a fey creature of the open air, an elfin figure given to the sudden eruption of melodies off her tongue that Malachi did not recognize. She began to seem like an otherworldly being to Malachi.

In the spring of 1887, two days after he lost his cow, the waters of the Hudson River, as usual, spilled over their banks and rose into the lumber mills, storage sheds, and piles of logs that were the elemental architecture of Sage's lumber yard, where Malachi worked as a handler. One log slipped its berth in the rising waters, knocked

William Kennedy

Malachi down, and pinned his left shoulder against a pile of lumber, paralyzing his left arm and reducing the strength in his torso by half, perhaps more. So weakened was he that he could no longer work as a handler, that useless left arm an enduring enemy.

He found work one-handedly sickling field grass on the Fitz-gibbon land, work that provided none of the fellowship that prevailed among lumber handlers. He worked alone, came home alone, brooded alone until the arrival of his wife, who grew more peculiar with every moment of Malachi's increasing solitude. He topped her at morning, again at evening after she returned from her communion with the birds of the field, and he failed to create either new life in Lizzie or invincible erectness in himself.

To test himself against nature he sought out the woman known to the canalers and lumber handlers as the Whore of Limerick, her reputation as an overused fuckboat appealing to Malachi's free-floating concupiscence. After several iniquitous successes that proved the problem existed wholly in Lizzie, Malachi abandoned the fuckboat and sought solace again in Lizzie's embrace, which cuddled his passion and put it to sleep. He entered heavily into the drink then, not only the ale that so relieved and enlivened him, but also the potsheen that Crip Devlin brewed in his shed.

Drink in such quantity, a departure for Malachi, moved him to exotic behavior. He lay on his marriage bed and contemplated the encunted life. Cunt *was* life, he decided. Lizzie came to him as he entered into a spermatic frenzy, naked before her and God, ready to ride forever into the moist black depths of venery, indeed even now riding the newly arrived body of a woman he had never seen, whose cunt changed color and shape with every nuance of the light, whose lewd postures brimmed his vessel. Ah love, ah fuckery, how you enhance the imperial power of sin! When he was done with her, the woman begged for another ride, and he rode her with new frenzy; and when he was done again she begged again and he did

238

her again, and then a fourth ride, and a fifth; and, as he gave her all the lift and pull that was left to him, his member grew bloody in his hand. When the woman saw this she vanished, and Lizzie wept.

The following morning, when he awoke, Malachi found not only his wife already gone from the house, he found himself also bereft of his privities, all facets of them, the groin of his stomach and thighs as hairless, seamless, and flat as those groins on the heavenly angels that adorned the walls of Sacred Heart Church. Here was a curse on a man, if ever a curse was. God was down on Malachi now—God, or the devil, one.

Malachi clothed himself, drained half a jug of potsheen, all he had, then pulled the bedcovers over his head. He would hide himself while he considered what manner of force would deprive a man not only of his blood kin, his strength, his labor, and his cow, but now, also, his only privities. He would hide himself and contemplate how a man was to go about living without privities; more important, he would think about ways of launching a counterattack on God, or the devil, or whoever had taken them, and he would fight that thief of life with all his strength to put those privities back where they belonged.

In the painting he called *The Conspiracy,* Peter Phelan created the faces of Malachi and Crip Devlin as they sit in Malachi's primitive kitchen with their noses a foot apart, the condiments and implements of their plan on the table in front of them, or on the floor, or hanging over the fireplace. The bed is visible in the background, a crucifix on the wall above it.

Malachi is in a collarless shirt, waistcoat and trousers of the same gray tweed, and heavy brogans, his left arm hanging limp. Crip Devlin wears a cutaway coat in tatters, a wing collar too large for his neck, a bow tie awkwardly tied.

These men are only thirty-four and forty, Malachi the younger of the two, but they are portraits of psychic and physical trouble. Malachi's face is heavily furrowed, his head an unruly mass of black curls, his black eyes and brows with the look of the wild dog in them. Crip is bald, with a perpetual frown of intensity behind his spectacles, a half-gray mustache, and sallow flesh. He is moving toward emaciation from the illness to which he has paid scant attention, for at this time he considers all trouble and trauma to be the lot of every man born to walk among devils.

Crip was in a late stage of his pox veneris, not knowing how close he was to death, when he brought his mystical prowess to bear on the lives of Lizzie and Malachi. He had studied for the priesthood briefly as a young man, and later taught primary school, but was unsuited for it, lacking in patience toward eight-year-old children who could not perceive the truth. In recent years he had worked as a lumber handler with Malachi, and in the winter they cut ice together on the river. But his disease in late months kept him from working and he lived off the sale of his homemade liquor, which, by common standards, was undrinkable, but had the redeeming quality of being cheap.

Crip had brought the recipe for the potsheen with him from Ireland, as he had brought his wisdom about the Good Neighbors, those wee folk who, he insisted, inhabited a hilly grove of sycamore trees and hawthorn bushes not far from Malachi's cottage. Crip was a widower who lived with his nine-year-old daughter, Mab; and he taught her all the lore of the Good Neighbors that he himself had learned from his mother, who once kept one of the wee creatures (a flute player) in the house for six months, fed it bread and milk on a spoon, and let it sleep in the drawer with the knives and forks. And didn't Crip's mother have good luck the rest of her life for her generous act? Indeed she did.

When Malachi listened to Crip Devlin talk, something happened to his mind. He saw things he knew he'd never seen before, understood mysteries he had no conscious key to. When Crip stopped talking Malachi also felt eased, relieved to be back in his own world, but felt also a new effulgence of spirit, a potential for vigorous action that just might give back a bit of its own to the foul beast that was skulking so relentlessly after his body and his soul.

In Ireland, Crip boasted, he'd been called the Wizard, the Cunningman who could outwit the Good Neighbors. And when Malachi heard this he confided to Crip that he had lost his privities.

"Did you ever lose them before?" Crip asked Malachi.

"Never."

"Was there pain when they went?"

"None. I didn't know they were gone till I looked."

"It's a shocking thing."

"I'm more shocked than others," Malachi said.

"I've heard of this," said Crip. "Somebody has put the glamour on you."

"Glamour, is it?"

"A spell of a kind. The Neighbors could do it. I read of a man who lost his privities and thought he knew who did it, and it was a witch and he went to her. He told her his trouble and also told her she had the most beautiful bosoms in the village, for he knew how witches love flattery. And she took him out to a tree and told him to climb up it and he'd find what he needed. When he did that he found a great nest full of hay and oats in the treetop, and two dozen privities of one size and the other lying in it. And the man says I'll take this big one, and the witch says no, that belongs to the bishop. So the man took the next-smaller size and put it in his pocket, and when he got to the bottom of the tree and touched the ground with his foot, the witch disappeared and his privity was on him. And he never lost it again."

"You're thinkin', is it, that a witch did this to me?" Malachi asked.

"It well could be. Do you know any witches yourself?"

"None."

"Have you had any in the family?"

"None that I know of."

"And your wife's family?"

"I've never heard it spoken of."

"They don't speak of it, don't you know."

"I'll ask her," said Malachi.

"I saw her up on the Neighbors' hill two days ago."

"Is that so?"

"It's so, and she was dancing."

"Dancing, you say."

"I do. Dancing with her skirts in the air."

"No."

"Didn't I see it myself, and the shape of a man in the woods watching her?"

"The shape of a man?"

"Not a man atall, I'd say."

"Then what?"

"One of the Neighbors. A creature, I'd call it."

"Lizzie dancing with a creature? You saw that. And were you at the potsheen?"

"I was not."

"Did you go to her?"

"I did not. You don't go near them when they're in that mood."

"What mood?"

"The mood to capture. That's how they carry on, capturing people like us to fatten their population. They like to cozy up to them that come near them, and before you know it somebody's gone and you don't even know they're gone, for the creatures leave changelings in place of the ones they take. But there's no worth atall to *them* things. They melt, they die, they fly away, and if they don't, you have to know how to be rid of them."

"You know how to do that, do you?"

"I've heard how it's done. I have the recipes."

Two books lie on the table in Peter's *Conspiracy* painting.

The first is the *Malleus Maleficarum*. Its subtitle, not visible in the painting, is *The Hammer of Witches Which Destroyeth Witches and Their Heresy as with a Two-edged Sword*. The book is a fifteenth-century theological analysis of the anarchical political forces that for centuries sought the overthrow of civilization through witchcraft, plus abundant remedies for this evil; and it is a work that had motivated Crip Devlin since the days of his priestly intent, for its divinely inspired misogyny conformed to Crip's own outlook, especially after his infection with the pox by his wife. And did she give it to him, the witch? Well, she did. Didn't she die of it herself, and die before Crip? Was that proof or was it not?

Malachi, when he listened to Crip's wisdom, handed down from the sages of history, felt like a chosen man, one who would yet again do battle with the dark spirits, the lot of the true warrior in every age. Malachi accepted the role without complaint, for its rules and its goals were as familiar to him as the streets and the fields of Albany. He agreed with them, he understood them, and he knew from his wound that he had been singled out for this challenge. As the *Malleus* pointed out so clearly, devils existed only with God's permission, and Malachi perceived that God had allowed these devilish things to happen to him, allowed his life to be taken away piece by piece, in the same way He had allowed Job and Jesus and the martyred saints to be warrior sufferers for His sake.

Without ever having heard the phrase, and with small capacity for understanding it if he had, Malachi had become an ascetic idealist, as obsessed by his enemy as Peter would be by his art; and when you look at the eyes Peter gave the man, you know that both Malachi and Peter understood that the world was inimical to them and to their plans of order and harmony, that their lives existed at the edge of disaster, madness, and betrayal, and that a man of strength and honor would struggle with the dark armies until he triumphed or died on the battlefield.

Malachi truly believed he would win this struggle with the black villain. He had done as the *Malleus* counseled, had said his Aves and his Our Fathers, had made the Stations of the Cross on his knees, had talked to the priest and confessed his sins (not his loss for that was an affliction, not a sin), and had gone to mass so often that the women of the parish thought he must be either very guilty, or dying. But, in truth, he was coming to understand that some sort of action that went beyond heavenly recourse was called for, action beyond what was known on earth—except by a chosen few whose courage was boundless and whose weapons were mighty.

The second book on the table in the painting is a slim volume that is open to a sketch of a plant with leaves and berries that any herbalist would recognize as foxglove. Also in the painting Crip is holding a chicken by the neck with his left hand and from its anus is receiving droppings in his right palm, some of these already floating in a bowl of new milk on the table.

Crip, before the moment shown in the painting, has enlightened Malachi on the things witches fear most, things that cure enchantment and banish the witch back to her own devilish world: foxglove and mugwort, white mullen and spearwort, verbena and elf grass, the four-leaf clover and the scarlet berries of the rowan oak, green and yellow flowers, cow parsnip and docken, a drawn sword, the gall of a crow, the tooth of a dead man, rusty nails and pins, the music of a Jew's harp, a red string around the neck, the smoke of burned elder and ash wood, the smoke of a burned fish liver, spitting into your own shirt, pissing through a wedding ring, and fire.

Crip mixed half a dozen potions for Malachi and he drank them; the two men burned ash wood and fish liver; they found foxglove and cow parsnip and made a paste of it and Malachi went off by himself and rubbed that on his groin. He thought of pissing through his mother's wedding ring, but then he remembered he had nothing to piss with. More things were done, all of them failing to restore Malachi's privities.

Crip then moved to the next logical step: an inquiry into the behavior and the physical properties of the women around Malachi (his sister Kathryn, the Whore of Limerick, Lizzie), for it was well known that witches sometimes assumed the shape of living people, especially women. Even so, they could be found out, for they always had marks and traits that were not human. Crip knew of one witch who had an extra nipple on her stomach, and another with nipples on each buttock. A third witch always lived with two creatures sucking her, a red one at her left breast, a white one at the inward walls of her secrets.

When Malachi heard these revelations he immediately undertook a thorough but surreptitious study of his wife, and for the first time he realized that she had shrunk in height by four inches, that the mark on her left thigh could well be an extra nipple. He remembered that she brought a succubus to their bed and encouraged him to copulate with it until he was bloody. Also, Crip swore to him that, on the night he watched Lizzie dancing on the Neighbors' hill, her partner, the shadowy creature, had the webbed feet of a goose.

And so Malachi made ready to launch his counterattack against the demon (and all its hellish consorts) that inhabited his wife's body.

BOOK FIVE

As the time grows closer for it, I'm becoming obsessed by the fact that Giselle is coming here, and that my life is about to change yet again. She now tells me she's pregnant, and that she didn't plan it. It's July, she's two months gone, and I did it to her in May, she says, when she came up to take the final photo of Peter for the *Life* profile she did on him. She was here all weekend, we went at it in my room, what, two, three times? And bingo! She left then to travel for two months, and I didn't hear from her until last night, when she said she'd be up today, with an enhanced womb, for the family meeting Peter had invited her to attend.

She also told me that, after five years of it, she's had enough and is leaving *Life*—as soon as she finishes her current project. She'll have a baby, then free-lance, giving *Life* first look at whatever she photographs. She no longer wants to be at the beck and call of magazine editors, now says she's willing to rejoin the nuptial bed, which she'd hinted at when last we bathed in the steam of our malfunctional wedlock.

I'd often given her my spiel, that the quotidian life is the most important element of our existence, and although she didn't accept that in the early days of our marriage, she now says I was right, that a career is indispensable, but it makes for a very sterile life if that's all there is. She says she envies me the family ties, and that she's come to understand she and I might be divorced now if it weren't for Molly.

Of course I don't believe much of what Giselle says. Such conversions are for minds more simple than hers. It will be a major change having her with me all the time, but it is true that she's grown closer to the family since the *Life* profile on Peter, and the book project that grew out of it. Walker Pettijohn suggested an art book on Peter, a book suitable for coffee tables, with Giselle doing the photos, me doing text blocks plus interviews with the artist (he thought the father-son link would enhance the book's appeal, but I pointed out to him the awkward disparity in our names), and a critic yet to be chosen analyzing Peter's work and putting it in historical perspective. Such is the man's fame, now that he's close to death (though not yet moribund), that this was one of four book offers prompted by the *Life* article. Peter has managed to jump through the flaming hoop of high art and come out the other side as a potential creature of the popular imagination.

I was still at the dining-room table, cheating at cards for Billy's amusement, when I heard Peter's hoarse voice call me.

"Orson, can you come up?"

And so I excused myself and went up. Peter was in bed, just reawakened after a mid-morning nap. He'd had his matinee with Adelaide, then attacked his easel until fatigue pulled him back to his pillow. He looked tousled and very old for his seventy-one years, his gray-haired torso going to bone, his hair and mustache almost solid white, and more scraggly than usual.

When I entered his bedroom he was sitting on the side of the bed gripping the sturdy blackthorn walking stick Michael Phelan had bought in Ireland. His room, the same one he'd slept in all his life in this house, was full of books, newspapers, and three unfinished sketches, this being his pattern: to keep incomplete work at his bedside, study it before sleep, and wake perhaps to find a solution that would let him complete it. I thought he might now be ready for a second go at the work-in-progress, but he had another plan.

"Anybody here yet?" he asked.

"Just Billy and myself."

"So you nailed him."

"He's here but he's itchy to leave."

"Keep his curiosity aroused and he'll stay."

"That's what I'm doing."

"Get him to help you move some paintings downstairs."

"He's got a cast on his foot."

"How'd he get here? You carry him?"

"He can walk."

"If he can walk he can climb stairs."

"Which paintings do you want?"

"*The Dance, The Conspiracy,* and *The Protector.*"

"Not the new one?"

"No, I don't want to shock them. Maybe later. Those'll do for what I have to say."

"Done."

I called Billy and he hobbled upstairs immediately. I took him through the rooms, which he hadn't seen since the day Sarah went crazy because Molly left her alone. Billy and Molly then had to repair all Sarah's damage and chaos, and that was the first Billy had ever been above the ground floor. He'd told me more than once he never wanted anything to do with the house, or its people, after his father's experience, the exception being Molly, who always gave him five dollars in birthday gold, as she gave others in the family. Like most people who knew her, Billy projected a ray of love toward Molly. "Good old dame," he called her. He liked to tease her about her hemorrhoids, a problem he also lived with.

"Christ, what a wreck this joint is," Billy said when he came upstairs.

"It's not a wreck. It's an artist's studio, all of it except my room and Molly's. And he's even moving things into her room, now that she's not using it."

"Molly's not livin' here no more?"

"Not for months. She's up at Saratoga with the Shugrues, living in the rooms I used to live in. She couldn't take care of Peter, couldn't go up and down the stairs twenty times a day. She's got all she can do to take care of herself these days, and so we swapped rooms. I came here, she went there. Alice Shugrue's her best friend in the world, great company for her."

"I didn't know Molly was sick. I don't hear what goes on."

"She's not sick, just weary. She's in good enough shape that she's cooking lunch for us. You like roast lamb?"

"Are you kiddin'?"

"Good."

"What's this lunch business all about?"

"About all the Phelans, and their ancestors."

"Not interested."

"Don't be so quick, Billy. We need you, and I really mean that. We need what you know."

"I don't know nothin' you don't know."

"You know about your father. You know when he came home in '42, and what he did. I don't know any of that. I was in the army already. You see what I'm saying?"

"I see what you're sayin', but I don't know what you're talkin' about. What's my father got to do with anything?"

So I showed him all my photos of *The Itinerant* series, in which Francis played the central role. I told him how Francis showed up all of a sudden, then fought with Sarah, and how Peter tracked him down and asked him to come back, and that I saw this with my own eyes.

"But he didn't come back," Billy said.

"No. He kept walking. He didn't come back to stay till the war. Do you know whether he ever came here in the war period?"

"He wouldn't put a foot on the stoop."

"Did he ever talk to Peter, or Molly, or Chick, or anybody?"

"Maybe Pete went to see him at a Senators game when he was coachin', but if he did my father never mentioned it."

"He saw you, and Peg, and Annie."

"That's why he came home. He called my mother and found out I was goin' in the army and he said he'd come home and be around if somethin' needed fixin'. He took a room up near the ball park. He'd come down to the house once a week and sit with my mother, bring her a pint of vanilla ice cream, or pineapple sherbet, talk an hour, have a meal with us, then disappear for another week. But he'd come by in a minute if Ma called him. He shoveled snow, cut the grass for her, put up screens and storm windows, fixed a busted asbestos pipe on the furnace."

"He was a strange guy."

"He was an *all-right* guy," Billy said with an edge to his voice.

"I didn't say he wasn't."

"Everybody else in this joint did."

"I just told you that wasn't true. Stick around, Billy. You'll learn something about your relatives you didn't know."

"Yeah," he said.

But I knew I'd hooked him. I took him into Peter's studio and found the paintings Peter wanted as props when he delivered his remarks to the assembled kin. Billy looked at the paintings the way he looked at everything else in the house: not interested. Then we carried them, one by one, down the hallway to the dining room.

That Malachi was still influencing our lives like this supported my idea that we are never without the overcoats, however lice-ridden, of our ancestors. This luncheon was going to be an expressionistic occasion, offering graphic imaginings of where we came from, what we might expect of ourselves (and our children), and what we might do to our greatest loves, given our inherited propensities. I tried to imagine whether and, if so, why Malachi was predisposed to disaster, and all I could do was project myself backward into my own disturbed history, into the isolation where I had been able to triumph privately in social, financial, marital, and artistic realms, no failure possible in that utopia where all eccentricity is justified, where ineffectuality is not only acceptable, but desirable as a badge of defiance, where there is no need to engage the actual world because the private world is always sufficient to the day. Reality conquered by the ego: Malachi's story precisely.

I now like to think that I am coming out of this benighted condition, and in my own peculiar way am again an engaged citizen of the bright day, working within the race. I see evidence of this in my ability to function in the publishing world without either the hem-kissing subservience of the acolyte, or the wound-licking reverie of the early failure.

I feel pride in my restrained reaction to Giselle's pregnancy, never once voicing those Strindbergian doubts that had dropped into my mind like henbane: never inquiring whether it truly was I who seeded her furrow; never offering the suggestion that it was perhaps an anonymous creativist at *Life,* or possibly Quinn the traveler who had left his enduring mark on her during one of his New York visits. Did I suggest, as the young Strindberg ruffian, Nojd, put it, that "it wouldn't be much fun slaving all your life for another chap's brat"? No, I did not. If it was Quinn who'd done the deed, then at least the Phelan ontogeny was now at work in Giselle's inner sanctum, and I might become father to my first cousin twice removed. But I am no more likely to have certitude on any of this than Nojd, or Peter Phelan.

Molly pulled the doorbell and stood on top of the stoop with her arms full of groceries. She turned to the curb, where Alice Shugrue waited behind the wheel of her Chevrolet, idling until Molly had gained proper access to the homestead; and then I opened the door and took a bag from Molly ("Be careful, there's breakables," she said). I hugged her and bussed her cheek, then waved to Alice.

"Come in and see us when you come back for her," I said, "and we'll catch up on all your news." Alice smiled and waved me down, saying, "You're not to be trusted with my news, now that you're writing a book," and off she went.

Molly stepped into the hallway and tapped the bag of groceries I was holding. "You're not to be trusted with breakables either," she said. "I've seen you with dishes in the hotel kitchen."

"There are things I never dropped," I said, "so get your dirty tongue off me."

Molly, kittenish, kissed my cheek with her arms full as we moved toward the kitchen. "I miss this house," she said.

"Well, come back to it, then," I said.

"Easy to say."

"Easy to do. There's change afoot in the world."

"Afoot me foot," said Molly. "All that'll change this place is an earthquake."

"Exactly what we've got planned for lunch," I said.

"It's a scheme, I knew it. What's he up to?"

"I'll tell you when it's time to tell you."

I thought Molly looked well, though a bit more frail than when I'd last seen her. Her north-country exile seemed to be sapping her energy, but she was wearing one of her dressy summer dresses, the pink one, so I sensed she was trying to rekindle her old self for the occasion. We put the groceries on the kitchen table and I then took her by the elbow and moved her toward the dining room and Billy. Her gaze went instantly to *Banishing the Demons* on the wall, then to *The Conspiracy,* which I'd leaned against the back staircase. She had seen, and fully understood, the content of both paintings, but made no comment on their presence. She turned and looked at Billy in his plaster cast.

"It's a long time since I've seen your handsome mug, Billy boy," she said. "I heard you might be here today."

"That's more than I heard. Who told ya that?"

"I'm no squealer, kiddo," Molly said. "And whatever did you do to your leg? Are you all right?"

"I can't kick," Billy said. "You're lookin' good, Moll. How's the old bareedis?"

"I'm fine in all respects, and I'll answer no more impertinent questions."

"How's Saratoga?"

"The hotel is busy. The track opens next week."

"But no more gamblin' casinos."

"None that I hear of. It's not like it used to be."

"Nothin' is," Billy said.

"How many are coming for lunch, Orson? We have to set the table."

"Us three and Peter, and Peg is coming with Roger Dailey, the lawyer, and Giselle. Seven."

"Giselle is coming?"

"Peter invited her. She's been up fairly often lately."

"How is she?"

"She's pregnant. I guess that makes it eight."

"Oh," said Molly, "oh." And she looked at me with that hybrid smile of hers: knowing smile of love, and comprehension, and loss.

"First tremor of the earthquake," I said.

"Hey," Billy said, "you gonna be a papa."

"Looks that way," I said.

"The lawyer," said Molly. "Why is the lawyer coming?"

"I'll tell you when it's time to tell you," I said.

"Well, I'll tell *you* what it's time for. It's time to make lunch. Bring me the potato dish, two big platters, a vegetable dish, and the pickle and jelly dishes. And the bread plate. And set the table with whatever's left of the good china."

Molly's reference was to the remnants of a set of china that Peter had bought for Kathryn with his mustering-out pay from the

first war, a belated acknowledgment that he had been partly responsible for Francis's fall into the china closet. And I wondered
how much of that episode in his father's life Billy knew, and I
decided he probably knew nothing at all.

"Have you taken a good look at these paintings?" I asked Billy,
indicating *The Conspiracy* and the *Demons*.

"Unhhh," Billy said, and he craned his neck to look at both,
then moved his chair for a better look, and he stared.

"That guy looks like my father," he said, indicating Malachi
in *The Conspiracy*.

"Right. And a little like my father too," I said.

"Yeah," said Billy. "What the hell is it?"

"It's Peter's vision. Your father's been important to him all his
life. He's painted him many times."

"This is the first one I saw."

"Not the last. He's in that one too," and I pointed to the
Demons painting.

"Who's that guy supposed to be? It ain't really my father."

"It's your great-uncle, Malachi McIlhenny."

"I heard of him. Wasn't he nuts?"

"Totally, but there's more to it."

"Yeah," Billy said, "when people go nuts they got a reason."

"You never uttered a truer word," I said.

I heard footsteps on the porch and went to see who was coming.
But it was only the afternoon paper, stuck between the jamb and
the doorknob by the thoughtful paperboy to keep it dry. It had
been cloudy for an hour and now a fine drizzle was beginning. I
was closing the door when I saw a taxi turning off Pearl Street onto
Colonie, and I thought, Giselle, accurately. She paid the cabbie and
slid out of the back seat with her arms full, offering me her knees
in the drizzle, constantly smiling, moving with small steps back into
my life. I held the door for her, and she kept going down the hallway
to the kitchen.

"Don't I even get a hello?"

"Yes," she said. "Follow me."

And so I did, as I always have, and in the hallway she gave me a serious kiss and went into the back parlor to deposit one of her bags next to the player piano. She said hello to Billy without introducing herself and delivered her gifts for the meal (goose-liver pâté, a wheel of Camembert, English tea biscuits, two bottles of Haut-Brion, and two pounds of Whitman's chocolates for Peter) to Molly in the kitchen.

"That's Giselle," I said to Billy, and I handed him the afternoon paper. He nodded and looked at the front page.

"They got a story on the shootin'," Billy said. "They picked up Johnny Rizzo at the railroad station, leavin' town, and Morty's in the hospital. He might lose a leg."

"That's a tough one."

"Yeah, but he loses a leg means the card game's off. That son of a bitch'll do anything not to pay me what he owes."

"If they have to reschedule the game let me know. I'll go with you anytime."

"Nah, forget that. I'll do it on my own."

"All right, whatever you say."

Giselle came in from the kitchen. "You're Billy," she said. "I've seen your picture."

Billy stood up and shook her hand.

"I'm Billy," he said, "and you're pregnant."

"My news precedes me," she said, and with both hands she arced a bulbous abdomen onto herself. I then took my first look at her body, which was sheathed in a smart white linen dress that gave no indication of the two months of new life that functioned beneath it.

"A kid in the family," said Billy. "That's something new."

Giselle had pulled her hair back tight in a ponytail, more severe than I'd ever seen her look. Was she already shedding glamour to befit her incipient motherhood? Throttling down her sex appeal for the sake of the family gathering? I heard the closing of a car door and then saw through the parlor window Peg getting out of a Cadillac convertible (its top up), abetted by a soulful caress of her elbow by Roger, the lawyer, that bespoke something beyond a lawyer-client relationship. I noted Peg's coy smile, the retreat of her elbow, and their mounting of the stairs together (Peg carrying a fat bag of fresh snowflake rolls and a strawberry pie from the Federal Bakery), and this instant gave me more insight into the femininity of my cousin Margaret than I had ever had heretofore. I could see the appeal she held for Roger, a man twenty-two years her junior, who was to be married in three weeks. But impending marriage was not an obstruction to fun for Roger, who en route to this luncheon meeting offered Peg an afternoon of pleasure at a hotel of her choice, a movie (*Indiscreet* was playing at the Strand), or an evening at an out-of-town summer theater (*Silk Stockings* was playing at Sacandaga, and he told Peg she had elegant legs, and she does).

Peg told me all this when I taunted her with what I had seen as they arrived, adding that she had declined the offers, even though she thought Roger was "a doll." And I believe her, cannot think of her as an adulterous woman, though of course what do I know? Also, I marveled at how quickly she offered up all this information to me, such frankness unheard of in this family, wherein affectionate elbow-stroking, had it been observed by Kathryn or Sarah, would have led to unexplained excommunication of both pairs of elbows from these sanctified rooms, not to mention the cancellation of lunch.

Peter came down the front stairs to the parlor and sat in his leather chair, which was still where I'd seen it in 1934, though hardly in the same condition. He had tried to transfigure his appearance, banish the scraggle by wetting and combing his hair, perhaps even trimming his mustache; and, despite the heat of the day, wore an

open-collared white shirt with a tan paisley neckerchief, brown corduroy sport coat with leather elbows, tan pants, and paint-speckled
dress shoes.

"Who's here?" he said as he was easing himself into the chair,
favoring his bad hip.

"Everybody," I said, and we moved toward him and took all
the available seats in the room. I brought a dining-room chair for
Molly, who came in wearing her apron, drying her hands on a
kitchen towel. Peter surveyed the assemblage with a constant smile,
then fixed on Giselle.

"And how is Mother Gigi?" he asked. I had never heard anyone
call Giselle Gigi before.

"She's sick every morning," Giselle said, "but otherwise fine."

"Margaret, how's the family?"

"About the same," Peg said, "except for Danny. He called me
at the office this morning to say he's getting married."

I looked at Giselle, who blinked at the news about Quinn. I
wonder why? She did not look at me.

"A Cuban girl," Peg said.

"New blood in the family," Peter said.

"Is she a Catholic?" Molly asked.

"Who gives a royal goddamn?" Peter said.

"All I know," Peg said, "is that he's very much in love."

"I should hope so," said Peter. "Roger, I'm glad you could
arrange your schedule to be here. And, Billy, it's good to see you.
It really is good to see you."

"Yeah, well," Billy said, and he worked up half a smile.

"Molly, you're losing weight, but you look grand."

"And so do you," said Molly, "with your kerchief."

"But you should take off that apron. A day of some formality
requires the proper costume." And as Molly untied her apron he
looked at me. "And you should have a tie on for your guests, Orson."

"I'll dress for lunch," I said.

I was wearing my usual shirtsleeves, slacks, and loafers; and who needs more in this weather? The answer is Peter, who was demanding proper tribute be paid to the patriarchal rite he was now conducting, and which I had organized. When it became clear that he would be getting a great deal of money for his *Malachi Suite,* he said to me offhandedly, "I don't want to keep all that damn money. I won't live long enough to make use of it. And when I go they'll probably take half of it in taxes."

"What's your alternative to being well off?"

"Give it away."

"To needy painters?"

"The family."

It began with that; then I called Peg to get a lawyer, for she had legal contacts I lacked. Enter Roger Dailey, perennial eligible bachelor, three-handicap golfer at Wolfert's Roost Country Club, a junior partner in one of the city's best law firms, member of an old Irish family with links to Arbor Hill when it was the neighborhood of the lumber barons and other millionaires. I talked him into coming to the house to see Peter, then left them alone. That was a month ago, and now here he was in his creamy Palm Beach suit, bringing us legal tidings.

I hadn't invited Giselle, for I'd evolved into thinking we were all but finished. But Peter took the matter out of my hands and invited her himself, which fixed the day of the event. It then fell to me to round up the others, which was a problem mainly with Roger, because today's visit cut into his golf schedule (the rain would have canceled it in any case), and with Billy, who, as we all knew, loathed this house. But I got around everything and here we were, wondering what was about to happen, imagining what was in Peter's mind, imagining Peter.

"You have the goods, Roger?" Peter asked.

"I do," said Roger, taking a document from the legal-sized envelope he'd brought with him.

261

"Then let's not drag it out, just go ahead and read it."

"This arrangement isn't unheard of, but it's a bit unorthodox," Roger began. "Then again we shouldn't expect conformity from a major artist like Peter Phelan, whose last will and testament I'm about to read to you. Peter has decided its provisions should be made public not posthumously but today, here and now." And then Roger read Peter's ideas translated into legalese:

"Because money has never been a source of anxiety in me, and because the pursuit of money was never what this family was about, I, Peter Joseph Phelan, have chosen to divide my modest, newfound wealth among my siblings, and the heirs of my siblings, for I do believe that my career turn toward financial reward and artistic recognition, which, however belated, has made me feel blessed with good fortune, has been a consequence of my knowledge of this family. And because I further believe that out of the collective evil to which so many members of this family have been heir, heiress, and victim (the scope of which I have only in very late years begun to understand) there can come some collective good, and because one known form of good is the easing of the financial woe that periodically besets us all, I therefore make the following bequests:

"To my brother, Charles Edward Phelan, the sum of eleven thousand five hundred dollars;

"To my sister, Mary Kathleen Phelan, the sum of eleven thousand five hundred dollars;

"To my nephew, William Francis Phelan, the son of my late brother Francis Aloysius Phelan, the sum of five thousand seven hundred and fifty dollars;

"To my niece, Margaret Mary Phelan, the daughter of my late brother Francis Aloysius Phelan, the sum of five thousand seven hundred and fifty dollars;

"To my former concubine, Claire Theresa Purcell, in acknowledgment of two reasonably good years, and two decades of thoroughly unsatisfactory relationships, the sum of two dollars;

"Further, concerning Orson Michael Purcell, my unacknowl-edged son by Claire Theresa Purcell, I do now fully and publicly acknowledge him as my true and only son, and appoint him the sole benefactor and executor of the remainder of my estate, after the bequests specified in this will have been distributed, and do invest him also with artistic and financial control over the future of all forty-seven finished, unsold paintings of mine, thirty-six other unfinished works of mine, and any new works I may undertake before my death, all profits from any sale or exhibition of these works, or any other of my worldly goods, holdings, or inheritances, to accrue to Orson alone, provided that he legally change his name to Orson Michael Phelan, and that he thereafter remarry, forthwith, his present wife, Giselle Marais Purcell, to insure that her unborn child of this moment, July the twenty-sixth, nineteen hundred and fifty-eight, will legally bear the Phelan name; and that if this issue be not a male child, that Orson pursue yet again the conception of a male heir with his wife of the instant, or, if that marriage is terminated, with a subsequent legal spouse, in order to insure at least the possibility of the Phelan name continuing beyond Orson's own demise, this latter contingent action thus ending his respon-sibility for the Phelan line; for more than this no man should be asked to do."

In the silence that followed the reading we glanced where we had to, me at Giselle, all the others at Peter; and Peg spoke up first to say, "Uncle Peter, thank you, thank you. I don't think you know how much this will mean to our family." Fifteen hundred down: easy as apple pie.

Molly walked over to Peter and kissed him on the cheek, said, "You have a good heart," and went back to the kitchen tying on her apron. Billy stared at Peter with what I took to be puzzlement: Why is this guy givin' money away? And why to me? But Billy made no statement except with his eyes.

I caught Peter's eye and I nodded at him. And then he nodded.

Giselle stared at me, and in her look I saw more comprehension of what the will had said about us than I myself possessed at this moment; for while I'd known Peter planned to dispense money, and suspected I would get a bit of it, no thought of a paternity clause ever crossed my mind. I believed he would die without acknowledging me, and I had decided long ago that that was all right. Who needed legitimacy? The answer again was Peter. He needed it now that he was going public. He needed to tidy up his life, organize his death.

He had not expected the professional and financial success that was now coming to him at such a late hour. But it happened that a few perspicacious gallery owners and museum people began to see that his work, despite the varied modes and genres in which he had painted and drawn, had about it a prevailing quality that now seemed to be singular. Recognition came to him as does the fixative an artist acquires at death: No more innovation for you, my friend; we read you at last. This handful of influential Peter-watchers saw him neither as sectarian of any art movement of his era, nor as yet another gadfly among trends. Now they saw an artist who had vaulted beyond his matrix, fused the surreal, the natural, the abstract, and the figurative, and produced an oeuvre that was as cumulatively coherent as his motivation had been in creating the work.

Peter Phelan, obsessive artist of Colonie Street, subsumed in the history of his family, all but smothered under his ancestors' blanket of time, had willfully engaged it all, transformed history into art, being impelled to create, and purely, what Picasso had called "convincing lies"; for Peter believed that these lies would stand as a fierce array of at least partial Phelan truths—not moral truths, but truths of significant motion: the arresting of the natural world at an instant of kinetic and fantastic revelation; the wisdom of Lizzie's lofted leg in her dance with the shadows; the wizardly acceptance of chicken droppings by the demented Crip Devlin; the madly collective flailing of arms in *Banishing the Demons*.

This latter painting, the largest in the *Malachi Suite,* treats of the collective Peter mentioned in his will. By the light of an oil lamp, a candle, and a fire in the McIlhenny hearth (shadowed homage to La Tour), the players in the Malachi drama are enacting their contrary rituals: Kathryn Phelan (abundantly pregnant with Peter, the arriving artist) is sitting on the bed in the background, holding the hand of the beset Lizzie, who is supine in her calico chemise, blue flannel nightgown, and black stockings, her hair splayed wildly on her pillow; and the Malachi minions—the wizard Crip Devlin; Crip's daughter, Mab (the image of the child who led me to Francis at the railroad tracks); Lizzie's father, old Ned Cronin, who badly needed a shave; Malachi's ancient cousin, Minnie Dorgan, with her dropsical stomach, and her stupid son, Colm, whose hair was a nest of cowlicks; and, central to it all, Malachi himself, with his wild curls and his wilder eyes, all these clustered figures pushing upward and outward with their arms (Colm gripping a lighted candle in his right hand and thrusting upward with his left), ridding the house of any demons that may have been summoned by the archdemon that Lizzie had become. The entrance door and two windows of the house are open to the night, and those errant demons, who well know that this room is inimical to their kind, are surely flying fearfully out and away, back to their covens of hellish darkness.

Malachi had gathered his counsel, his blood kin, and his in-laws about him for a communion of indignation at what was happening to Lizzie, and also to people his house with witnesses to his joust with the evil forces. He'd begun that joust with interrogation of Lizzie.

"What is your name?"

"Lizzie McIlhenny. You know that."

"Is that your full name?"

"Lizzie Cronin McIlhenny. In God's name, Malachi, why are you asking me this?"

"We'll see what you think of God's name. Why are you four inches shorter than you used to be?"

"I'm not. I'm the same size I always was."

"Why are you asking her these things?" Kathryn Phelan asked.

"To find out who she is."

"Can't you see who she is? Have you lost your sight?"

"Just hold your gob, woman, and see for yourself who she is. Don't I know my wife when I see her? And this one isn't her."

"Well, she is."

"Are you Lizzie McIlhenny, my wife?"

"Of course I am, Malachi. Can't you see it's me? Who else do you think I am?"

"Do you believe in God the Father, God the Son, and God the Holy Ghost?"

"I do, Malachi, I do."

"You do what?"

"I believe in God the Father, Son, Holy Ghost."

"She didn't repeat it exactly," said Crip Devlin.

"Let me ask her," said Ned Cronin. "Are you the daughter of Ned Cronin, in the name of God?"

"I am, Dada."

"She didn't repeat it," said Crip.

"Repeat it," said Malachi.

"Dada."

"Not that, repeat what he said."

"I don't know what he said."

"Ah, she's crafty," said Crip.

"You'll repeat it or I'll have at you," said Malachi. He grabbed her and ripped her nightgown, then pushed her backward onto the bed. When she tried to get up he held her down.

"Ask her where she lives," said Crip.

"Do you live up on the hill with the Good Neighbors?"

"I live here with you, Malachi."

266

"Who are you?"

"I'm Lizzie, your wife."

"You're four inches shorter than my wife."

"I'm not. I'm this same size since I was a girl."

"You really are insane, Malachi," said Kathryn. "You're torturing her."

"We'll see who's insane. Do you believe in Satan?"

"I don't know," Lizzie said.

"Crafty again," said Crip.

"By the Jesus," Malachi said, "we'll get the truth out of you," and from the table he took the cup of milky potion he and Crip had prepared for this encounter, set it on the bedside table, and lifted a spoonful to Lizzie's mouth. "Take it," he said.

She smelled it and turned her head. "It's awful."

"Drink it," Malachi said, lifting the cup to her lips. Lizzie pushed it away and some of the potion spilled onto her nightgown.

"Oh you'll take it, you witch," Malachi said, shoving the cup to her lips and pouring it. Some of the fluid entered her mouth and she screamed and spat it out.

"She won't take it," said Crip. "And if any of it falls on the floor she's gone forever."

"She'll take it or I'll break both her arms," said Malachi. "Hold her legs, Colm." And the dimwit flung himself crosswise on the bed, atop Lizzie's legs.

"Like this?" Colm asked.

"That's it," said Malachi.

"There's rewards in heaven for them that beats the devil," said old Minnie Dorgan, rocking her body on a straight chair in the corner, plaiting and unplaiting two strips of cloth as she watched the exorcism. She blessed herself repeatedly, and dipped her fingers into a jar of holy Easter water she had brought with her. She sprinkled the water at Lizzie and then at Malachi.

"If you get the drink into her, the witch is dead," said Crip.

"We'll get it," said Malachi.

"That's enough of this crazy talk," Kathryn said, putting herself between Malachi and Lizzie.

"Get out of my way, Kathryn."

"I'll get out and get the police if you don't leave her be."

Malachi walked to the door, locked it, and pocketed the key.

"You'll go noplace till I say you will," he said. "And neither will anybody else in this house. Build up the fire, Mab." And Crip Devlin's child, silent and sullen, threw twigs and a log on the dying fire. It crackled and flared, creating new light in the bleak room, into which not even the faintest ray of a moonbeam would penetrate tonight.

Kathryn whispered into Lizzie's ear, "I won't let him hurt you, darlin', I won't let him hurt you." And she stroked the distraught Lizzie's forehead and saw that her eyes were rolling backward out of their rightful place.

"You're a vile, vile man to do this to her," Kathryn said.

Malachi looked at the women and walked to the hearth. He picked up a long twig and held the end of it in the fire until it flamed; then he pulled it out and shook out the flame and walked toward the bed.

"You bring that near her," said Kathryn, "you'll have to burn me too, Malachi," but he quickly put the stick between his teeth, grabbed his sister with his good right arm, and flung her off the bed and into the lap of Minnie Dorgan, who sprinkled holy water on her. "Mother of God," said Minnie. "Mother of God."

"You'll not be burning her, Malachi," said Ned Cronin. "You won't burn my daughter."

"It's not your daughter that's here, it's not the wife I married. It's a hag and a witch that I'm sleeping with."

"It's my daughter, I'm thinking now," Ned said.

"Have you no faith, man?" said Malachi. "Don't you know a demon when it's in front of your eyes?"

And he had the twig in his hand again, and he lighted it again, blew out its flame again, and put it in front of Lizzie's face.

"Now will you drink what I give you?"

When she threw her head from side to side to be rid of the idea he touched her on the forehead with the burning stick, and she screamed her woe to heaven. "Now you'll take it," he said, and with terrified eyes she stared at the madman her husband had become; and she knew no choice was left to her.

"Leave her be!" screamed Kathryn, and she tried to move toward Lizzie. But Minnie Dorgan and Ned Cronin held her.

"Give her the drink, Mab," Malachi said, and the child raised the cup to Lizzie, who stiffened at the odor of it and, retching dryly, said weakly, "Please, Malachi."

"Drink it, you hag, or I'll kill you."

And she took the cup and drank and screamed again as the foul concoction went down her throat, screamed and spat and drank again, then fell back on the bed as the cup's remnants splattered on the floor.

"It's done," said Malachi.

"And it's spilled," said Crip. "There's no telling what it means."

Colm, lying across Lizzie's legs, sat up. "I'm goin' home now," he said.

"Indeed you're not," said Malachi. "You'll stay till we're done with this."

And Colm fell back on the bed with a weakness.

"When will we be done?" Ned Cronin asked. "For the love of Jesus end this thing."

"We'll end it when I've got my wife back," Malachi said.

"How will you know?" asked Ned.

"We'll see the demon leave her," Crip said. "But time is short. Ask her again."

"In the name of God and heaven," Malachi said, "are you Lizzie McIlhenny, my wife?"

All in the room watched every inch of Lizzie, watching for the exit of the demon. But Lizzie neither moved nor spoke. She stared at the wall.

"We've got to go to the fire," said Malachi. "We've no choice."

"It'll soon be midnight," said Crip, "and then she's gone for sure, never to come back."

"We'll carry her, Colm," said Malachi, and the dimwit rolled off Lizzie's legs. Then he and Malachi carried the now limp figure toward the hearth as Mab stoked the fire with a poker. Lizzie's nightgown was off her shoulder and Malachi ripped it away and it fell on the floor. Mab moved the grate back and Malachi sat Lizzie on it so she faced the fire.

"Are you goin' to make a pork chop out of me, Malachi?" she asked. "Won't you give me a chance?" And on the dark side of the room the women fell on their knees in prayer.

"Do you know what I'm doin' here, Ned Cronin?" Malachi called out.

"Jesus, Mary, and holy St. Joseph," said Ned, "I pray you know what you're doing." And he knelt beside the women.

Malachi leaned Lizzie toward the fire and when it touched her it set her calico chemise aflame. Kathryn Phelan wailed and screamed at her brother, "You'll live in hell forever for this night, Malachi McIlhenny. It's you who's the demon here. It's you that's doing murder to this woman."

Malachi let go of Lizzie and she fell away from the fire, burning. He watched, with Crip beside him, and Colm holding the now unconscious Lizzie by one arm.

"Away she go, up the chimney," Malachi said. "Away she go!" And he waved his good arm into the flame.

"I saw nothing go," said Crip.

"Hail Mary, full of grace, the Lord is with thee, blessed art thou amongst women," said Kathryn on her knees.

"Come home, Lizzie McIlhenny!" yelled Malachi, waving his

arm, watching his wife's body. The room was filling with smoke from Lizzie's burning clothes and flesh.

"Beast!" screamed Kathryn.

"Do you think that's Lizzie that's lyin' there?" Malachi asked.

"I saw nothing leave her," said Crip.

"More fire," said Malachi, and Colm leaned Lizzie back toward the flames. Another edge of her chemise caught fire and now half her torso was exposed, the flesh charring from below her left breast to her hip.

"Let her down," said Malachi, and from the floor beside the fireplace he took a can of paraffin oil and threw it onto Lizzie's stomach. Her chemise exploded in flame.

"Away she go!" yelled Malachi, waving his arm. "Away she go!" And he threw more oil on her.

Kathryn Phelan ran to the wildly flaming Lizzie and threw herself on top of her, snuffing the fire, burning herself, and sobbing with the grief known in heaven when angels die.

The last painting Peter put on exhibit for his luncheon guests was *The Protector*, a portrait of Kathryn Phelan smothering the flames on Lizzie's clothing, her own maternity dress aflame at one corner, the smoke obscuring half her face, the other half lit by firelight. Kathryn's burns were not severe but her act did precipitate, two days later, the premature birth of Peter Phelan, child of fire and brimstone, terror and madness, illusion and delusion, ingredients all of his art.

I had asked him why he chose to resurrect Malachi, such a dreadful figure in the family's life, and he said he could not answer with any accuracy, that the Malachi he was painting wasn't the Malachi of history, that, in whatever ways his paintings reflected reality, they would fall far short of the specifics of that reality, which was always the fate of anything imagined. "We try to embrace the universe," Peter said, "but we end up throwing our arms around the local dunghill." And yet he felt that whatever he imagined would somehow reflect what was elusive in the historic reality, elusive because its familiarity and its ubiquity in real space and time would make it invisible to all but the imagining eye.

In this context, what he had intuited from the Malachi story was the presence of a particular kind of thought, a superstitious atmosphere aswirl with those almost-visible demons and long-forgotten abstractions of evil—votive bats and sacrificial hags, burning flesh and the bones of tortured babies—the dregs of putrefied religion, the fetid remains of a psychotic social order, these inheritances so torturous to his imagination that he had to paint them to be rid of them.

He had always rejected as extraneous any pragmatic or moralistic element to art, could not abide a didactic artist. Nevertheless, his work already had an effect on the moral history of the family, and would continue to do so through the inevitable retellings of the story associated with the paintings; and these retellings would surely provide an enduring antidote to the poison Malachi had injected into the world. The work would stand also as a corrective to the long-held image of Kathryn in the family's communal mind.

"As much as we loved her, none of us can undo the two generations' worth of trouble and anguish she caused," Peter said, and he quoted Francis as saying long ago, "She didn't really know nothin' about how to live." Peter agreed there was some truth in this, but he added that Kathryn surely knew how *not* to live under the mad inheritance that had destroyed Malachi and Lizzie; and that the thing she knew best was denial, the antithesis of Malachi's indulgent madness. After Malachi, Kathryn had even denied herself the pleasure that had probably been hers with the conception of Peter (the subsequent children were conceived under duress).

And, by convincing her husband to make the deathbed request to Sarah, she had imposed on the girl the scullery-nunnery existence that made Sarah deny and eventually destroy her own life rather than admit that lives of sensual pleasure were not only possible, but sometimes eagerly pursued outside the cloistered innocence of this house. She became a mad virgin, Sarah, the dying words of Michael Phelan her dungeon, the courage of her saintly, sinless mother the second-generational iron maiden of her fate.

No chance at all to rescue Sarah. No bequest for Sarah.

No chance to rescue Tommy either. His spinal injury turned into a plague of unpredictable immobility and, when he went back to his job as a sweeper at the filtration plant, the pain struck him so severely that he collapsed and rolled into the thirty-five-foot depths of one of the plant's great filtering pools; and, having been unable to learn to swim any more than he could learn to think, he drowned, another martyr to the family disease.

And not much of a chance to lure the maverick Chick out of his Floridian indignance and back to the family circle. He telephoned Peter from Miami Beach, acknowledged the bequest, offered lively thanks for what he said would be his hefty down payment on a sporty inboard motorboat he'd been longing to buy, invited his brother to come down and go ocean fishing, said Evelyn sent her best, and hung up, maybe forever.

By the time lunch was about to be served, the light rain had become heavy, a storm gaining strength, according to Peg's reading of the weather story in the *Knickerbocker News.*

"It's going to rain all night, and some places might get floods," she reported. She was at the table, where Peter had told her to sit. The rest of us were standing half in, half out of the dining room, waiting for Peter to seat us. Molly was still in the kitchen, organizing the meal.

"The Senators won't play ball tonight," Billy said.

"George's Democratic picnic must be rained out too," Peg said.

"Democrats like the rain," Billy said.

"The Irish like the rain," Peter said. "Three days of sunshine and they start praying for thunderstorms."

The roast lamb lay in slices on the platter in the center of the table, and on the sideboard the leg itself, on another platter, awaited further surgery. Molly had asked me to carve but before I could begin Peg suggested Billy do it, for he did it so well. And so he did, and when only half finished he asked Molly, "You got any mint jelly to go with this?"

Molly looked in the pantry and the refrigerator, reported back, "No mint jelly, I'm sorry, Billy."

"There's mint jelly in the cellar," I said, and I took the flashlight, opened the trapdoor, and found dusty jars of mint jelly and straw-berry jam.

"Sarah put those up," Molly said, "after the war. We got the strawberries from Tony Looby's store, and Sarah grew the mint out in the yard."

"You certainly know your way around this house," Peg said to me. "How'd you know they were down there?"

"I was fixing something one day and I saw this stuff."

"This house would fall apart if it wasn't for Orson," Molly said. "He also kept the Lake House from collapsing around its own ears. Orson is a treasure."

"Just waiting to be dug up and spent," I said.

"You'll never be spent, Orson," Giselle said.

"Oooh-la-la," said Peg, and everyone looked at Giselle, who smiled at me.

"Orson," said Peter, "take control of your wife."

"I would prefer not to," I said. "I like her the way she is."

"We're ready to eat," said Molly, coming in from the kitchen with the potatoes, hot from the oven.

And then, one by one, we sat where Peter placed us, and we were seven, clockwise: Peter sitting where his father had always sat, in the northernmost chair in the room, the first formal resumption of the patriarchal seating arrangement since Michael Phelan died in 1895; Giselle next to Peter to have the impending grandchild in the closest possible proximity to the grandfather, then Roger, Peg, me, Molly in Sarah's chair (her mother's before it was hers) nearest the kitchen, and Billy at Peter's right, completing the circle.

Giselle's pâté, Camembert, and English biscuits lay in tempting array on the sideboard, forgotten, and alien, really, to the cuisine of this house. But we made ready to devour Sarah's mint jelly on Molly's leg of lamb, with the marvelous gravy made from the drippings, small new peas out of the can, the best kind, potatoes mashed by Peg (she said Billy mashed them better), bread by Peg out of the Federal, and the two bottles of the rich and robust Haut-Brion 1934 (a momentous year for both the Bordeaux and the Phelans) that the extravagant Giselle had brought. Peter contributed the saying of grace, which he pronounced as follows: "Dig in now or forever hold your fork."

I suggest that this luncheon was the consequence of a creative act, an exercise of the imagination made tangible, much the same as the writing of this sentence is an idea made visible by a memoirist. If Peter brought it about, I here create the record that says it happened. If, through the years, I had been slowly imagining myself acquiring this family, then this was its moment of realization, and perhaps the redirection of us all.

I think of Peter's creative act (though I am not so modest as to deny my own contribution to the events) as independent of his art, a form of atonement after contemplating what wreckage was left in the wake of the behavior of the males in the family: Malachi's lunacy, Michael's mindless martyring of Sarah, Francis's absence of so many years, the imploding Chick, Peter's own behavior as son, husband, father: in sum, a pattern of abdication, or flight, or exile, with the women left behind to pick up the pieces of fractured life:

a historic woman like Kathryn, an avant-garde virgin renegade like Molly, a working girl like Peg, and, to confirm this theory with an anomaly, there is the case of Giselle.

"I have to say it," Roger said. "This is the most unusual lunch I've ever been to."

"Perfectly normal little meal," Peter said. "Last will and testament with lamb gravy."

"Those here, we've never sat down together like this before, never," Molly said.

"That's hard to believe," said Roger. "You look like such a close family."

"Get your eyes examined," Billy said.

"Don't mind my brother," Peg said. "He's a perpetual grump."

"What this gathering is," I said, looking at Roger, also at Peg to discover where her eyes went, "is the provisional healing of a very old split in this family."

"What's that mean, provisional?" Billy asked.

"For the time being," I said. "More to come later. Like having the first horse in the daily double."

"Yeah," said Billy.

"And it's about time," Molly said. "We should have done this years ago."

"The point is it's done," said Peg. "I love you for it, Uncle Peter," she said, and she blew him a kiss.

"I'm not takin' the money," Billy said.

Peter looked my way, caught my eye, chuckled. I'd predicted that Billy would say this.

"Don't be hasty, now, Billy," said Peter.

"Don't be stupid, you mean," said Peg.

"The hell with stupid," Billy said. "My father couldn't live here, I don't want no money outa here."

"It's Francis's money as much as it's mine," Peter said. "I made it in good measure because of him."

276

"I showed you those photos," I said to Billy, "*The Itinerant* series, and you know Francis inspired that. Peter only painted it." Peter gave me a sharp look. Nothing worse than an ungrateful child.

"And Malachi's face is the face of Francis in the new paintings. You've seen that for yourself," Peter said. "And that's where the money for these bequests really came from."

"So you paint his picture? What the hell is that? He wasn't welcome here and all these years neither were we."

"I came here plenty of times," Peg said.

"I didn't, and neither did he," Billy said.

"You're gonna ruin it," Peg said. "You'll be like Sarah, spoiling it for everybody else."

"I ain't spoilin' nothin' wasn't spoiled years ago," Billy said.

"Have some mint jelly, Billy," said Molly. "Sweeten your disposition."

"I'm sayin' my father never got nothin' outa this house and neither did we, and I don't want nothin' now."

"You told me Molly gave you gold on your birthday," I said.

"Yeah, that's right."

"And she gave me gold too," Peg said.

"You know where I got that gold, Billy?" Molly asked.

"You never said."

"You remember Cubby Conroy?"

"I remember his kid, Johnny," Billy said. "They shot him over highjacked booze and dumped him in the gutter."

"Cubby was a good friend of your father's. They grew up together on this block." Molly paused, looked at Roger. "Mr. Dailey," she said, "do lawyers keep secrets?"

"If they don't, they're not very good lawyers."

"I can't tell my story unless you keep it a secret."

"I'll carry it silently to my grave," Roger said.

"Good," said Molly. "Cubby Conroy was a bootlegger."

"Right," said Billy. "He was also a con man. He and Morrie

Berman got badges and flashed them at Legs Diamond and convinced him they were dry agents. They almost copped a truckload
of his booze before he caught on."

"I did hear that," Molly said. "And then somebody shot Cubby.
Perhaps it was Mr. Diamond, who was upset by what they did."

"Maybe so. Diamond was like that. But how do you know all
this tough stuff?"

Billy was smiling, and I marveled at the way Molly had turned
him around so quickly. She was wonderful at human relationships
and I loved her.

"Well, you know, don't you," Molly said, "that they killed
Cubby up in Glens Falls in one of those roadhouses. Then they
killed Johnny, and the only one left was Charity, Cubby's widow,
who had a collapse of some sort, afraid they'd come after her, I
suppose, or maybe just living alone and drinking alone. I used to
cook her a dinner every day and bring it over, but it didn't help
much. She got sicker and sicker and one day she told me she had
this bootleg money she wanted me to have. All her relatives were
dead, she didn't know where Cubby's people were, but wherever
they were she hated them, and so the money was mine. I thanked
her a whole lot and took it home."

"Where'd she have it hid?" Billy asked.

"Inside an old mattress in the cellar."

"How much?"

"Twelve thousand dollars," Molly said, and we all wheezed
our awe.

"She let you take twelve thousand home?" Billy asked.

"She did. I had to make six trips in the car with my suitcase.
Maybe seven."

"Wasn't she afraid of goin' broke?" Billy asked.

"She wasn't broke."

"How'd you know that?"

"When she died," Molly said, "I found another fifteen thousand in two overstuffed chairs and a sofa. That took twelve trips."

We all wheezed anew.

"Twenty-seven grand," Billy said.

"Very good arithmetic, Billy," Molly said.

"What'd you do with it?" Roger asked.

"Everything I wanted to do," Molly said. "I went to Philadelphia for two weeks to visit our cousin and I looked at the Liberty Bell, and I bought curtains for the house, and I went to Keeler's twice a month and had oysters and lobster, and I paid for the new oil furnace when the coal furnace cracked in half, and I gave money to special people, and I turned it all into gold and put it in safe-deposit boxes because I didn't trust paper money."

"You have any of it left?" Peter asked.

"If I do will you take back my bequest?"

"Of course not," said Peter.

"I have nineteen thousand."

We all looked carefully at Molly now, a woman worth scrutiny, the true and quixotic mistress of this house, the secret financial power behind Sarah's imperious, penurious throne, the self-sufficient dowager, ready with the quick fix for family trouble, the four hundred dollars she gave me a case in point.

"You know, Billy," said Molly, "when your father came home during the war I called and invited him for dinner, lunch, anything, just to get him back in the family. But he hung up on me and wouldn't answer my calls."

"I went to see him at the ball park," Peter said. "He told me he was too busy to talk to me. He wasn't a forgiving man, your father. Always difficult."

"I got along with him," Billy said. "So did Peg."

"I'm glad somebody did," Peter said.

"He gave Billy his old baseball glove," Peg said.

"Sure, why not?" said Peter. "Can you imagine him telling Billy not to take this money?"

Billy fell silent.

"I'm going to take some pictures of the table," Giselle said with perfect timing. "I'll use your camera and tripod, Orson," and she went up the back stairs, knowing exactly where my camera equipment was.

"I feel like an interloper," Roger said, "but I might as well get it straight. What was Francis doing at the ball park? I thought he lived on the road."

I pointed to Billy for the answer, and he gave me the back of his hand.

"Don't bug out on us, Billy," I said.

"Who's buggin' out?"

"Francis came home in 1942 to help the family when he thought Billy was being drafted," I said. "Francis stayed close to Annie till he died, didn't he?"

"Yeah, he did," Billy said.

Giselle came down with the camera and flash and set them up on the tripod in the back parlor. Nobody spoke while she did this. We waited for her to say she was ready, but she'd heard our conversation and she left the camera standing and came back to the table.

"Francis lived up by Hawkins Stadium, the ball park," I said, "isn't that so, Billy?"

"Hoffman's Hotel," Billy said. "Eight rooms with a saloon. Old-timey street guys and barflies, newspapermen with no teeth and dyin' ballplayers, an elephant graveyard. But Francis was in good shape for a guy who bent his elbow so much, and he went to all the Senators' home games. Johnny Evers was one of the bosses of the club and he and Francis both played big-league ball at the same time, so Evers gave Francis a season pass. Those were tough days for baseball, all the young guys gettin' drafted, and you hadda fill their shoes with kids, or old guys, or deaf guys, or guys with one arm, or one eye. Francis tells Evers he knows a guy doin' short time in a Buffalo jail hits the ball a mile and does Evers want him? Evers says hell yes and hires the guy when he gets out and hires Francis as a coach. Francis, he's sixty-two and he suits up, ain't played a game of ball for maybe twenty-eight years and he's out there telling kids and cripples never to swing at the first pitch, and how to steal bases and rattle the pitcher, when to play close in, when to go deep. Ripper Collins is managin' and he pinch-hits Francis, puts him in for the hit and run, or the sacrifice, because Francis can still bloop it to right once in a while, and he's champ with the bunt, lays it down the line, soft, easy, never lost the touch. He runs like a three-legged goat, takes him two weeks to get to first base but it don't matter. He's out from the go but the runner gets to second or third. I seen him do this half a dozen times before they drafted me, December, and I'm gone eight months I'm back out with a bad eye. Francis is coachin' third, and they're writin' stories about him, and the con he talked Johnny Evers into signin' is knifed dead on a dance floor hustlin' somebody's wife. Dangerous game, baseball. And there I am in a box behind third and there's the old man, movin' like a cricket, and while I'm watchin' him he falls over in the baseline. You can't get up? I'm up and over the fence, on the field, and they got a stretcher comin', take him down to Memorial. I'm in a cab behind the ambulance but it don't make no difference. He's dead before his chin hits the dirt."

Giselle said, "The chocolates," and got up from her chair and went to the kitchen. When she came back with the box of candy I saw she'd been crying. Molly saw it too.

"Everything all right, dear?" Molly asked.

"Oh, sure," said Giselle.

"What is it?" Peter asked.

"Nothing," she said.

"It's Francis," I said.

Giselle opened the candy and put it in front of Peter. "There's

281

strawberry pie for dessert," she said, "but I know you love chocolate."

"Francis?" Peter said, looking at her.

"It was more Billy," she said. "The image I had of him climbing the fence to help his father."

"Wire fence," Billy said. "Keeps you from swallowin' foul balls."

"Nobody in my family would've done that, climbed a fence, or even thought about it," Giselle said. "We were so full of hate for one another."

"Your mother?" said Molly. "Your father?"

"When my mother died my oldest brother cremated her the same day with no funeral service, so no friends or family could see her."

"Stuff like that happened here," Billy said.

"But today everybody's at the same table," Giselle said. "That never happened in my family after I was six and it never could. Hate is a cancer, and even when it fades, something awful takes its place. I know, because I hate my brothers. I hate them."

When no one chose to ask her why, she said, "So I want to take a photo now. Turn your chairs and look toward the camera."

"Oh, good, a picture," Peg said. "Danny raves about you. He says you take wonderful pictures."

"Danny is just being friendly," Giselle said, and I agreed. Danny was compulsively friendly.

"You should be in the picture," Peter said to Giselle.

"I will be."

And so another formal photograph in modern Phelan family history came into existence; my second with my father, Peter's first with Billy and Peg, and so on. The new combinations were quantifiable. Giselle, eminently photogenic, set the shutter, hurried back to her chair, and imposed a smile on the film that was as natural as sunshine and equally radiant.

282

We were a family soon to disappear from this form, from these chairs, from this place. The diaspora would be complete in, what, four, three, two years? Barring a miracle, Peter would die in the months ahead. Molly could go on for years, but even with a house-keeper (and she could afford one) she wouldn't stay here alone. And Giselle and I? Ah, now, there's a rub.

Whether or not we would now stay here for an extended time was a new question. But she was responsible for my being here (I see no need to run through the tissue of causation) and therefore obliquely responsible as well for this day of reunification, this time of our dawning into unity (as Keats put it), if indeed it was unity, if indeed it was dawning; and perhaps she would also be responsible for us reordering the house to accommodate a modern married couple, with nursery. The very thought of these things was so ex-otically afield of my present consciousness that I could only look at it all as a freakish turn of fate. The lives we had known for five years were about to be superseded. But by what?

My personal agenda was to finish the book on Peter's art, and finish also this memoir, of which Walker Pettijohn had seen two-thirds. He professed to admire it, this time with editorial associates supporting publication, but a contract awaited completion of the manuscript, and I detected no confidence in Walker that the book would sell more than forty copies. I no longer needed survival money, but I yearned for proof that I was not chattering to myself in the forest, making no sound.

Giselle said the book made her weep, a rare occurrence (her weeping at Billy climbing the fence was the only time I'd ever seen her in tears). She'd read it the weekend I threaded her needle's eye with such rare, if unverifiable, significance, and told me this book was the fulfillment of the intuition that had helped convince her to marry me: that she knew, without understanding why she knew, the value of the way I wrote and thought about this family. I'd shown her the early version of the book and talked to her about the family as if I'd owned it, when I was actually drawing out unknown, unspoken impressions of people to whom I had only tenuous connection, none of my impressions really authentic, all of them as much a creation as one of Peter's sketches. Yet this talk insinuated itself into some receptive corner of Giselle's imagination, and she concluded that one day I'd write a meaningful work about the family; and she wanted to be part of that. And all along I'd thought it was my romantic charm that got her.

"Why didn't you tell me you liked what I wrote?"

"I didn't know how to say it. Maybe I didn't like it so much either. Maybe I only liked how you talked about it. But now you write better. And I think I think better."

"My artistic soul drew you to Colonie Street."

"You might say that."

It ran through my mind that I might also say it was her desire for a safe haven in which to ride out the pregnancy that drew her here; or the lure of this new money coming my way (in fair measure because of her work) as a cushion for the future; or her weariness with being a pioneer feminist in a man's world; or the realization that one-night stands only exacerbate solitude; or perhaps she'd had advance knowledge that Quinn was about to settle down with one woman. ("Does that change your mind about him, now that he's getting married?" she asked me, to which I replied, "Why should it? It didn't change his when I got married.")

There was always the possibility that she genuinely perceived her psychic transformation into motherhood as an idea whose time had come. But even if she *was* luxuriating in it (Mother Giselle: it landed with an oxymoronic bounce in my consciousness), what was her view of remarriage? Perhaps it was as ambivalent as my own view of this particular paternity.

The proposed renaming of the putative grandson, the unnamed fetus, would be the occasion for reaffirming the matrimonial vows and the sacrament; but a year or more ago I had decided that

284

fathering a child with Giselle could turn into a crime against the unborn, predestining trouble for the product of this all-but-doomed union. I had also anesthetized my anguish glands, had learned how not to be a Giselle addict, how not to fall into a neurasthenic droop when she left the room. I had, in reaction, found abundant, even raucous solace with other women, for, without ever having proof of Giselle's infidelity, I believed in it. How not to, knowing her as I had? "I never did anything bad," she once said with moderate conviction, but that changed nothing for me; and this vast unknown, this black riddle, I do believe, was the erosive element that had destroyed my acceptance of the marriage as a temporary game of long-distance singles.

But now here she came with her renovated interiors, telling me that she had learned how to think, had learned how to be a mother; in effect, that she had grown into the marriage the way a child grows into a garment two sizes too large. But she could know little of how her physical condition would transform her in the months ahead, or what it would be like not to work at what she did so well, or what remarriage and the fusion with this family in the name of a name would do to her, or what our arm's-length connubiality had done to me. She might even come to think of her own name (Gisel in Old English, Giall in the Old Irish) as her fate: for the word means "hostage."

The ring of the telephone broke our concentration on our communal photographic image, and Molly answered it. Alice Shugrue.

"She can't pick me up," Molly said when she hung up. "It's raining so hard the sewers are backed up and the streets are flooded. Her engine got wet and they had to tow her out of a huge puddle. She's at her cousin's in the North End, and she's not even going to try to go home tonight."

It was truly a fierce storm. Great sheets of water were flowing off the roof past our windows, and you could barely see Pearl Street.

"So you'll stay here tonight," Peter said to Molly.

"If it keeps up we'll all have to stay," Peg said.

"If it keeps up," said Peter, "it won't come down."

"Oh dear," said Molly, "my brother is telling Papa's jokes."

"As paterfamilias he's entitled," I said.

"As what?" Billy said. "Whataya givin' us all these twenty-dollar words."

"Just means the 'father of the family,'" I said, "Also means he's liberated from his own father—and mother too, you might say. Am I right, Father Peter?"

"I hope we're all liberated," Peter said.

"I'm liberating Molly from the kitchen," Peg said.

"Don't be silly," said Molly.

"I'll help in the kitchen," Giselle said.

"No you won't," Peg said. "You take it easy. I'm drafting Roger to dry dishes." And I said silently to myself, "Ah ha, Margaret, ah ha."

"It rained like this," Peter said, "the day I left home in 1913. You remember that, Billy?"

"You mean the rowboat?" Billy said.

"Right. You and your father rowed down to rescue me."

"I remember," Billy said. "We took you to the railroad station. Where were ya goin'?"

"New York, but anywhere would've been all right with me. I was just getting out from under. And yet I never really left this place."

"It can be a trap," Molly said, and she turned to Giselle. "So be careful, my dear, if Orson decides you should live here. You *are* going through with the second marriage, aren't you?"

"It's not for me to say," Giselle said. "Are we, Orson?"

"It somehow seems as though deuterogamy is an idea whose time has come," I said.

"There he goes again," Billy said.

286

Molly smiled. "Why am I not surprised?"

Peter was nodding his head at the completion of something, the beginning of something else. It seemed facile to think of the remarriage as a beginning when it was merely the supercharging of an old steam engine that might or might not make it over the next rise. The new name, the child, the remarriage as confirmation that the first marriage was a bust, which it was, these thoughts also saddened me: the sadness of the completion of anything, a book, a marriage, a life. Or a sad painting.

"There's one more painting," Peter said. "It's upstairs, and it's not a pretty picture. I warn you against it, but Orson will show it to anybody who wants to see it."

"Have I seen it?" Molly asked.

"No," Peter said. "Only Orson."

And so we all, including Giselle, who had photographed it two months ago when it was embryonic, went up to Peter's studio to see *The Burial,* his major unfinished work. If he lived on, it would very probably not be his last in the *Malachi Suite.* He'd already made several sketches of Malachi and Crip in hell, and was trying to assign a fitting punishment for them; but as of today, *The Burial* was as far as he'd gone with his great graphic leaps through those abominable events.

It is raining in the painting, and Colm Dorgan, with the point of a spade, and Malachi McIlhenny, with his muddy right brogan, are pushing the half-folded corpse of Lizzie into her muddy grave, which is too short for her. The grave's borders are a sea of mud and Malachi and Colm are drenched. Lizzie is naked except for her black stockings and a burlap bag over her head. Colm is pushing her feet into the grave. Malachi is stepping on her right breast with his foot. The left side of her chest is a broad, raw crevasse of flesh, her charred rib cage and parts of her internal organs protruding, the flesh burned off two fingers of her left hand, leaving the burned bones visible.

William Kennedy

A small cottage, Malachi's, wherein the other witnesses to Lizzie's burning are locked and awaiting the return of Malachi, is visible in the distant background, as are a sky and a landscape full of demonic figures, including the lithe form of Lizzie dancing on a hill with a web-footed creature with the head of a goat.

Piles of dirt beside the grave will be heaped on Lizzie and on the secluded grave, which is at the side of a ditch, with a high fence on one side and trees on the other. When the grave is covered with dirt it will be hidden by leaves and twigs, and Lizzie will lie scrunched in it for five days before searchers find her corrupted body, tortured even in death.

Upon his return from the grave to the cottage, Malachi will, with a long knife in his hand, swear all present to secrecy, and will invent the story to be circulated: that Lizzie ran away from the house in a crazed condition the previous night. Malachi will be especially threatening to his sister, Kathryn, whose throat he swears he will cut if she peeps a word of what happened. When Kathryn swears this out of fear, Malachi will then scrape his trouser leg with the blade of his knife and say, "Oh Kate, that's the juice and substance of poor Lizzie I'm scraping."

And Kathryn will say, "Malachi, even if you scrape off your skin, God will not let the stain be off you. You're damned, my brother, and I hope the devils in hell never let you draw a painless breath."

Upon public revelation of this story, neighbors will sack and burn Malachi's house, and Malachi and Crip Devlin will be tried and convicted of murder and sentenced to twenty years in jail. Colm Dorgan will be sentenced to ten years, will serve all ten, and emerge toothless, hairless, mindless, and without a family. Ned Cronin will be given, and will serve, one year in prison, and live six more months before dying of public shame. Minnie Dorgan, though guilty of conspiracy to murder, will be set free because of her advanced age, and will sell all that she owns to move away from Albany.

In the first six months of his incarceration Crip Devlin will sicken from the pox, develop intolerable headaches and lightning pains to the legs. He will vomit and become incontinent, will develop ulcers of the heels, soles, toes, and buttocks, blockage of the penis, and rubbery tumors in the testicles. At the moment when his memory vanishes and he can no longer remember who he is or what he did to Lizzie, he will die of suppressed urine and an exploded brain.

In 1890, during the third year of his sentence, Malachi, with leather thongs he created in the shoe shop of the Albany penitentiary, will hang himself in his cell, swearing to the moment of his death that it was not Lizzie but a demon that he burned, and he will be buried in a potter's field. On the day after his burial his grave will be violated and his corpse stabbed through the heart with a wooden dagger in the shape of a cross, a suitable implement for destroying the soul of a heretic.

Kathryn Phelan will be the chief witness against Malachi. Already the mother of Francis, Sarah, and Charles, she will give birth to Peter within two weeks of Lizzie's death. She will also have three subsequent children, in this order: Julia, Mary (Molly), and Thomas.

Mab Devlin will become a charge of the city, but will escape confinement and become a vanished child.

The family's mood, after viewing the painting and listening to my recounting of the details, was so bleak that Giselle suggested putting on some music, and she then unwrapped the gift she'd found in a second-hand store and bought for the house: three player-piano scrolls of the songs "They Always, Always Pick on Me," "After the Ball," and "Won't You Be My Little Girl." I put on the first one under the hopeful gaze of Julia, whom Peter had etherealized in the sketch of her at the seashore, about age twenty-one, a year away from death, abounding in her virginal glory; although I noted Peter had emphasized the ample bust line that was common to all the Phelan girls. But even with Julia as a prod, I could not bring myself to pump the piano's pedals, could not so easily turn my mind from Lizzie to music.

George Quinn called to tell Peg he had asked Patsy McCall for work, something he had never done before; for city and county jobs paid only pittances, and George always believed that the ban on gambling was temporary, that the okay would come down from on high one sunny day and all the gamblers in town would go back to work. But he could afford this fantasy no longer, and so he finally popped the question, and Patsy told him to go down to Democratic-party headquarters in the morning and talk to Tanner Smith, and they'd probably put him to work canvassing the Ninth Ward for the next election. Peg said the prospect of a political job so excited George that when she told him about her bequest from Peter and her plan to buy the house he said only, "That's great, I gotta go. Patsy's giving me a ride to my car."

Peter finally relaxed, took off his neckerchief and his coat, and sat alone at the table, smiling. I leaned across and asked him, "After all these years, what do I call you? Papa?"

He considered that, then shook his head no. "Sounds like an alias," he said.

Billy stood up from the table and, with cane and gimp leg, hobbled into the front parlor.

"Shall we adjourn?" I said to Peter.

"You go ahead. I'll sit here a minute with the chocolates."

So I joined Billy, and when I did he said, "I ain't even gonna collect my elephant bet if they take that bum's leg off."

"You were pretty sure they weren't elephants."

"One of the workers was up there came by Brady's saloon. All them guys knew the bones was owned by a mastodon, whatever the hell that is. It's big like an elephant, but it ain't an elephant."

"You're pretty shrewd, Billy. You shrewd enough to use that money to get married? Money *was* the main obstacle, wasn't it?"

"Who said I was takin' the money?"

"Nobody."

"Right," Billy said.

"Maybe we could have a double wedding," I said, and that made Billy laugh.

Doing people favors isn't always easy.

If I really was a magician and could command the spirits the way Malachi thought he could, I'd build a skeleton that would have Lizzie's ribs and fingers, Tommy's chipped backbone, Francis's all-but-gangrenous leg with the bone showing, Billy's broken ankle, Sarah's near-fleshless arms with bones pushing through skin and with tubes dangling, Peter's arthritic hips, Walter Phelan's partial skull, Meister Geld's toe and thumb, the handless armbone that my sugar whore loved to suck, and I'd have the creature dance to the 1911 tune Giselle brought us to lighten things up with music from the past. Remember the lyric?

> They always, always pick on me,
> They never, never let me be.
> I'm so very lonesome, I'm so sad,
> It's a long time since I've been glad.
> I know what I'll do, bye and bye.
> I'll eat some worms and then I'll die.
> And when I'm gone, just wait and see.
> They'll all be sorry that they picked on me.

It's about four o'clock in the afternoon now, and outside the rain is as torrential as it was at three. Colonie Street is a river. Here, in the midst of this performance by nature, we have no reversal, no ironic sunshine about to dawn. The day is crepuscularly gray, as it seems to have been forever in the life of this family; and there is something so profound in that grayness, in that cloud of unexpungeable horror and loss, that, even when the sun finally does come our way, we grieve at the change, and we pray for thunderstorms.

Poor hubristic Malachi, think of it. When you cross the border out of the real world, as he did, the way back, if you can find it, is perilous, at best; and not only for yourself. I think of the itinerant Francis, walking abroad in a malevolent world, never knowing what lay beneath the exile his mother and sister had forced upon him; and of the subterranean Molly, burying and resurrecting her sins, and living on to regret everything forever; and of myself, Orson Phelan-to-be, fugitive from the isolato's disease, about to reinvent marriage with an ambiguous wife of a second dubious dimension; and of all the others in this family: collective of the thwarted spirit, of the communal psyche that so desperately wants not to be plural.

I am one with the universe, we Phelans say; but I am one.

The universe answers us with black riddles of the past that refuse to yield their secrets: lost faiths and barren dogmas that weave the web and the winter that the poet of order had seen: the web is woven and you have to wear it, the winter is made and you have to bear it . . . It is all that you are, the final dwarf of you.

I remember Molly telling me that her mother was always afraid her daughters would meet someone, and in a single night would ruin their lives. But it takes longer than that.

I left the contemplative Billy and walked to the dining room. I watched my father choosing between a chocolate-covered nougat and a vanilla cream. In the kitchen I saw Giselle drying the dishes alongside Molly and Peg and Roger, the four of them discussing a prolonged kiss that Cary Grant had given Ingrid Bergman in a movie, and I took my cue from that. I gripped Giselle's face in my right hand and kissed her, did the same to Molly, kissed the radiant Peg, shook Roger's hand, and I then said to them, "It's all that we are."

They looked at me as if I had gone back into isolation, but when I smiled at them they knew I was as sane as any of them.